SPEND GAME

We'd seen his flying body leave the car and hit the roadside tree, to flip brokenly aside towards the ditch. All those unlit country by-roads in East Anglia have ditches lined by hedgerows, though they were no shelter. Sue's blonde hair was straggling across her face from the rain. We couldn't get any wetter. The sheet lightning showed us how poor Leckie lay crookedly in the glistening mud, folded into the splattering ditch water, his left shoulder humped under a grassy overhang and his overcoat crumpled up above his waist. Leaving Sue's hand I slid down towards the muddy bottom and reached along Leckie's arm, thinking, where the hell do you find a pulse? His hand felt warm. Dead, but warm. For a minute I pressed anxiously around his wrist, with no real hope of knowing what I was doing.

Also in Arrow by Jonathan Gash

THE GRAIL TREE
THE JUDAS PAIR
PEARLHANGER
THE SLEEPERS OF ERIN

SPEND GAME

A Lovejoy narrative

JONATHAN GASH

ARROW BOOKS

Arrow Books Limited
62–65 Chandos Place, London WC2N 4NW

An imprint of Century Hutchinson Limited

London Melbourne Sydney Auckland
Johannesburg and agencies
throughout the world

First published in Great Britain by
William Collins (The Crime Club) 1980
Hamlyn Paperbacks edition 1980
Arrow edition 1986

Printed and bound in Great Britain by
William Collins Sons & Co. Ltd, Glasgow

ISBN 0 09 947080 2

To
To Wu Ch'ang, ancient Chinese god of
wealth and good luck who hands out
gold mountains to the humble and
pious of heart, this book is humbly and
piously dedicated.

Lovejoy

For
A story for John and Julie, Susan, Julia
and the Port Sunlight Players, Pat and
Roy, Elizabeth.

1

No matter what people say, you can't help getting into trouble. And the antiques game is nothing *but* trouble – beautiful, lovely trouble all the bloody time.

This story starts where a pretty but terrified woman was holding my hand in a thunderstorm. We were looking down at the dead man in the ditch, and I was frightened too. In fact, I bet I was more scared than she was, because I knew roughly why he'd been killed. She didn't.

The rain was hurtling down in great falling clouds. We were soaked and it was pitch black. Occasional sheets of lightning washed the silent night sky into sudden silver, letting us see his face and our own aghast paleness. It was my friend from the auction, all right. We call him Leckie. The rumble of thunder from the east seemed to shut the light away and Sue and I hung on to each other's hands for dear life. We slithered down the embankment from the road, calling out to see if he gave any sort of answer, though I think we both realized he was killed the moment he was flung clear of his tumbling car.

'A torch, Lovejoy,' Sue said frantically. 'We need a torch.' I was impressed. Women are so much more practical. Often useless, but permanently practical. She kept on about a torch, getting me mad.

'I've not got one.' I was literally shaking.

She sounded snappy. 'Everybody with any sense keeps a torch in their car.'

'I've not got one,' I said back doggedly.

'You should always keep –'

'Shut up.' I needed to think.

'Headlights!' Sue exclaimed, tugging at me. 'Lovejoy, your headlights! You can turn your car this way with the lights on –'

' – Then we can see what we already know,' I finished for her. 'That he's already dead.' She was getting me madder, as well as more frightened. What if the big car came back? It had been deliberate, blundering into a lunatic swerve and chucking Leckie's little car into the air like that.

'Have you a lighter?'

'You know I don't smoke.'

'Then feel his pulse.' This sort of thing turns my stomach over, but Sue might be right. You never know till you make sure.

We'd seen his flying body leave the car and hit the roadside tree, to flip brokenly aside towards the ditch. All these unlit country by-roads in East Anglia have ditches lined by hedgerows, though they were no shelter. Sue's blonde hair was straggling across her face from the rain. We couldn't get any wetter. The sheet lightning showed us how poor Leckie lay crookedly in the glistening mud, folded into the spattering ditch water, his left shoulder humped under a grassy overhang and his overcoat crumpled up above his waist. Leaving Sue's hand I slid down towards the muddy bottom and reached along Leckie's arm, thinking, where the hell do you find a pulse? His hand felt warm. Dead, but warm. For a minute I pressed anxiously around his wrist, with no real hope of knowing what I was doing.

'Well?' Sue whispered down.

'Well what?'

'His *pulse,*' she hissed.

'I don't even know what a bloody pulse is,' I hissed back, though why we were whispering in a downpour at the bottom of a ditch with the nearest village six miles away God alone knows. Death does it, makes whispers. Sue clucked from exasperation and slid down beside me with a muddy splash.

'I'd better do it. You're *hopeless,* Lovejoy . . .'

I pressed Leckie's hand towards hers. She gave a small gasp as her fingers touched the cooling skin but gamely stuck to the task. Every so often I listened for an approaching car just in case. There had been two men in the sleek motor that had seen Leckie off. They had seemed casual enough to come driving coolly back with the intention of 'finding' the accident and reporting it to the police. They might have enough nerve, but would they be so stupid? They'd performed a swift, silent search, very businesslike and rather sinister.

'Lovejoy,' Sue whispered.

'What?'

'I can't feel his pulse.' A pause. 'He's dead.'

I pulled her up on to the tall roadside grass. We sloshed back to where my contraption was parked in the muddy gateway of a large field. The lightning was still busy battering the low valley. On the underbelly of the stormclouds to the south you could see the orange glow from our local town's lights, some miles of wet fields and woods away.

'What do we do, Lovejoy?' she asked.

'We go back.'

'Back? To Medham?' I'd attended the antiques auction in

Medham that afternoon. It's my game. I'm an antique dealer.

'No, Sue. To the main road.'

'But the police, Lovejoy.'

I opened the door and pushed her in. The trouble with women is they think everybody else is law-abiding and peaceable. Their belief happens to be untrue but I usually go along with them to save bother.

'You *will* phone the ambulance, Lovejoy?' Sue demanded as I climbed in beside her.

I pretended to reflect a split second, then gave her a smile I hoped was reassuring. In that instant, dwelling on the relative usefulness of honesty and untruth, I settled swiftly for falsehood. It's more predictable, especially when you're in adverse circumstances like now. I've found that.

'Of course,' I said. I switched the engine on and gunned my archaic little bullnosed monster into creaking action. I drove for a few hundred yards by memory and the occasional lightning flash, one hand on the wheel and peering out into the driving rain, until Sue could stand it no longer.

'*Lights,* Lovejoy. For heaven's *sake.*'

'Silly me!' I switched them on and notched up to an aggresive twenty, which for me is flat out with a following breeze.

'What is the matter, Lovejoy?' Sue was eyeing me sideways as I drove.

'It's the shock, love,' I said. It was that all right, because I knew something about Leckie. The more I thought, the more I remembered. We'd known each other on and off for some years.

'They didn't even go down to see if he was all right,' Sue said angrily. 'Those two men. Just getting out and walking over like that, looking in the car and on the grass. They didn't even seem to *care.* You should report them.' (Note: not we, nor I. You, Lovejoy. *You* should do the reporting. That's a typical woman for you – essential but woolly-minded.)

'Well . . .'

'You should, darling,' she urged me earnestly. 'Why, they seemed more interested in the poor man's car than –'

I didn't want her dwelling on that aspect too much so I broke in hastily. 'Do you suppose *they* reported the accident?' I asked innocently. After that we drove on in silence. Sue's not daft. She didn't think so either.

I got back to the main road, thankful for the absence of that powerful car's immense staring lamps and the pair of cold malevolent lunatics that drove it. The storm was still on, but there was plenty of traffic now, switchback lines of headlights undulating in the darkness, buses full of singing football supporters beering their way homewards from the big match, and juggernaut lorries unerringly finding pools to spray over my windscreen.

We drove back to the motorway café. Sue leaves her car there. It is convenient, only a few miles or so from where we live in our respective dwellings in apparent mutual disdain. Her car's one of those long low things the size of a small bungalow, so we mostly use hers for our nocturnal discussions among the hedgerows. This particular night, though, some kind guardian gremlin had nudged me into insisting that we use my own elegant conveyance, a mercifully nondescript little banger I'd painted dark blue to disguise the scrapes. Of course Sue grumbled like mad, but I get these stubborn moods. In summer there's lovely sweet grass to lie on. I could see her point. I telephoned from a booth in the hallway while Sue waited outside. The police station asked my name and address. I obligingly invented the name of a mythical Mr Witherspoon of Solihull, poor chap, and reported finding an overturned car and a man probably dead.

'I stopped four cars for help,' I lied to confuse the issue in case Old Bill got a rush of blood to the head and started filing our footprints. 'They're waiting there for you.'

'Where are you?'

I gave the name of a distant pub at Kelvedon. 'In the taproom,' I told him briskly. It was overdoing it a bit, but I like touches of local colour.

'Wait there, please, Mr Witherspoon,' the constable said, all efficient. 'One of our cars will be with you shortly.'

'Anything to help.'

'You didn't mention me, darling?' Sue checked as I returned to the car. I said of course not. When we're together in public she develops that reserved ultra-cool look of the secret sinner, a woman ever so polite but who obviously can't really be bothered with this nerk opposite transparently boring her to death.

It was time to go, Sue being due back home. I raced out with her into the rain. We ran stiff and hunched, holding hands.

'I'm still shaky,' she said in her car.

'Me too.'

'Drive safely, Lovejoy.' The accident was on her mind.

'Don't I always?'

'No, love,' she said. 'Do try.'

We said a protracted farewell. Sue's husband would be home about ten. She had a safe hour to spare when we finally parted, which is our usual safety margin unless passion's particularly rampant. Sometimes we cut it pretty fine.

I waved her off into the streaming traffic and splashed back into the café's brittle glare, but only when I was sure she wasn't going to turn round with some afterthought. I still had some change. The emergency call had cost nothing. Tinker Dill would still be sober so early in the evening, thank God, even at the weekend. I'm so used to phoning him at the White Hart its number's engraved on my cortex.

I got through first time. The public bar sounded crammed and noisy. Some charitable soul amputated Tinker from the bar and dragged him to the blower.

'Whatcher want, Lovejoy?' He was peeved as hell. 'You seen me all bleeding day at the auction.'

'Just listen, Tinker,' I said, putting my threatening voice on. 'And don't radio what I say all round the pub.' I felt his sulks come over, force five.

'Have I to go out?' He hates leaving a pub.

'No. Today's auction. Leckie bought an escritoire, right?'

'Yeah, and –'

'Shut up,' I snarled. 'I told you. Say nothing, just tell me if I missed anything.' The White Hart's one of those rambling old East Anglian pubs where antique dealers congregate in droves. Even the woodworms have ears.

'Don't get shirty, Lovejoy,' Tinker whined. He has a specially humble stoop for whining. I could see him doing it now.

'And a crummy doctor's case, Victorian?'

'Bleeding horrible it was,' Tinker cackled indignantly. 'Bloody prices –'

'And that book.' We paused, thinking. There had been seven hundred items auctioned at Virgil's auction house in Medham that day, a long stint relieved only by ecstasy, beauty, excitement and the scent of profit. A typical country auction in a typical country town. I avoided mentioning Leckie's accident. They would hear at the White Hart soon enough, preferably when I was there. And I'd make certain I looked as astonished as everybody else when the bad news came.

'That's all, Lovejoy.'

'Sure, Tinker?'

'Yeah.' Another pause while his brain swam out of its alcoholic fog. 'Here, Lovejoy,' he croaked in what he imagined was a secret whisper, 'we in trouble again?'

'No, Tinker. See you in a minute or two.'

I left the caff and drove with the rest of the traffic towards the orange sky-glow. The rain was easing now and the cars fewer. I would reach the pub a bit later than usual but the other dealers wouldn't notice because we turn up at all hours. First I had one job to do.

Leckie's one of those people who never seem much while they're knocking about, yet when they depart leave a rather depressing space. We'd been in the army together for a spell, in one of those nasty little wars we used to have going on simultaneously in a dozen places. Leckie and I were in the same artillery unit. He's one of those odd calm Englishmen you get now and then who look great on camels and are naturally full of linguistics whether they come from the slums of Moss Side or a duke's stately home. Leckie always managed to convey the impression that no matter how accurate the desert snipers were the main problem was having sherry trifle properly served when the bishop called for croquet on the lawn. I was posted to a snowbound war as punishment for getting malaria. I never saw him after till he turned up here.

I found myself smiling as I drove, remembering his arrival. He was a Keswick man, thin and pleasant. He took as naturally to tweeds and hand-sewn leather shoes as a duck to water. It was a noisy Saturday night when he'd sailed in, found me and strolled across. We said hello and chatted. He was out of a job.

'What's the local industry, Lovejoy?' he'd asked, forcing himself to like the gin. It was labelled 'Best London Brands Blended', but only for the sake of appearances.

'Well, we're mostly antique dealers,' I told him. He grinned, shrugged and looked us over, in that order.

'That'll have to do,' he said casually, as if the whole of East Anglia had made him an offer and he hadn't much else on that day.

'Know anything about antiques, Leckie?' Mind you, most antique dealers are utterly clueless about antiques. And the good old public comes a close second.

'No. What does one do?' He watched me grin and shake my head. I told him he hadn't changed. 'I suppose it's buying and selling, something in that line?' he'd gone on, still not batting an eyelid.

That was Leckie all over. Didn't care much about difficulties, knowledge and education. He just knew his attitude would carry him through. Most times he'd been right. Like the time our platoon went into a high scrubland plateau where the tribes spoke a weird private language of clicks, hisses and croaks. Within a week he was our official translator, having absorbed the language by a sort of osmosis.

We were never really very close once he started in antiques, just casual competitors in a fierce trade. I don't think I had any special affection for him, even though I'd known him some years. You just don't get many Leckies to the pound, not these days.

I turned off the motorway into town. Our two cinemas and

fifty-seven pubs were still hard at it, but the shops had that benign retirement look which all showy glass fronts get after the Saturday rush. A few people strolled, or waited for the buses to take them out into the countryside or down along the estuary to their cold sea-sprayed cottages on the harbour walls. Our town's one official tart was already out, well wrapped, by the furniture shop. I wagged an arm and shouted 'Wotcher, Jo,' to show I wasn't biased, then put my ancient little crate, every erg agog, hard at the slope below the preserved cathedral ruins. It spluttered bravely up towards the garrison.

We're a garrison town; in fact, never have been anything else since Cymbeline did his stuff and Claudius landed. You wouldn't think it, though, because the barracks are now tidied away between the football grounds and encroaching woods, and in any case low terraced houses submerge much of the evidence. You can see the layout of the barracks and spiderhuts from the train, but only if you know where to look. I hurtled at a breathless fifteen into a small street near the barracks and jerked my horseless carriage to a wheezing stop outside a quiet little pub. There were three other cars by the pavement, all innocent. I made sure nobody was in the street as best I could – there are only four or five street lamps there, and they're still those old gas-mantle standards kids can climb up or use for cricket stumps. I hurried round the back street and went into the little stone-flagged yard of the house next to the pub. A knock on the window like a clandestine lover.

'It's Lovejoy,' I said. The light came on over the yard door. Val let me in, her face disapproving.

'You know the time?' she said. I nodded and shook rain all over the carpet.

'I'll not be a minute, love. Has Leckie been?'

'No.'

'Not to leave anything? No messages?'

'No.' She was right to look puzzled. 'Should he have called? You didn't tell me. Is anything wrong?'

She gave me a nip of rum for the cold. Val and I had been friends in the roaring days of youth, learning our adolescent snogging techniques in joint training sessions in school lessons quaintly called 'Agriculture: Methods and Theory.' Education's gone downhill since then. She'd married George, who's the barman at the next-door pub, an arrangement which saves on fares and leaves Val sufficiently free to run an antiques sideline. She does no dealing herself, only guards what's given her until it's collected. Posh London dealers have their own depositories. Lone antique dealers either do without or have a safe lock-up arrangement with

11

some trustworthy soul like Val.

'Can I look?'

'I'll get the key.'

These older terraced houses are admittedly small, but whoever built them had his head screwed on. There's a narrow stone-flagged cellar under each. You enter through a doorway set below a few steps leading down from the yard. There's no window, only a solid wooden door. Val had persuaded the publican to have it metalled with iron strips and linked by a warning bleep in case he ever needed it for extra storage of bottled spirits. When I met up with Val again and incorporated her in my famous arrears system of payment I let Leckie use the same facilities. Antique dealers call this sort of arrangement a 'cran', just as other gangsters call it a drop.

Val and I went down with a flashlight. She always takes time fumbling with the lock because there's no outside light. Only a few weeks before George had rigged up a light bulb on a perilous flex to cast a feeble glimmer on our valuables. My phoney eighteenth-century oak chest was ageing usefully still. Unless my luck changed I'd soon have to auction it, a terrible admission of failure for any self-respecting antique dealer. There was an ebony flute in its case, distinguished by that grim little-finger D-flat key, the size of a small springboard, they had before the Boehm system let the modern instrument makers have some restful nights. Flautists must have had digits a foot long before 1850. And there was my famous non-painting, an oil copy of Il Sodoma's 'tailor' portrait, of that skilled type which abounds in the country areas of England. I'd bought it for a song from a German tourist who had paid the earth. (Tip: never buy a painting without measuring it. If the size of the real thing is well known, and the painting you're considering buying is thirty square inches too small, it follows that the latter is probably a copy — a legitimate copy perhaps, but still a copy.)

Leckie had a few pieces of lustreware on the one shelf we'd rigged up and two of those Lowestoft jugs I hate. But no escritoire, no doctor's bag, and no book. Now there's a thing, I thought. How very odd.

'Lovejoy. Is anything the matter?'

'Eh?'

'What's wrong?' She pulled me round to face her. 'I've never seen you like this, except for that time.' That time was a dust-up everybody ought to have forgotton by now. Only women remember fights, their own included.

'Nothing, love,' I said jovially.

'Lovejoy?' She kept hold of me. I saw her eyes change. 'Dear

12

God. Is . . . is it Leckie?'

I felt my chest fall a mile. Her face was suddenly white as a sheet. Things clicked horribly into place. I now remembered that holiday she had taken last year with an unnamed friend to the Scillies. Leckie had been away too, by an odd coincidence. After that he'd had more money to buy with. His trade had looked up. Twice he hinted at a silent partner. Christ Almighty, I thought, suddenly weary as hell. It never rains but what it pours crap. Sometimes I'm just stupid. Val and Leckie, for gawd's sake.

'Tell me, Lovejoy.'

'It might have not been him, love,' I said desperately. She drew back and looked at me, up and down and up and down. She shone the flashlight.

'That's mud.'

'There was an accident . . .'

'Leckie?'

'It . . . it looked like him, love, but – '

She walked away towards the wall and stood there a minute.

'It was a car, Val. He got . . . got . . .'

'Killed,' she said, turning. She fumbled for the key and held the door. 'And the first thing you could think of was what antiques he'd left here, in case there was a chance of making a few pounds.' Her eyes were streaming.

'Not really, Val,' I began, but she wasn't having any and gestured me up the steps.

'Take your stuff out of here first thing tomorrow, Lovejoy,' she said in a monotone. 'You're not nice any more. Don't come here again.'

'Look, love,' I tried desperately. Val and Leckie. How was I to know?

She dropped the key on its string and went into her house, just let the key fall there on to the steps and walked off, leaving the cellar door open and me standing there like a goon. I had to feel around before I could find it, and even then it took a while to lock up. I put the key on the lintel. I knocked a couple of times, half-hearted. She must have heard but didn't come to the door.

The rain had eased off. I cranked my zoomster into feeble bronchiectatic life and rattled back through town towards my own village. It's three miles off to the north-west. Three-quarters of an hour before closing time, the town hall clock said as I trundled past. It would be touch and go, because two miles are uphill. My old crate sounded worn out. It feels these sudden strains, same as me.

13

2

There's nothing so welcoming as a good pub and nothing so forbidding as a bad one. We've some repellent ones, but the White Hart's as kindly as they come. I stood in the porchway pretending to be preoccupied with my coat, but really sussing out who'd got back from the auction. Tinker Dill was there looking like a derelict straight off the kerb in his tattered mittens and rubbishly old greatcoat. He was standing among a group of other thirsty barkers, all runners for us dealers. Tinker might be the shabbiest barker in the known universe, but he's the best by a street. He's also the booziest. He saw me and came weaving through the crowds, not spilling a single drop. A barker only lets go of his glass under anaesthetic.

'Hiyer, Tinker.' I spoke quietly. 'Get my stuff from Val's.'

'Eh?' He goggled.

'You heard.' My eyes were everywhere. 'First thing tomorrow.'

'*Sunday*: Bleeding hell.'

'That's what she said.' We fought to the bar. I chipped out for a refill and snatched at the barman's eye for my usual. Tinker grumbled, but that's nothing new. He hates merely shifting stuff. His job's sniffing out antiques wherever they lurk.

'Where do they go?'

'Tell you later when I've arranged something.' The four people crammed nearest us were dedicated anglers talking about massacring the next bream run on the Ouse. Ted was a mile down the bar and his wife Jenny sprinting between the two bars. It looked safe enough, but I kept my voice down. 'Don't gape about, Tinker,' I said casually, 'but tell me who was here when you arrived.'

Tinker measured the clock and turned round to lean his elbows on the bar. There's never any problem about space round Tinker, not with his pong.

'Helen?' I began, smiling and nodding at the familiar faces in the bar mirrors. I like Helen, long of leg and stylish of manner, shapely of fag-holder and quick of mind. She saw my eyes and nodded a quizzical smile. She does English porcelain mostly, and does it well with profit. Her eyebrows said, Come over here a minute, Lovejoy, but I was busy and frightened.

'She was here,' Tinker growled. 'She's asking for you.'

14

'Aren't they all?' I looked round some more. 'Jean?' Jean Plunkett's a middle-aged woman who suddenly metamorphosed from a mild housewife into an aggressive dealer about four years back. Continental silver and tooth and nail. Big Frank from Suffolk's been after her for a while now, seeing her as a potential third spouse to add to his bigamous affairs which litter the surrounding countryside. He was busy now, plying her with clever alcoholic combinations. Both Jean and he were smiling happily. He'd bought a copy of a Ravenscroft glass at the auction — unusual, because he's mostly silver and furniture.

'Her and Frank reached the pub before me,' Tinker said jealously. I said to keep calm, we'd buy a helicopter.

We seemed to have the usual crowd, in fact. A score of dealers and barkers, with a couple of tough-looking vanmen to do the lumber in case any dealer infarcted at the thought of having to do any lifting.

'The vannies, Tinker?' I suggested. He grinned a no.

'They came straight here — with Jill.'

Worn out with the worry over Leckie as I was, I just had to smile. Jill was talking slagware to Brad, a real mismatch if ever there was one. Brad hasn't thought of anything except Regency flintlocks since he learned to read and write, and Jill couldn't tell one from a ballistic missile. She'd been at Medham and bought a good pair of blue saltboats in that odd opaque slag glass which you either hate or crave. Early Victorian furnace workers were allowed to skim off the metalled surface 'slag' at the end of the working day. They used to make what they called 'foreigners', little pieces of art to sell or give. The artistry is often pretty cumbersome and really rather crude, but sometimes varies between the merely natty and the exquisite. It was the only perk glassworkers got in those days besides silicosis. Jill has an eye for such knackery, especially when prices are blasting off as they are at present. She also has an eye for the male of the species. In fact she's known for it. I've never seen her on her own in ten years, nor with the same bloke twice. She carries a poodle the size of a midget mouse, the focus for many a ribald jest.

'She's buying,' Tinker said in a gush of foetid breath from the side of his mouth, still grinning. He nudged me, cackling. 'They've got some shovelling to do later.' One of the vanmen was tickling the poodle's chin. A lot of meaningful eyeballing was going on. I could see Brad was rapidly getting cheesed off. Soon the vannies would have Jill all to themselves, lucky lads.

Good old Tinker, I thought sardonically, still sorting through the crowd. Alfred Duggins was in from down the coast. He's a benign little chap underneath a bowler. Never animated, never interrupts, just incubates thoughts behind his split lenses and sucks on the rim of a quart tankard. He'll do prints and hammered coinage up to the Civil War. He gave me a nod and pulled a comical face at the clock. A laugh. For some reason we haven't yet fathomed he hates going home.

A huddle near the fire caught my attention, gin drinkers all. Two were strangers to me. The man looked a contented sort who had to be a Londoner.

'Was Happiness at Medham?' I asked Tinker, carefully looking away from the extravagant bloke.

'Yeah. You must be blind, Lovejoy.'

'I didn't mean her. I meant him.' The blonde woman had been noticeable in the auction all right. She'd sat on one of the chairs crossing her legs till we were half out of our minds. The auctioneer had even started stuttering and losing control at one point. She happened to glance up as I looked again at her through several layers of pub mirror. Thirty or so, smiling between earrings màde of gold-mounted scarabs, original trophies from ancient Egypt. Even without them she'd have been gorgeous. Neat clothes, light fawns and browns. The shoes would match, million to one. Our eyes met. I turned away, but noted the startled air she conveyed. Perhaps it was finding herself lusted at by the peasantry. Maybe I looked as sour as I felt. I liked her. She didn't care much for me. Well, that's the way the Florentine crumbles.

'That grotty escritoire,' Tinker told me. 'Leckie outbid him, remember?'

'So he did,' I said. So he did.'

Tinker stared hard over the bar and wagged his eyebrow for another pint. Ted streaked up with it. I watched all this, peeved as hell. I have to wave and scream for service. The slightest gesture from Tinker Dill's like a laser. My eyes got themselves dragged into the mirror by awareness of the woman through the noise and shouts and smoke. She looked carelessly away just in time, back into the huddle of people she was with. Happiness was tapping knees and cracking jokes. The others were falling about obediently with displays of false hilarity. It had to be sham because antique dealers are like a music-hall band — they've heard it all before. Other people in the bar were looking round at them with each gust of laughter and smiling.

'Who is he?'

'Fergus, London. They call him Fergie.'

Fergus, Black Fergus. I'd heard the name. Some trouble a few months back about possession of a silversmith's 'touch', a metal marker for hallmarking. I've heard it's quite legal in the States. Here our magistrates go bananas if you're found with one. The

16

fuss hadn't done Fergus any harm, though. If there'd been any bother he looked well on it.

He was sitting on a fender stool. Facing him was Sven, a Scandinavian originally. Sven was literally washed ashore after one of those terrifying winter storms we have here on the east coast. His ship was a diminutive freighter plying across the North Sea. They put our lifeboats out, and Sven and six others were saved. Sven refused to go home once he was ashore, just simply refused point blank to cross either by air or boat. 'I'll go home when they've built the bridge,' he jokes when people ask what does he think he's playing at. They say he's still got a wife and two kids over there, writing the same sad questions to him in every Monday post. He scratches a living as a free-floating barker, side-trading as a flasher. A flasher's not what you're probably thinking. Nothing genital. He'll go around antique shops sussing out what he supposes to be a bargain – say it's a necklace of carved rose quartz. He agrees to buy it as a present for his girl or wife (note that: a flasher *never* says he's buying for himself). He then gives the least possible deposit, or perhaps 'pays' by a dubious credit card or cheque, and goes into a nearby pub where he tries to sell it at a profit to a tourist or a dealer. If he's successful he returns to settle up, and simply keeps the balance. If not – and it usually is not, especially with Sven – he brings it back complaining the woman doesn't like it or it won't go with her new orange blouse. If necessary he'll break a link and claim he's returning the goods as faulty. That's a typical flasher. It's a hopeless game, operated entirely by useless goons who have even less clue than the rest of us. Sven's the world's worst, but I've a soft spot for him. He got me out of some complicated trouble I was having with a woman once, so I owe him a favour.

Madge was with them, dark-haired, swingly and flouncy in a bluish swingback swagger coat and those shoes that seem nothing but thin straps. She's furniture and porcelain in her shop on East Hill near the Arcade and is probably the wealthiest dealer in town. Her husband has this trout farm to the north of Suffolk. Why he sees so little of her nobody knows. Madge is what we call a 'tea-timer' in the antiques game – she'll take up with a knowledgeable bloke, using any means in her power, until she has assimilated most of his expertise. Then she'll ditch him for a different interest and never again give him the time of day. It's a very novel and worthwhile form of apprenticeship. So I've heard, that is. She currently had Jackson in tow, a rather sad thin elderly man who wears a waistcoat and makes models. He used to do a thriving business in militaria and engineering prototypes, including buying and selling the original designs – now a very profitable line I urge you to buy into as fast as you can. Then he threw himself into Madge's promotions, scattering all caution to the winds. He moved in with her for a spell and the inevitable happened. He was rumoured not to have done a deal in months, at least not on his own account. Madge has thrived.

'They friends?'

'With Sven? No.' Tinker looked about for somewhere to spit but I held up a warning finger just in time. I'd rather him gag than pollute the rest of us. 'I heard Madge introduce him to Blackie at the auction.'

'When did they come?'

'Oh, ten minutes before you.' He lit one of his home-made fags and coughed. The taproom paused respectfully. One of Tinker's specials takes a full ten seconds and starts a mile down the road. He subsided. Conversation picked up again.

'What car?'

'A bleeding great Humber.'

'They know Leckie?'

'Dunno.' Tinker nudged me. 'What's it all about, Lovejoy? You and Leckie had a dust-up over Val?'

Sometimes people amaze me. I stared at Tinker till he grew uncomfortable.

'Well,' he said, all defensive, 'she's got Leckie going because of you and Janie. Everybody knew that.'

Janie and I had our last holocaust three weeks before all this. She stormed back to her husband in her expensive solid-state Lagonda in a livid temper for reasons no longer clear to me. She was always storming somewhere. We'd been together a long time on and off. Very critical of a man, Janie was. She'd found out about Magdalene staying at my cottage for a few days. Wouldn't believe she was only helping me to redecorate. Now how had Tinker Dill spotted the Val-Leckie affair when it had taken a killing to push it into my thick skull?

Suddenly I had a headache. It had been a hard day and tomorrow wouldn't be any easier. There didn't seem to be any clues here, I thought in my stupidity and ignorance. This was all too much to sort out just now. I cast a final glance round and saw Margaret, a cool middle-aged woman who has a neat corner in the town's antiques arcade. I mouthed a request for a lift home. She nodded, smiling to her companion, a tall thin priestly-looking character I'd never seen before, and started to fight her way to the door. I gave the keys to Tinker.

'I don't feel so good, Tinker. Drive my crate back to the cottage, there's a pal.'

Outside, the night air was like a cold flannel on my face.

Margaret came limping out – some childhood injury that, curiously, makes her fortyish roundness more intriguing. She told me I was white as a sheet. In her motor I lay back and closed my eyes as we moved off and the pub noise receded.

'You look terrible, Lovejoy.'

'I've got a bad head.'

'I'll make you a hot drink.' She drove us out of the pub yard into the narrow lane between the hedgerows. 'Come back with me?'

'Yes, please,' I said, astonishing myself, but I couldn't face the Old Bill calling on everybody at all hours asking when we'd last seen Leckie.

'Good heavens!' Margaret cried suddenly. 'Whatever's Patrick doing?'

Patrick's paintings and early Victoriana. He was hanging from his car on the other side of the road, flashing his lights and waving his handbag at us to slow down. We could see him being all dramatic in our headlights. He'd seen us come out of the pub yard and stopped to shout across.

'Carry on, Margaret,' I said. She slowed and started to pull in, winding the window down.

'But Patrick wants to tell us something – '

'Carry on.'

'Oh.' She dithered and we jerked a bit, then picked up speed. 'What was all that about, Lovejoy? It might have been important.'

'It would only have been bad news,' I said, and closed my eyes again to shut the horrible world out. The more you remember the more you remember, especially about a bloke like Leckie. Ever noticed that?

3

That night was odd, really weird. Margaret made me up a bed in her other bedroom and produced some men's pyjamas. I've more sense than to ask. I hate bathing at night because I never sleep after, so I sat reading Keppel's voyages till Margaret came out all clean and brewed up for us both. She smiled and called me lazy. It's not true that I'm idle – only her coffee's a bit less lousy than mine. She made it plain that our past, er, friendship was not to be regarded as much of a precedent for tonight. We had some cheese on toast to fill odd corners.

'Are you in one of your moods?' she asked me.

19

'No, love. Tired.'

The phone rang about midnight. Margaret went down to answer it and was kept talking there for a long time. I heard her come up the stairs eventually and heard my door go. I was still into Keppel and didn't look up.

'Lovejoy?' She was in the doorway.

'Mmmh?'

'There's some news,' she said carefully, standing there.

'Go to bed, love,' I told her. 'There's time in the morning.'

'You knew.'

'Good night, Margaret.'

You'll have gathered we antique dealers are a varied bunch. Most of that night I lay awake going over the auction in my mind. Leckie wasn't really a dedicated dealer, not half as good as Patrick, our world-famous pansy, or a tenth as lucky as Helen, or anything like as careful as Margaret. He never had the learning of Big Frank, nor Brad's dedication, Black Fergus's money-backers, or the inside knowledge of the Aldgate mob who are said to bribe half the barkers and auctioneers in the known world. Just a dealer, reasonably good.

I stared at the ceiling, wondering a little about that curious expression. Reasonably good. Leckie is – all right, *was* – a reasonably good antique dealer. Funny, but I'd never thought how very odd it was until now. 'Reasonably good' in the antiques game means really pretty shrewd and very adaptable. Moderate antique dealers go to the wall in a millisec. Hopeless ones never even get off the ground. Now here was the odd thing: I couldn't for the life of me think of a single thing Leckie was *bad* at. How odd. He had even helped Bill and Jean Hassall, friends of mine who deal in furniture and historic maps, to decorate their new house down on the sea marshes at Peldon. Word went round it was a stylish job, though they seemed ordinary colours to me. He was good with engines, too. Thinking about it, with most mechanical gadgets. And his small garden actually grew things, vegetables and flowers and bushes that managed to keep their berries weeks after birds stripped mine clean. He was good at everything.

Dozing sounds easy till you're desperate to do a bit, then it's the hardest thing in the world. Half the trouble was that I was missing Lydia, my enthusiastic and bespectacled trainee. Prim as any nun, she'd finally moved into my thatched cottage for the best of all possible reasons. Like a fool I'd spent my last groat to send her on an antiques course in Chichester, still thirty days to go, so just when I needed her she was missing. See how unreliable women are? I suppose I ought really to have been longing for the wealthy Janie, but I've found that some women creep into your bones.

Funny how things go round and round. I slept fitfully until the sky turned palish. A car revved distantly. I got up and padded over to draw a curtain. Margaret lives in a flat right in the town centre. You could just see the shops. Yellow street lights were being doused in strings. A bobby stretched an extravagant yawn on the cobbled shopwalk below, probably thinking of a warm bed.

It was the hour when Chandler's private eyes light cigarettes, but I don't smoke. Just my luck. A clatter, suddenly muffled, told me Margaret was up and about. Val's face misted into my mind. Her and Leckie. Tinker said because I'd taken up with Janie that time. Dear God. If I'm good at antiques, how come I am so bad at everything else?

Margaret came in, smiling at my modesty as I hurtled back into bed. She left the light off.

'You've forgotten I'm part of your Dark Past, Lovejoy.'

'I've not,' I said. 'I remember you. Rapist.'

'Cheek.'

She put the tray on a chair and faced me from the bucket seat. Oho, I thought. Here it comes. Coffee and grill.

'Leckie's dead. Tinker phoned to tell you last night.'

'That's terrible,' I said, even-voiced, taking the cup carefully. Margaret goes mad if you spill things.

'A road accident.' Her eyes never left my face.

'Shame.'

'Will the police be round?' she asked, too casual.

'Late as ever, I suppose.' I can be as casual as her any day.

She rose and twitched the curtains back for more light. 'Are you in trouble, Lovejoy?'

That's all people ever say to me. I shrugged.

'How did you know?' she pressed.

'Who says I did?'

'Me.'

I slurped her gunge and collared all four biscuits to avoid her challenge.

'Do me a favour, Margaret,' I said. 'If Old Bill calls, act suprised.'

'How did it happen, Lovejoy?'

'When did Leckie leave the auction?' First things first.

'He was still there when I left.'

'Talking to anybody?'

'Loading his stuff, like always.'

I'd forgotten that. Leckie took his purchases with him after auctions, the big stuff strapped under plastic covers on his roof rack. But he hadn't put them in Val's cran, and he didn't have them when he'd crashed. The two tough nuts had gone off empty-

21

handed. So where had Leckie been, between leaving Medham and hitting the tree? Answer: where his escritoire, book and doctor's case now reposed. But where the hell was that? Val's was his only cran.

'Come back, Lovejoy.' Margaret adjusted the curtains and put the lights on.

'If you played your cards right,' I said fluttering my eyelids temptingly, 'you could have me. I'd not tell.'

'Cheek,' she said. 'Breakfast in twenty minutes.'

'Then drive me,' I called after her. She paused to ask where. 'Past a ditch I know,' I said.

Margaret went quiet at that, but finally said all right.

St Osyth village has pretentions to class, but its recent marriages of styles show, so to speak. Bungalows designed in 1930 council meetings, hopeless wartime forgetfulness in architecture and latish 'fifties concrete styles are jumbled about the feet of great Tudor houses and this ancient Priory, making a posh shambles. People go there for holidays, presumably under sentence. There are lovely walls, though, flint and mortar. I got Margaret to take me to Leckie's house. I knew where it was from dropping something off there for him once, but that was all. It's a windmill. It's not as daft as it sounds. It is set back from the road on an ancient mound, looking vaguely like a large dome-topped shed with a rectangular base and steps up to its one door. It only has two sails now, projecting at right angles to the main building. They never go round. Margaret tried dissuading me from going in but I wasn't having any.

'The police, Lovejoy,' she tried soulfully.

'You've missed the point, love,' I said unpleasantly. 'They're not here.'

I swarmed up the struts to the door, to save leaving any signs of me on the steps. Leckie's alarm's the same as mine. I unkeyed it easily and stepped inside the place. I waved Margaret up but she wouldn't come, which was a pity. Women have this instinctive ability to judge if anybody's been in lately, if anything's out of place. I'd have to manage on my own.

Apart from a small Continental clock with a rare platform escapement (you can still pick them up for less than a day's wages) there wasn't an antique in the place. And it hadn't been done over, either. Neat, fairly clean; signs that some resident obsessional woman came in to dissect the joint every morning. There was a note from a daily help explaining something complicated about the groceries and wanting a weighty decision on the fish delivery next Thursday. I read it for background, but got nowhere.

I must have been in there an hour. Margaret was on tenterhooks all this time, and hooted her horn several despairing times. Nothing. I re-set the alarm and swarmed my inelegant way down the windmill's running struts to ground level.

'Ta, doowerlink,' I told her. She was mad at me for taking the risk, but drove us back to the side road where I'd seen Leckie done in last night. We went in silence, me staring politely at the countryside and Margaret changing gears noisily to show me how mad she was at me.

There was no sign of Leckie's motor. One ugly set of tyre burns marked the camber. A horrible whitish scar showed vividly on the elm trunk. Two bobbies measured and mapped. I told Margaret to stop, and wound the window down. We were the only vehicle except for a police car blinking its blue light for nothing, as usual.

'Good morning,' I called, 'Can I help?'

'What are you doing here, Lovejoy?'

Oh hell. I'd not seen Maslow, lurking behind the car. Burly, aggressive, and being all geriatric macho with a pipe and overcoat.

'No, Maslow.' I stayed pleasant. 'Let's begin again. What are *you* doing here?'

'Leckie had an accident.' He peered in at Margaret and walked round to memorize her number. I seized my opportunity, quickly got out and went over to the ditch. A photographer clicked away in the undergrowth. I was beside him in a flash, trampling about among the white tapes laid carefully along the ditch bottom. He yelped and tried to push me off.

'Keep back there . . .' A bobby flapped his arms hopelessly.

I tut-tutted and trampled a bit more before climbing out. Maslow was glowering. He does it really well.

'You stupid burke, Lovejoy. We're photographing the footprints.'

'Where is Leckie?' I asked innocently.

'It was last night. Leckie's dead.' He paused, glanced shrewdly at the ditch. I saw it coming. 'Where were you — ?'

'Don't be daft, Maslow,' I said. 'You couldn't sound like a proper detective in a million years.' He's head of our local CID. 'I've alibis even — ' I smirked — 'even for breakfast.'

He glanced towards Margaret as she got out of the car.

'You aren't very surprised to hear the news.'

'I'm more than that. I'm astonished. Why is the head goon doing spadework for a routine crash?'

He smiled, bleak. Margaret had joined us nervously.

'I know you, Lovejoy, you bastard,' he said, all ice. 'You're always bother, and I don't like it, lad. I have more trouble with you than all the antique dealers in the kingdom. Tell me what you know.'

I thought a bit. 'No,' I answered calmly. He eyed me.

'Then you're in trouble, Lovejoy. And I'm nasty.'

'I know.' I paused. 'Oh. One thing, Maslow. You must make a real effort to find the baddies. Otherwise . . .'

'Yes, Lovejoy?' Quiet and dangerous. The constables were suddenly still, listening.

'Otherwise keep out of my frigging road,' I said over my shoulder. 'While I do it for you.'

'One day, lad, one day.'

'Don't fret,' I told Margaret loudly. 'He's all talk.' She made a shaky start, but that didn't stop me squeezing my eyes at Maslow in coy friendliness as we passed. He watched us go between the tyre marks.

'Why do you *do* it, Lovejoy?' Margaret was furious, slamming her gears. 'Why?'

'Shut it.' I watched the trees flit past. 'Leckie's not going to be shelved in some crummy office file and forgotten. The poor sod's taxes paid Maslow's wages. It's time Maslow earned some of it.'

'You frighten me.' She was quite pale.

'Then get out and let me drive.'

We coursed into town like tiffed lovers, lips squeezed and not speaking.

Margaret dropped me by the War Memorial. I'd seen Tinker as we passed, waiting outside the Sailor's Return on East Hill, twenty minutes before opening time. I wonder where he waits if it's raining.

'Wotcher, Lovejoy,' he croaked, a horrible lazaroid spectre so early. It looked touch and go whether he'd last out.

'Get my crate from the cottage, Tinker.'

'Bleeding hell. Right now?' He kicked the pub door in distress.

I relented. 'In half an hour, then. Look. Who told you?'

'About Leckie? Patrick. I phoned Margaret.' He was peeved I'd taken no notice.

'Where'll he be now?' Knowing this sort of thing's a barker's job. He rummaged around in his mind.

'Just left Lily's,' he decided finally. 'You'll catch him at St Nicholas.'

That was odd, but I know better than argue with Tinker's mental radar. I hesitated.

'Black Fergie,' I said. 'Suss him out, eh?'

'And that bird?' He was grinning all over. 'Her with the big knockers?'

24

'Charmingly put, Tinker. Her too.'

I left him thirsting and cut across by the remains of the Roman Wall. Pneumatic drills were going. Another car park, more progress. St Nicholas is a late-Saxon church, rescued from destruction by conversion into a museum. It specializes in farm crafts and rural occupations. I'd given it a set of three ladies' decorated clay pipes, seventeenth-century, to help get it started. I must have been off my rocker. They're worth a fortune now.

Patrick was there as Tinker said, arguing in the foyer and stamping his foot. I don't know how Tinker does it. I waited impatiently for Patrick's tantrum to subside. Lily was catching it good and proper for buying some old Indian playing-card counters of mother-of-pearl made for some officer in the days of the Raj.

'You won't be told,' Patrick was wailing. He spoiled the effect by seeing how dramatic he was being in his handbag mirror. 'I said don't pay more than sixty quid.'

'But, darling — '

'Don't.' He closed his eyes and reeled about a bit. Lily gasped and propped him up. 'I can't *bear* it.' They're partners. She's married to this engineer but loves only Patrick — and so does Patrick. I'd explain further but it's too complicated.

I lost patience with all this drama, partly because sixty quid for a complete vintage set of officers' 1878 counters is a gift.

'Look, girls,' I interrupted. 'About Leckie.'

Patrick recovered and shook Lily off.

'Lovejoy.' He glared and shook a finger. 'I've a good mind to smack your wrists. You and that cow Margaret *ignored* me last night. You — you barbarian.'

'Who told you about him?'

'You don't deserve to know,' he pouted. He's like this all the time. Lily thinks he's marvellous. Why women go about looking for a crucifix to carry heaven knows. Life's difficult enough.

'Speak up,' I said, not smiling. 'Or I'll be narked.'

He looked at me. 'Well. It was Bill, Bill Hassall.'

'Where?'

'Lovejoy,' Lily cut in. 'Patrick's emotionally disturbed about Leckie. Couldn't you leave it to some other time?'

'Where?' I said again.

'The King Hal at Medham. I went back for some stuff and popped in for drinkies.' He vapoured again, tottering on to Lily's arm. 'And you're a heartless beast, Lovejoy, so there.'

'Come on, darling. Rest.' Lily gave me a reproachful glance. I left them doing their thing, thinking, well, well. Bill.

Bill Hassall. Now, how did he come into it? He'd been at the auction too but I'd a vague idea he left early. His was the house I told you about that Leckie painted. I crossed to Woody's nosh bar for a cup of his outfall. Tinker would be bringing my zoomster in a few minutes. I decided I'd go to Peldon and maybe see if Leckie's colours had faded.

Tinker was in a flaming temper delivering my old wheezer opposite the post office. The pub had been without him a full half-hour. I gave him a quid. For once he didn't sprint off.

'Here, Lovejoy. Are we in trouble?' That old refrain.

'Not more than usual. Why?' He'd left the engine running so I wouldn't have to wind it up. Rust sprinkled the roadway from the vibrations.

'That bleeding grouser niggled me on Bercolta Road.' Grouser is dealers' slang for a policeman of nasty disposition. He meant Maslow. 'Stopped me and asked where you were last night.'

'*Bon* appetite,' I said, ferreting into the stream of eastbound cars. There was no sense in stopping to explain to Tinker.

Half a mile and I was past the turn-off and heading out into horrible open country where no antique shops exist. Most traffic swings due east there towards the Clacton coast. I settled down at a pacy 18 mph on the switchback rural road due south to Peldon marshes. Driving gives you a chance to think.

I'd been to yesterday's auction because of the Kashan carpets, a lovely pair. The auctioneer – dumber even than us antique dealers, which is mindboggling – had written them up as Isfahan. The luscious deep red gave the Kashans away, that and the fine knotting, the double borders, the lustrous feel. See the carpet-dealers in Persia price an antique carpet worth its weight in gold. They do it by a cigarette, counting the number of knots per single fag length. The more knots, the greater the price. Kashans will have two, maybe three times as many as Isfahans. And the coarser Isfahans are usually three times the size, often fifteen by twelve feet. These little darlings were six by four. Helen told me I stood no chance. I said who cares and I wasn't interested anyway. Seeing them go to a quiet Manchester dealer broke my heart. He paid a brave price, knowing how exquisite they were.

I swung past the football ground, tears in my eyes at the memory. Other than that the auction had been pretty uneventful. I'd seen Leckie win the escritoire, bidding against Helen, Jill, Patrick, Brad and a couple of others including Fergie. I'd gone out at that point to talk over an alleged Estonian parcel-gilt tankard by Dreyer, 1780 or so. It was a fair copy, modern of course. Nodge, a "thin" dealer from the antiques Arcade in town, had been trying to unload it for weeks. Thin means holding only low-grade antiques, mostly junk. That must have distracted me because I hadn't seen the rest of the auctioned items close to. I'd eventually got fed up and streaked off for some of Sue's special consolation. I hadn't even seen the things Leckie bought, though I'd heard Helen say she'd tried for all three.

The road to Peldon seems downhill, through woods and receding fields. After a dozen miles the sea glistens and the estuary's before you. Mersea Island's a mile off, with the Strood road straight as a die across sea marshes then climbing the island's dark green shore. It floods with each tide. When that happens you follow the marker posts, but it's safer to wait for low water. Peldon's the village this side.

Bill and Jean Hassall had married, to general astonishment, only a month before. They'd been lovers and antique-dealer partners for six years. Patrick shrilly called them obscene exhibitionists, then insisted on choosing Jean's wedding outfit. He drove us all crackers, phoning everybody at all hours asking if beige clashes with yellow, stuff like that. We'd all gone. A boring business, enlivened only by Big Frank trying to do a deal with the vicar for his sixteenth-century reredos.

Their bungalow stands back from the narrow rutted lane. Bill keeps geese and chickens. Jean does folksy handloom weaving, using invented patterns she says look Gothic. Bill's car was missing when I bowled up. He usually leaves it by the gate. Just my luck to find them out. Timothy sprinted up, barking furiously, then halted sheepishly when he recognized me. He rolled over on his back.

'Look,' I said as I passed, 'Let's come to some arrangement. You don't scratch my belly, and I'll not scratch yours. Okay?'

He followed me round the back, wagging happily. Why these animals are always so pleased at me I don't know. Jean was in, clacking away at her loom. I knocked on the open window.

'Is that supposed to be medieval?'

'Lovejoy.' Her eyes were wet. 'Did you – ?'

'I heard.'

'He decorated our bungalow,' she said, weeping steadily.

'Your woof's a mile out,' I couldn't resist telling her. 'Early English weaving's characterized by – '

She gave me a half-incredulous laugh and shook her head. 'Come in, Lovejoy. You're good for the soul.'

Timothy hurtled ahead of me into the little kitchen, obviously delighted at the digression.

'Bill's gone into town. Inspector Maslow phoned.' She mechanically started to fill a kettle.

'Did Leckie call here last night, Jean?'

She paused, looking tearfully at me. The kettle overflowed but she took no notice for a moment.

'No.' She suddenly became careful, slow in her actions. I watched, thinking, oho. The match, the stove, the coffee bit. 'How did you find out, Lovejoy?' she asked quietly.

I almost said find out what, but turned it into a shrug just in time. I stirred Timothy absently with my foot to gain a second. My mind blared *What the hell's going on around here?* Suddenly I felt completely out of touch with everything.

'Oh, just two and two,' I said casually.

'Do the rest know?'

'Well, no.' *Know what?*

'It was my fault, not Leckie's.' Jean stared out of the kitchen window, swirling a spoon round and round in the same cup, her eyes fixed on nowhere. 'Bill has no idea, Lovejoy. Please.'

I nodded, avoiding her by playing with Timothy. Now it was Jean and Leckie, as well as Leckie and Val. Gawd, I thought, Leckie put it about. Nearly as bad as me.

'We broke it off a dozen times,' she went on absently. 'I think Bill occasionally suspected. You know how Leckie was − self-sufficient, independent. He never really needed me, not really. I don't know why he bothered. Now this.' Jean wept steadily, stirring away.

I gave her a minute, then interrupted. 'The auction. You saw him at the auction?'

'Yes, but not like that.' She sniffed and dabbed her face. 'Only with the others. We left before him.'

'Why did Maslow phone you?'

'Our address was in Leckie's car.'

Which all seemed fair enough and quite tidy. Now, Bill Hassall's a cheerful pleasant sort of chap. He wasn't the sort to do Leckie in because of Leckie and Jean. At least, so I thought. Anyway, the point didn't arise because Bill hadn't known. Jean said so, and women are famous for being pretty shrewd about this sort of thing.

'Where did Leckie leave his stuff?'

She swung round, ready to accuse me of greed the same way Val had. Then she paused, tilted her head quizzically.

'You clever bastard, Lovejoy. You didn't know.' She examined me some more. 'So I gave myself away. Lovejoy, it − it *was* accidental?'

'What else?' I rolled Timothy about. He was in ecstasy. Dogs never seem to worry like us.

'Leckie takes − took his stuff with him. Isn't it to some place in town?'

The problem seemed clear, yet more obscure. Leckie had loaded his items from yesterday's auction. They'd now vanished. Then Leckie got done, with precision, by two hard lads who'd searched his car and found nothing. Apparently he'd been late leaving Medham.

I decided not to wait for Bill. There was an antiques fair at the King George in town. Everybody would be there sussing out the exhibits, and so would I. Timothy accompanied me reproachfully to my crate. Jean waved me off from her window. I heard the clack-clack of her handloom begin. Some consolation.

As I pulled away I had a sudden curious thought. Forget for a moment the problem of where Leckie had *been*. The mystery then changed into: Where was Leckie *going*? That narrow lane where Sue and I snog leads hardly anywhere, maybe a farm or two. In fact, it's one of these purposeless loop roads the ancient Britons were expert at creating, which is why I invariably choose it for seeing Sue and other birds.

I swung left on to the town road, the estuary behind me, now worried sick. Did Leckie know where I'd be snogging busily in the rain last night? Maybe he did, and came haring that way because the hard lads were after him.

I felt ill. If so, Leckie had been racing to find me. For help. And I'd sat there safely out of the rain contentedly rutting and watching him get done. Not good enough, Lovejoy. Nil out of ten, and no star for effort.

'Do better next time.' I gave myself the stern order in the clattering car. Only there would be no next time for Leckie. I normally feel quite proud of myself, even if nothing happens to justify the feeling. This time I drove miserably on, feeling a louse, I tried eating my reserve pasty which I keep in a cardboard box under the seat, but threw most out of the window. I felt I didn't deserve it.

4

Tinker was in the sixth pub I tried. By then I was hot and irritable. He was surrounded by a clique of mournful barkers each sourly trying to avoid buying the next round and whining in unison about the lack of antiques. Finding them's supposed to be their job. They live on commission, which ranges from a single pint to ten per cent of the purchase price. Tinker, the filthy old devil, was swilling and whining with the rest but I knew his instinct was still there, his brain still tuned for the slightest stray hint of an antique. I'd been screaming for a Regency model of any local East Anglian church, but he'd not come up with one. And I had a beautiful delicious buyer – actually an irascible retired colonel, but you know what I mean. These models are often done in real stone, complete with gargoyles and real stained glass, real slate and real lead. And when I say 'often' you'll realize by now that term's relative. Cost? Oh, nowadays you'd have to sell your house and car to bid for a good one. Points to look for: named modellists (especially those who *dated* their creations); named churches; whether the model is of a church now destroyed and (last but certainly not least) the model's provenance – that is, who's had it all this time. Remember you're not looking for something tiny – one will cover the average coffee table, doll's house scale. Exquisite things.

'Tinker. Your wally's in,' somebody called, meaning me. A wally is a barker's dealer. I'm good to Tinker. I'm always a mile behind with my payment but I never default. Other dealers 'slice' their barkers' commissions all the time. That's why I'm poor and other dealers aren't. Honesty's a real drag.

I gave Tinker the bent eye and he carried his pint over.

'Just having me dinner, Lovejoy. No dinkie yet.' For dinkie read antique and authentic scale model.

'Sod it. Sit down.' Normally I'd have gone over and joined them. I made sure nobody could overhear. 'Concentrate. About Leckie, women, and me.'

'Eh?'

'Did Leckie know about Sue?'

Tinker's stubby face opened in a cadaverous toothy grin. 'One day you'll catch it, Lovejoy. Everybody knows you're a randy swine.' I held my breath as his cackle wafted over me in a foetid alcoholic spray. 'Sure he did.'

'Did he know *where*?'

'Not from me, Lovejoy.' He began to get my drift and became wary. 'But they call it your loop. That by-road you park in.' This seemed suddenly hilarious to him and he couldn't resist falling about some more. 'Lovejoy's loop. Leap's more like it, eh?'

'Very witty, Tinker,' I gave back gravely. 'So Leckie knew where Sue and I go?'

He sank back into his whining position. 'I told nobody, Lovejoy. Honest. It weren't me.'

'Calm down,' I said testily. 'I've a job for you – find Leckie's stuff.'

He stared puzzled. 'It's all at Val's. I shifted your stuff. His is – '

'No, lad.' I let the fact sink in. His face unscrewed suddenly.

'Hey! You're right! From the auction – '

'Shut up, you burke,' I hissed, throttling him with a hand. He wheezed as I let go. The barkers were listening hard, pretending to chat still; they go all casual, the only time in their lives they seem off-hand.

'His Medham pickings,' Tinker whispered, as if he'd thought of them and not me. 'They weren't in Val's cellar. Where are they, Lovejoy?'

I gave him a sour grin. 'Off you go.' I could see the penny drop.

'Oh. How soon, Lovejoy? Next week?' he asked hopefully. My smile dimmed his expression.

'By tonight, Tinker. Come to the cottage. No phoning.'

'Lovejoy.' He flicked the quid I gave him out of sight like a frog does a gnat. 'Why's Maslow sniffing about?'

'We tell him nowt,' I said curtly.

'And Val's all burned up about you,' he warned.

I shrugged and left Tinker to saunter back to his cronies while I set out to walk over to the King George by the cattle market. That didn't mean Tinker was being idle. If anything could be sniffed out between now and midnight about Leckie's secret cran Tinker would find it. More important still, he'd make it seem he wasn't actually looking for anything in particular. That was vital. I didn't want those two heavies coming after me, but I badly needed to find Leckie's stuff before they got their hands on it. After all, you don't go killing somebody for *cheap* antiques, do you? Only for valuable, pricey items. And things hadn't been going too well for me lately. I was uncomfortably near the bread-line. I was mad at myself for having missed spotting the stuff he'd bought. In fact, I couldn't quite understand it because I'm what's known in antiques as a 'divvie'. Put me near a genuine antique and I gong like a fire bell. And the more brilliant the antique, the more I gong. Sometimes I can't hear people speaking for the beautiful clanging of my hidden bell. So I was shaken by all this in more ways than one. If there had been anything at all at Medham yesterday I ought to have sussed it out just by standing there looking daft. As it was I'd only felt a few minor chimes. Leckie couldn't have got blotted for mere junk, could he? Vaguely possible, but a hell of a mistake for somebody to make. I could hear street music up ahead, and went between the narrow gabled houses towards the sound.

The other thing which intrigued me was that the two heavies had not even glanced about in the lane, nor shone a light. Therefore they didn't know it was Lovejoy's famous loop. But Tinker said all our local dealers *did* know, which suggested that the pair weren't locals. Anyhow, I hadn't recognized them. Nor would I, in the dark. They had lacked the feel of familiar figures, which was good enough for me, but I was sure they were men. Could Fergus have been one?

Our brass band was playing tipsily in the old coachyard of the King George as I walked in. People milled about. I like Sunday antique fairs because only the nicest kinds of people are about. The cold thought clanged somewhat as I went in through the arid saloon bar – only the nicest kinds of people plus two. And if Tinker managed to find Leckie's escritoire, old leather bag and book, those two horrible purposeful killers would come knocking on my door, sure as God built trees.

I waved to a few other dealers, beaming like an ape. There's nothing so unprofitable as gloom in our game. Margaret was there, inevitably at the porcelains. She was wearing a new green dress, simple and fetching. That's why I like older women. They never make mistakes the way younger ones do. She beckoned me across. I pushed into the smoke, elbowing the noisy crowd and giving out big hellos everywhere.

'Brought your cheque-book, Lovejoy?' Sven cracked.

'Mine's empty. I fetched yours instead, Sven.'

A laugh all round. Margaret pointed with her eyes. One porcelain leapt into clear view and suddenly I could hardly breathe. Bustelli's porcelains are always on too shallow a base which is uninterestingly level. His cavaliers and ladies, though, are superb. He modelled them mostly from the Italian stage, gestures and all. After he died in 1763 – he barely reached middle age – the Nymphenburg factory in Bavaria was never the same. The most valuable of his porcelains is the Coffee-Drinkers, a Turkish chap swigging with his bird, all rococo. And this was such a piece, genuine, by the master. I could feel the blood drain from my face.

'No,' I said, pretending away. It took all my strength. 'Did you think it was Bustelli?' I chuckled a shrill badly-acted chuckle at her folly.

'Well . . .' Margaret hesitated, knowing me.

The thirty or so stalls were set out around the rectangular dance hall, mostly draped trestle tables pushed as far back as they would go. It costs a few quid to rent one for the day. An antiques fair usually brings more dealers than collectors. Today we were here in force. This particular stall was a real miscellany of stuff; Victorian fob-watches, spoons, playing-cards, old embroidery samplers and pottery. And in the middle this luscious piece of Bustelli. You never see his Coffee-Drinkers without their background of delicate scroll-work, invariably beautifully done. It was Nodge's stall, the 'thin' dealer I mentioned.

'Thought you had me there, Nodge?' I said affably, putting it down. I didn't even shake. He looked at me.

'It's Bustelli,' he said doggedly.

'Not even Nymphenburg, lad.'

'Get knotted, Lovejoy.'

'Charming.' I made to turn away, desperately thinking of something to say to keep the chat going, paused. 'Oh. That other copy – parcel – gilt thing. You get rid of it?'

'Which?' He looked suddenly shifty.

'You showed me it. Medham. The auction.' I grinned, my antennae still fixed on the Bustelli porcelain.

'Did I?' He glanced uneasily about the room.

'Not like you to forget, Nodge,' I joked. In fact it's not like any dealer to forget. I gave Margaret that look which meant we'd split the price and profit and she picked the Bustelli up casually.

'Oh, er, yes. I sold it,' Nodge said.

'What's the asking price?' Margaret began the deal.

'Take my tip, love,' I told her, moving off. 'Save your gelt. I could make you six copies by tea-time.'

'But I like it,' Margaret said, on cue.

'Women,' I gave back, shaking my head, and nodded a farewell to Nodge. 'Good luck with your crockery, Nodge.' He said nothing, just watched me go.

I drifted about, wondering. During the next few minutes I occasionaly glanced casually back at Nodge, to catch his eyes just averting by a millisec. He was definitely uneasy at seeing me. And reminding him of the Medham auction had made him worse. I was suddenly irritable. No antique dealer ever forgets a deal, for heaven's sake. Not ever. And here was Nodge trying to avoid any mention of that Medham auction. Why?'

'Lovejoy.' Helen appeared at my elbow. 'Coins, now?'

'Er, no.'

'They're going up. So they say.' Her joke.

'I wish they'd take me along with them.' I'd been staring at a tray of coins belonging to Chris, a hopeful Saxmundham dealer.

'I've hammered silvers, Lovejoy,' he said.

'You're too dear, Chris.'

I was ready to begin a brief enjoyable heckle, to take my mind off worrying, when Helen said the words which changed everything and caused people to start dying all over the bloody place. And none of it was my fault, honest. Not any part of it. I'll swear to that. Hand on my heart, if ever I find it.

'Lovejoy,' Helen said in my ear.

'Your Norman mints are cheaper in London,' I was saying cheerfully, hoping to nark Chris.

'Lovejoy. I've a message.' Helen

'Mine are finer,' Chris shot back, successfully narked, to my delight.

'*Lovejoy.*' Helen pulled me away in inch. 'I said I've a message for you.'

I let Chris off the hook a second, still smiling. 'Who from, love?'

Helen put her lovely mouth against my ear to whisper. 'From Leckie,' she said.

'Who?' My face tightened. I felt my scalp prickle and could swear the room turned full circle.

'I tried to give it to you last night.'

Cain Cooper saw us talking and deliberately barged us apart, his idea of fun. He's a big puppy, all action and no sense.

'Stop that, you two,' he yelled. General laughter, with people looking our way and nudging and grinning. 'Lovejoy's at it again, folks.'

I managed a grin, with some effort. I was damned near fainting.

'Don't mind Cain,' I told Helen loudly. 'It's time for his tablet.' More laughs as I pulled Helen aside. Nobody more casual than Lovejoy, as Cain returned to his collection of paintings – some even genuine – and we drifted over to see Alfred Duggins, commercial as ever under his bowler.

'I've some good prints, Lovejoy.'

'Lend me one, then, Alf.' Keeping up the wisecracks was giving me a headache. The room seemed suddenly unbearable, stifling. A message from Leckie, when Leckie's dead?

'Let's get out of here, Helen.'

'I tried to phone you all evening.'

'I'd gone to earth.'

Jill bore down on us with her poodle outstretched like a figure-head. It licked me while she tried to interest me in some loose portabilia.

'See you in the bar in ten minutes,' I lied, shamming interest in the set of household gadgetry. Women used to carry them around the house in a small handbag.

'Lovejoy, you're an angel,' she carolled. 'Take good care of him, Helen. Come along, Charles.'

Charles looked knackered. He's one of the vannies. He trailed her back into the smoky oblivion while Helen and I slipped out. Jean Plunkett was still being propositioned by Big Frank from Suffolk in the foyer. We passed them just as Black Fergus arrived, complete with the luscious bird, with a thin cadaverous bloke in tow, incongruous in a bright check suit. I'd seen him before somewhere. Helen and I got out of their way by stepping aside to examine the books. They always set up a bookstall in the downstairs lobby, new collectors' publications and suchlike. Fergus passed us like a carnival and added to the hullabaloo inside. The blonde woman now had an elderly Wedgwood cameo, her scarab

34

earrings presumably back in the family vault. Her eyes had flicked at me, again with that same startled air, before she gave Helen a cool once-over, the typical critical hatred of any two women passing each other. Women don't like other women. Ever noticed that? When we got outside Helen still had her lips thinned out, recovering from having given the blonde tit for tat.

We crossed the road, dicing with death among the traffic. I bought two ice-creams at the entrance to Castle Park, Helen laughing and shaking her head. 'You're like a big kid.'

'Here.' I collared a spot on the low wall near the rose-garden. People were milling here and there.

'This is hardly my scene, Lovejoy.' She examined the wall distastefully. I can't see what's wrong with sitting on a wall.

'Don't muck about, love.' Women get me down when they go all frosty. 'The message.'

'Couldn't we go into the Volunteer?' There was a bonny breeze blowing, which always makes a woman think of firesides.

'The message.'

She sighed, nodding and perching reluctantly on the wall beside me.

'He gave it me just as I left the sally.' Dealers' slang for auction.

'What did he say?'

' "Give it Lovejoy," he told me. "Nobody else, Helen." It's written down.' She rummaged in her handbag while I held both ice-creams. 'Here.'

An envelope, and the words, 'In case' written on in pencil. I felt sick because I'd seen the words before and in the same handwriting.

'Was he okay?'

'A bit preoccupied.' She put her hand on my arm. 'I'm sorry. You look so shocked. But I did try to get you all last night, and I told Tinker – '

'It's all right.' I remembered now. Tinker had said Helen wanted a word with me in the White Hart. But that was before they'd known Leckie was dead.

'Aren't you going to read it?'

'Not yet.'

I made Helen describe what happened at Medham. She'd been among the last to leave Virgil's auction warehouse, hoping to do a cash-adjusted swap with Cain Cooper. He'd got a Pembroke table and she had a Regency snuffbox. It came to nothing. Cain roared off in his Aston-Martin while Helen settled up for the two little Georgian watercolours she'd bid for. Leckie had come over and given her the letter.

'Did you see Leckie leave?'

35

'No. He just stopped to have a word with the whizzers.' They are the lumber men who set out the items for auction.

'Here. You Lovejoy?' This lad was leaning on the wall, his eyes all over Helen's legs. He wore the clobber of the modern trainee psychopath – studded leather, wedge-heeled boots and a faint sneer between pimples.

I gave him the bent eye. 'Yes.'

'What a crummy name.' He snickered. Two of his mates snickered behind him. I looked them all up and down.

'Your gear's out of date, lads.' I watched the consternation show for a second before he turned sulky and cut his losses.

'Clever, clever. Val says call.' They melted among the people going into the Park gates. Helen gazed at me.

'Word is, Val banished Lovejoy from her cran,' she murmured. Despite my worries I couldn't take my eyes off her tongue as it took the ice-cream in lick by lick.

'Word's right.' So now what makes Val change her mind, I wondered.

'I'm dying to know what's going on, Lovejoy.'

'Me too, love.' I gave her a peck on the cheek and dropped down. She moaned away about gallantry, reminding me to come back and lift her down. I wasted more time waiting while she brushed imaginary contamination from her skirt, though Helen even looks good doing that.

'Here, love,' I said. 'Got any change? I could ring Val now.' There's a phone booth near the path to the High Street. She lent me some and I rushed off. I find borrowing's cheaper.

'Val? It's Lovejoy.' A pause at the other end. 'This lad – '

'I sent him.' She sounded world-weary. 'Young Henry from next door. He's a good boy. Going through one of these phases.'

'What is it, love?'

'Oh.' She summoned nerve and rushed the words out. 'Leckie's cousin Moll phoned. She's got a cupboard. Leckie dropped it off last night.'

Now Val can't tell an escritoire from a circus tent. They are all cupboards to her. I got her to tell me Moll's address. We then rang off, full of hesitations and politeness. It was Val's way of making up. I find that conversations with women are crammed full of significant pauses. It's a hell of a strain sometimes. I was shivering despite the watery sunshine, and the envelope in my pocket weighed a ton.

I sat in Woody's nosh bar, remembering.

The letter was brief, a few words on a crumpled invoice, the sort of paper that accumulates in pockets in spite of good intentions to clear it out. Leckie's hand had scrawled on it hastily:

Lovejoy, Take care. The side walls are even worse this
time, older but of course they couldn't be as deep. No
running, though. Keep faith, Leckie.

I struggled not to understand, but I knew right enough what he
was referring to. I sat staring sightlessly over my tea out at the
crowded pavements. The whole lot vanished. I was in a hot,
sweaty, hilly land and frightened out of my skin.

Leckie had been an explosives man in the army. Though I was a
gunner — so they told me — I was put on a job with him and four
other soldiers.

A railway ran perilously high across this plateau, over two
gorges, on spindly trellis bridges made of bamboo. Even to think
of it now gives me heartburn. We climbed on to the ridge among
the vegetation. It had taken us four days to reach. From there we
could see the first gorge and the rickety bridge swooping into the
tunnel opposite. We saw a hoop of distant light in the blackness
where the railway emerged from the hill on the far side. I'd never
been so scared in all my life, but Leckie just gave one glance at the
scene and stood up, not even using his field-glasses. 'Should be all
right, chaps,' he said, and strolled down.

That was Leckie all over. With my scalp prickling I stumbled after
him. The corporal carrying the radio transmitter was immediately
behind, the three yokels to the rear making more bloody racket
than a football match. At least I was always quiet in the jungle,
more from terror than training. I never did find out how Leckie's
sixth sense worked. Other times he'd give the same quick glance,
then signal for us to lay low. I'd never even see the sniper till our
riflemen got going. This time he was right again, of course. He
strolled across the creaking bridge into the tunnel, while I tried not
to look down at the river gorge a trillion miles below.

'We blow the tunnel, chaps,' Leckie informed us as if announcing a rather dull menu. We hadn't known till then.

This we tried to do, only the side walls had some concealed
internal buttresses made of concrete. We only saw them after our
first small explosive charge revealed them among the settling dust.
It was a clear mistake, probably unavoidable, but Leckie felt bad
about it, especially as he knew we were all petrified. The echoes
were still reverberating round the chasm, and the bridge behind us
was creaking like an old floorboard.

'Sorry about that, chaps.' Leckie was casual as ever, always
casual. 'It needs a second go.'

We looked at each other. Leckie was amused.

'My turn,' he said apologetically. 'Sorry, but I insist.'

It should have been me, but I could hardly stand upright from fright. I'd have run like hell except they'd have shot me for desertion.

That's when the tunnel began its noises. Our first explosion must have weakened the mountain's innards. Have you ever been *under* a mountain, especially one that has half a mind to crumple? It complains, whines, groans, even hums and hisses, full of noises. I'd heard one old geezer from our street talk about it when I was a kid. He'd got out of the Pretoria pit disaster as a young miner. Luckily his dad, also a miner, had told him how to listen to the rock on his first day and he'd made it back to the surface. 'The sound of the rock's breathing changed,' this geezer explained to me years later. I'd always thought him daft. Until our first explosion the tunnel had seemed empty, quiet. Now it crackled and twanged as the mountain above shifted uneasily. The lads began to back off, but Leckie only struck a match to light a cigarette. His sudden action made me jump a mile.

'Er, isn't it going to cave in, er, anyway?' I croaked, my voice an octave higher than normal.

'Possibly.' Leckie smiled. 'But possibly is also possibly not.'

We got his point. If the tunnel didn't crumple, a few of their side's diehards could clear the debris and shore it up in a few hours. Risky, but simple.

'What about blowing the bridge instead?' I suggested helpfully. Leckie laughed and wagged a finger.

'That's a different game, Lovejoy.' He was telling me our orders were the tunnel, so the tunnel it had to be.

He sent two of the lads, both riflemen, back to the ridge to hold it for us. The corporal was to wait just below them and to radio independently as soon as the tunnel blew. The spare rifleman was to stay on the safe end of the bridge, watching with Leckie's glasses, to report back should things go awry. I helped Leckie. He wouldn't let me come into the tunnel while he laid the charge up.

'Some other time, perhaps,' he joked, smiling. I'd tried to smile confidently back, but my teeth chattered and he finally had to untangle the wires for me. Thank Christ the other lads hadn't seen my hands shake.

By now the mountain was making incessant noises. It sounded like a distant orchestra tuning up. Cymbals crashed and instruments ravaged scales. Once the rock actually screamed, a real living scream which chilled my spine. Even Leckie looked down the tunnel as that terrible scream echoed and echoed. 'My word,' he murmured. 'Do you think it knows what we're up to?' I was pouring sweat. My fingers were too slippery to be any use. Leckie did it all, occasionally sussing out the surrounding hillsides with a rapid glance. As I scooped the instruments into my pack I dropped the pliers. They hurtled into the void below. For the life of me I couldn't take my horrified eyes off them — until Leckie pulled my arm and jerked me back.

'Off you go, Lovejoy,' he said amicably, as if nothing had happened. 'All set. Oh'. He pulled out a sealed envelope. 'Could you hold this for me?'

I stuffed it into my battledress.

'Er, am I not supposed to stay?' It took three swallows to get the words out. It's the hardest sentence I've ever said in my life.

'Not just now, Lovejoy.' He nodded towards the far side of the bridge. 'Scoot over there. We might need a third go and you'll have to do it.'

There'd be no chance of a third go. We both knew that. I nodded anyway and crossed over, drenched with sweat, trying to walk like Leckie, but all the wrong muscles kept going tight. The blast came as I crouched beside the bridge's five splayed holding struts where our first rifleman was lying beside a small overgrown outcrop of rock.

You could see nothing over there except dust. The narrow-gauge railway lines ran into a haze of suspended dust where the tunnel mouth had been. Leckie's end of the bridge was obscured by a brownish cloud. Rocks tumbled and crashed in the gorge below. The bridge was switching from side to side like a twitched rope under the impact of the blast. To my horror I found myself running and stumbling along between the iron rails across the bridge towards the tunnel, several times having to scramble upright from catching my boots on the sleepers. I must have had some daft idea about seeing what had happened to Leckie, maybe helping him back. Small rocks spattered about me as I ran. It couldn't have taken more than a few seconds. As I reached the cloud Leckie came hurtling out of the dust at me, choking and spluttering as he came. His white eyes peered from his blackened face.

'Get back, Lovejoy!' he yelled, floundering towards me. 'Get back. *The bridge is going!*'

I dithered for a split second, abruptly realized where I was and the lunatic thing I was doing, and tore back the way I had just come, wondering what the hell I was playing at. Leckie was on the safe mountainside nearly as quickly as I was.

'Come on, you two,' he said, waving us. 'Run.' The rifleman was off like a Derby starter, scrabbling up the hillside ahead of me. Leckie brought up the rear. We made the ridge, where the radio man waited with the other pair, having done his stuff. I halted and looked back then. The bridge hadn't gone after all but the tunnel was filled solid and part of the mountain face to one side of it had been stripped clean away in a miniature landslide.

'Settle down, chaps,' Leckie told us, hardly out of breath. 'Let's wait a bit and see what happens. Fag?' He offered them round, and we stretched out on the ridge, watching.

It was an hour later that the bridge wobbled and tottered finally into the gorge. It hit the bottom with hardly a sound. I went quietly off into the undergrowth and was spectacularly sick at the sense-less risk I'd taken, running back over the bridge just to get Leckie like that. Sometimes I think I'm off my stupid head.

It was on the trek back that Leckie reminded me. 'One thing, Lovejoy,' he said casually over his shoulder. 'Got that envelope?'

'Eh? Oh, here.' I found it and passed it forward. We were moving in single file.

'Good of you, Lovejoy. Coming back like that, I mean.' He gave me a grin, turning on the narrow track. I can see him now, doing it, as I write. 'Always good to meet a chap who'll keep faith.'

I mumbled something. We got to our base about eight o'clock one morning four days after, only Leckie always called time some-thing hundred hours. And Leckie never mentioned the tunnel or the envelope again. That was the last real soldiering I did, and if I have any say at all it's the last I'll ever do. The reason I've told you all this is that, as I'd passed Leckie his envelope back, I'd noticed the two words scribbled on the front of it. They were *In Case*, same as on the scribble Helen had given me.

I didn't need to be told in case of what.

'Lovejoy.' Tinker Dill was sitting opposite me, already half-way through a revolting mound of egg and chips. 'Why you saying nuffink?'

'Eh? Oh, wotcher, Tinker.' I put the note away. 'Sorry. Miles away.'

'Sauce.'

I passed him the sauce. He cascaded it over his grub. It's not a lovely sight. I wish he'd take his filthy mittens off while he eats. I'd wish the same about his tatty greatcoat and his greasy cap, but God knows what sights lurk underneath. He tore a chunk off a bread roll, one of Woody's special cobbles, and slopped it through his tea. A bit never made it. It plopped into the sauce, but Tinker just scooped it up with his stained fingers and rammed it into his mouth.

'I found out where Leckie's stuff is, Lovejoy,' he said.

'So have I.'

You can see the door of the King George from Woody's. I

40

watched idly through the window. Fergus, the blonde and their thin pal were emerging, chatting and obviously in a festive mood. He must have done a good deal. I guessed Cain Cooper's paintings.

'Here, Tinker. That thin bloke.'

'Him? Jake Pelman. Clacton. Silver and Continental porcelain.' He ate noisily on. 'Just gone partners with Nodge, word is.'

I'd not heard that before.

'Any reason?'

Tinker shrugged. 'Why not?' I realized that Pelman was the bloke I'd seen chatting to Margaret in the White Hart the night before.

A sudden thought struck me. 'One thing. How did you know Leckie left his stuff at his cousin Moll's?' I hadn't even known he'd got a cousin living locally.

He grinned, all brown crags and gaps. 'I didn't because it's not there.' He cackled away, nodding at this fresh evidence of my dependence on his ferreting skills. 'It's still at Medham.'

'*Eh?*' But Val said it was at this cousin's. What the hell?

'Medham.' He wiped his stubbly chin on his sleeve and belched. 'He never took it. Left at the sally. Virgil's.'

'But . . .'

Tinker eyed me pityingly. 'You're losing your touch, Lovejoy. Leckie got an old three-ply post-war piece. Gave that whizzer Wilkinson a quid for it, all of a sudden, and dashed off with it on his car. But the stuff he'd bid for in the auction's still there.'

I gaped. A decoy. Leckie knew they were waiting outside for him to leave. So he'd done the best his gentlemanly soul would allow – message to me via Helen, a decoy piece of grotty furniture strapped to his car to his cousin Moll's, and then coming to find me. Me. The one pal Leckie had who would keep faith and help a friend in need. Who had watched him get done.

'Thanks, Tinker,' I said as normally as I could.' 'You did well.'

'Keep your hair on, Lovejoy.'

He watched me go in silence. The trouble with people who are on your side is they always know what's best. They give me heartburn sometimes.

I slammed the door and took no notice when Woody bawled after me. He's always wanting to be paid.

I left town then, and drove to Moll's like a bat out of hell. Well, nearly twenty. But there was bile in my mouth and I've never had indigestion in my life.

5

I didn't know it then, but my peaceful days had ended. Looking for Leckie's stuff was, until I drove out of town on the coast road that Sunday, a sort of innocent instinct.

From then on it was war.

Moll turned out to be thirtyish, fair-haired, squeaky and excitable. Plump, as any man in his right mind likes them. The odd thing was that she wanted to draw me, draw as in sketch. She was a water-colour artist, amateur without aspirations. I realized I'd vaguely heard of her but never considered her real. It's like that with people you never expect to meet.

'And you're Lovejoy! I simply must take a sitting.'

'Er — ' I'd only said hello so far.

'Sit!' she commanded, pushing me on a chair and rushing about with a lamp standard.

'The cupboard . . .'

'You're exactly as I imagined! So positively . . . *lived in!*'

'Look, Moll — '

She shut me up and trotted about the room looking for shadows. It was definitely her room, flowery wallpaper and dazzling curtains, prettily decorative. In other circumstances I'd have reached for her. Paintings hung everywhere, crummy modern stuff. Sitting there like a nerk, I felt how modern her bungalow was. Not an antique in the whole place. Disgusting.

'Stay absolutely motionless!' she cried, tilting her head to see me sideways. 'How atrociously sensual! How excruciatingly, totally sensitively . . .malign!' I can never understand words artists use.

'I've come about Leckie's cupboard,' I said doggedly.

Her eyes instantly filled with tears. She flopped down on a sofa and wept, lamp flex trailing.

'Poor, poor Leckie. And he'd called only *minutes* before!' She pointed at the door. 'He put a cupboard in the garage — '

I was out of the back door and in the garage before the next breath. It stood there, ashamed and 1948 utility. Pathetic repro door handle, rusting screws. The inside was horrible and cheap.

'You're not even furniture,' I told it critically. 'Never mind antique.'

42

A voice said, 'No clues there, Lovejoy.'

I turned. What the hell was Maslow doing in Moll's garage? He'd wormed in behind me.

'Get lost, Maslow. You've no business here.'

'Oh, but he has,' this other geezer said. A taller version of Maslow, but smiley and brisk. He looked a good footballer.

I looked from him to Maslow, then back again. Hell-fire. Different faces, but very very similar. That's all I needed, Leckie's trail of clues obstructed by a family full of coppers.

'Are you Tom? Moll's husband?'

'That's me.'

'How do. I'm Lovejoy. I . . . I knew Leckie. I came to see his stuff.'

'Come inside.'

And Maslow even followed us in, greeting Moll casually and sitting down without being asked. Tom and him had a stronger resemblance indoors. Moll recovered fast with a flurry of greetings. She called Maslow Jim. My heart sank. Brothers.

'I've been on duty,' Tom explained to me. 'You're the friend I heard about.'

'He's the friend everybody's heard about.' Maslow grinned without humour. 'What you here for, Lovejoy?'

'I'm going to outline his face,' Moll put in eagerly.

'Leckie's cupboard,' I said. Coppers speak of being on duty. So Tom was not only Maslow's brother. He was in the peelers with him. Two coppers and a sketching wife. What a bloody family.

'Typical.' Maslow went colder still. 'Trying to make a bob or two, and Leckie not even stiff.'

I kept my temper. One day I'll rupture Maslow. He knows it, too. Still, it does no harm to mislead the Old Bill. On principle I let it go.

'Maybe,' I said, cool. Moll's eyes filled.

'And I thought you were Leckie's *friend*. How *could* you?'

'His sort's always the same, Moll.'

'If that's all Leckie brought . . .' I said, rising. It's times like this I wish I'd a hat to fumble with.

Nobody saw me off. I now knew why Maslow had gone to the loop road in person. Leckie was vaguely related through his brother's wife. Not that it made any difference to me, or to Leckie any more.

I took the south road into town. It was time I went home and did a few things. The Medham auction warehouse would be shut on Sundays, or I'd have gone straight over there and searched for the escritoire. It's a miracle I didn't run anybody over, weaving my preoccupied way through the strolling families on the riverside that links with the village road. All I could think of was Leckie, suddenly aware he was being watched in an emptying warehouse by the bad lads, and with no friends around save Helen, desperately passing her a note and then trying to reach me for help. He'd even tried leaving a dud cupboard at his cousin's as a decoy, probably hoping against hope that her stolid husband Tom the copper was home.

I slammed the gears up and down on the Bercolta road, making some afternoon drivers honk at me, but I didn't care. Leckie was too much of a gentleman to protect himself with women, say by cadging a lift with Helen or staying at Moll's. I'd have sheltered screaming behind the nearest woman quick as a flash. That was typical. Leckie couldn't be a mean bastard if he'd tried.

'But Lovejoy's one already,' I said aloud, full of resolve.

The shadows were already lengthening when my crate gasped clanking into my garden. Sue was in the cottage porch, posting me a message by the looks of things. I cut the engine and shrugged. My crusade would have to wait till tomorrow. I waved to Sue. We went towards one another, smiling. Anyway, I excused myself, Sunday's a day of rest for everybody, even the two killers.

Sometimes I just make one mistake after another.

I knew there was something wrong the minute I clattered into the warehouse yard the next day. Virgil's is one of these ancient auctioneers which litter East Anglia. As the rest of the world evolves, they stay immutable. They may behave all modern and efficient, even to the extent of having computers around the place, but in reality they are Queen Anne, and no nonsense about change.

For a start they have their own night guard. He hadn't done much good last night, judging from the sober faces of the four people standing near the double doors. Nodge was there, funnily enough. My crate fitted neatly between a furniture van and a police car. For the only time in recorded history the bobby wasn't Maslow. Wilkinson, the auctioneer's chief whizzer, gave me a wave. He's one of these long, loping men who can't stop their arms from dangling about. Tinker says whizzers have telescopic arms for taking bribes faster.

'Trouble, Wilkie?'

He came over, smoking a fag. His fingers are black from nicotine. 'Vandals done us over, Lovejoy.'

'Anybody hurt?' I couldn't avoid glancing over at Nodge. I knew what Wilkie was going to say.

'No. Old George didn't hear a sound.'

I thought, oh, didn't he, and crossed the yard to see the broken window, glass crunching underfoot. Whoever it was had split the double doors at the top of the loading ramp as well. All in all a neat crowbar job. Old George was giving his version of the raid to the young red-faced stammering copper, who looked fresh out of the egg. Nodge listened, shaking his head sadly at the deplorable sinfulness of mankind.

'Can I go in, Wilkie?'

He shrugged and glanced at the copper. By the time he had phrased the request I was inside. The warehouse is one large ground-floor rectangle of plank flooring. An auctioneer's stand is positioned against one long wall opposite the doors, and a curtained space shows burglars unerringly where to search for next week's accumulating stock of dubious antiques. I switched on the lights, because an auctioneer's natural preference, like Dracula's, is towards an all-concealing gloom. The light from the two bare bulbs just made it to the far corner, where an Edwardian copy of an escritoire had been split and practically shredded by aggressive but meticulous hands. I crossed over and sorted the bits. A real hatchet job, done in a hurry by people bent on plunder. The only recognizable piece was a Bramah lock still stuck to its wood.

'They came with the right tools,' Wilkie grumbled, which was just what I was thinking.

The quack's bag was a small elongated leather job, very like a bowling bag. Its contents were scattered and the base was slit lengthways.

'Don't touch. The Old Bill's going to look, just as soon as he's ready.'

I grinned at Wilkie's sarcasm. One way and another our local antique whizzers like Wilkie and his merry crew have pulled off more illicit deals than the rest of the world put together. They do it naturally, like breathing. I crouched down and began assembling the doctor's gruesome instruments.

'Here, Lovejoy – '

'Shut up.'

I replaced them in the bag. The clip had been broken, so it couldn't fasten. By the time I straightened up Wilkinson was on tenterhooks, but was wisely keeping watch on the uniformed lad. Nodge was hovering on the ramp and trying to peer in at us while the bobby scrawled away. A book, marked with a sticker to show the same lot number as the bag, lay underneath the pedals of a decaying piano. I scraped it out with my foot. The binding had been expertly split down the spine, whether from spite or as part of a search I couldn't be sure. A name was written on the flyleaf, Doctor Chase of Six Elm Green.

'Wilkie.' I gave him the bag and book, keeping my back to the daylight in case Nodge's bleary vision reached this far. 'Into my crate on the sly.'

'Here, Lovejoy,' he croaked, furtive eyes instantly on the doorway. 'I don't want no trouble – '

'Money,' I interrupted pleasantly, which shut him up. I find that word calms the most troubled seas. 'One other thing. Was anything nicked?'

'That Cruikshank picture.'

'Big deal.'

Some things you can be absolutely sure of in antiques. One is that minor artists will get copied and faked from now till Doomsday. Virgil's chief auctioneer Cecil Franklin had been exhibiting the Cruikshank picture for three weeks, boasting of its authenticity. It was allegedly a Georgian print done by Bob and George Cruikshank, showing two elegant blokes playing a prank on a night watchman in a London street. The faker had got their clothes wrong – the commonest mistake a forger ever makes in manufacturing this sort of print. The two characters were Tom and Jerry. Not the cartoon creatures, but the originals, Jerry Hawthorn and his cousin Corinthian Tom, who were pranksters widely publicized in Georgian London. Their favourite trick was creeping up on a dozing watchman 'Charley' and up-ending his sentry-box, laying face down so he couldn't get out, and then running like hell. A lovable pair.

'And give me the address of the vendor,' I added. 'Slip it in the book.'

'Watch out,' Wilkie hissed, sensing the policeman's approach. I broke away and went forward, smiling and full of those questions a perturbed member of the public naturally asks when confronting mayhem. Wilkie would get the stuff undetected into my car boot somehow. The fact that it's always locked would be a mere detail to an honest whizzer like him.

I didn't give Wilkie or the warehouse another glance while I asked the bobby and Old George more questions than they asked me. The young peeler finally drew breath and went into the warehouse to defend law and order now the crooks were miles off. Nodge, hands deep in his overcoat pockets, seemed anxious and morose, on the fringes of everything.

'Cheer up, Nodge,' I told him happily. 'You're in the clear.'

He gave a sickly grin. I had a sudden strange idea. Wherever I'd been lately I'd seen Nodge's apprehensive face. And he'd seemed so odd yesterday at the antiques fair. I glanced about. We were all alone in the yard. Old George's quavering lies were still audible from inside the warehouse.

'Look, Nodge.' I tried to keep it casual. 'What the frigging hell's going on?'

'Eh?' He shuffled nervously.

'And what are you doing here?'

'Just passing,' he muttered. 'No law against looking in, is there?'

'You look hunted, comrade. Where's the happy Nodge of yesteryear?'

'Nothing wrong with me, Lovejoy,' he said, still shifty.

'You've got my phone number.' I shrugged and went inside with him to tell the others good morning.

As I pulled out of the yard I saw another familiar face across the road among the early shoppers. Jake Pelman was standing in a butcher's shop opposite, hesitating between the veal and lamb counters while a couple of women offered advice. He swung away abruptly on seeing my crate, but not before I'd made sure it was him.

Medham village is quite big for East Anglia, three thousand people or so. Maybe it's even a town. There was a lucky phone box near the Yew Tree pub. I had to sort a few things out or I'd go bananas. To save my ulcer perforating from worry I phoned Margaret first.

'Lovejoy here, love.'

'Where've you been?' she sounded as though she'd just got up.

'Shush. You were talking to Jake Pelman that night in the pub. What about?'

'Well, honestly . . .'

'*What about?*'

'Don't be so rude, Lovejoy.' She unbent slowly. 'About Leckie. Jake was asking what sort of things Leckie collects.' We politely ignored the wrong tense. I thought, most dealers aren't collectors, otherwise they'd be collectors and not dealers. Right?

'And you replied . . .' I prompted, knowing Leckie didn't collect anything at all.

'Relics.' Margaret was all patience.

'*Eh?*'

'Relics. Church relics. Saints' bits and bobs.'

'Oh. Right then,' I said lamely. This was all news to me. Later on I was to wish I'd heard it earlier. And clearer.

'Can I be of any further assistance?' Margaret asked sweetly into the pause. 'Take a message to Sue? Tell Helen you're on your way, perhaps?'

'Er, no thanks. See you, love.'

'Well, really — '

Isn't indignation ridiculous?

I found another coin to ring Helen. She'd be into her second fag of the day. Monday morning's her nightie-and-coffee dreamtime among last week's antique-collecting journals. She answered on the third ring. This is the best luck I've ever had with a phone box, two successes one after the other.

'Lovejoy,' I told her.

'You all right, Lovejoy?'

'Look, Helen. The night Leckie got . . .'

'I remember.'

'You had this message.'

'I gave it you.'

'But you didn't give it me *then*,' I pressed. It was one of these details which were beginning to get on my nerves. Outside I saw Jake Pelman standing on the corner. The blighter must have followed. He was peering uncertainly towards my phone box. All this was making me irritable. What sort of nerk wears a green suit like that, for God's sake?' 'Why not, Helen?'

'I gave you the eye,' she complained. 'But you didn't come over.'

'But Leckie told you it was urgent. Why didn't you shout you had an urgent message from him for me?'

'How did I know you'd take off so suddenly with that old bitch?' She meant Margaret, women being like this about each other. 'Anyhow,' she said with finality, 'I couldn't. Not with Leckie's wife there.'

'*Who?*'

'Leckie's wife. With Fergus.'

We read the silence like mad for a minute.

'Leckie's ex-wife, then.' Another pause. 'Didn't you know? That showy blonde, wrong shoes and that ghastly handbag.' She mistook my stunned silence for an invitation to continue her invective. 'She's never had a proper hairstyle in the three years she's lived here. And her make-up's like a midden. I don't know why she bothers — '

Jake Pelman was still at the corner as I clattered past in my zoomster. He'd a parcel of some unspeakable meat under his arm, and was ever so casually inspecting an extinct bus timetable. I honked my horn. He started guiltily, but didn't look round, not even when I shouted, 'Wotcher, Jake!'

Near Medham there's one of King Cymbeline's earth-works, only we call him Cunobelin round here. It's an oval rampart about seven feet high, swelling from the ground of a small forest and curving for half a mile. Normally I'm not one for countryside and trees and bees and all that jazz. I like towns, where people and antiques are. For once I relaxed my rule, which is to get the hell out of the beautiful countryside and back into a smelly noisy town as quick as my beat-up asthmatic cylinders can haul me. This particular morning I parked among the roadside trees and struggled knee-deep in filthy leaves until I reached the crest of the overgrown earthworks. My head was splitting. Since when had Leckie a wife? And she was with Black Fergus and Jake Pelman that night in the pub. And . . . and . . .

I sat there in the silent forest in a patch of sunlight while birds and squirrels aped about like they do. Resting is hard work for a bloke like me, but gradually I calmed down. It was an hour before my headache went. I was no nearer making sense of any of it but at least I was able to drive home. I stopped at the station for a plastic pasty, and this time ate it all.

6

Next morning the cottage looked like a battlefield. Living as I do, occasionally without a woman's assistance, I can tolerate most shambles with good grace. It's only when such as Sue are too tired to go home that the fur flies in the dawn. Honestly, I just can't see the point of moving things to a fixed spot for the sake of mere tidiness. Things only wander about again. I find it more sensible just to stay vigilant, simply keep on the lookout for essentials like towels and the odd pan. In fact, I'd say neatness is a time-waster.

My cottage is a thatched reconstruction, the sort modern architects deplore as inefficient. The place is not very spacious. There's a little hall, a bathroom, and a living-room with a kitchen alcove the size of a bookcase. I kip on a folding divan. Sue says it looks suggestive, but she's only joking.

Today was my laundry day. Sheets, pyjamas, towels and shirts. I do socks and underpants in separate bits. They have to come round every day or you get uncontrollable mounds if they're left. I put some wood under the old copper boiler in the back garden and got it lit third go by a fluke. Luckily the cottage is set back from the country lane on its own, so there's nobody nearby to complain about the smoke. Filling it takes ten buckets. I usually feed the birds before breakfast, otherwise they come tapping on the windows and I get no peace. Today they got some of Sue's Battenberg cake. I'd been trying to get rid of it for days. Her marzipan's a foot thick. She has this thing about wholesome food.

That done, I scrambled two eggs and brewed up. On good days I sit outside, though the birds pester me and hedgehogs are always on the scrounge. Today it looked like rain. Anyway, I had several reasons for noshing indoors. They were laid on the carpet beside the doctor's bag.

Wilkie had got them into my car as I'd asked. I had some daft idea of leaving them a day or two to collect my thoughts, but I'm not strong on resolution. I'd stayed up half the night looking at this crummy book and the contents of the bag, and I was still no wiser.

The doctor's instruments turned my stomach over. Even clean and shiny they'd have been gruesome. Patchily rusted as they were now, I could hardly look. Some of the needles were five inches long. And they weren't your average darning needle for lovely innocent cotton. They were for people, and seemed to be triangular in section, with cutting edges along the length like those frightening short Land Pattern socket bayonets collectors are all after nowadays. Some were curved, others slender and tiny. The old quack also had a mask, rather like a fencer's, covered with gauze. For dropping ether anaesthetic, I guessed. I'd seen one of those before in the medical museum in Euston. A pair of curved forceps big enough to . . . I hate to think what they fitted round. Lancets, all shapes and sizes. And some scissors that curved and others that didn't. A stethoscope like an ear-trumpet. A group of lenses in a leather slot-box, with one spare lens coloured like you see in those children's kaleidoscopes. I tried fitting it into the slots with the others but there was no room for it, so I chucked it into the bag and forgot about it. With instruments like this bagful I'm glad the old doctor was on the side of health.

As I mopped my plate with some bread I read the card Wilkie had slipped in the bag. The same address as inside the doctor's bag. I knew the village, having been on the knocker round Six Elm Green during one of my bad spells. Old Dr Chase's ageing widow, I guessed, had put her late husband's effects up for sale to eke out the groats during her winter years. I'm naturally full of sympathy of these cunning old geezers but I'm usually poorer than they turn out to be.

The book was only twenty years old, privately printed for the author. It was that well-known world-shattering best-seller *Structural Design of Experimental Carriage-Ways in Nineteenth-Century Suffolk*, by none other than that famous quack Dr James Friese Chase, MD, whose medical bag I now possessed. I'd flipped through it last night, but decided I'd wait for the film. No hidden messages, no beautiful marginal notes by the author which might have increased its value, and no handwritten letters from Shakespeare skilfully concealed in the end papers.

I laid it aside and sorrowfully repacked the bag. Nothing. After all that, nothing. So Leckie had been killed for nothing. Some tearaways had believed Leckie had a real find, a priceless antique among the day's items bought at auction. They'd probably asked him to sell. He'd said no, sealing his doom, and for nothing. You can buy old medical instruments for practically a penny a ton. And a tatty copy of the world's worst-seller like Dr Chase's book is even more piteous.

Outside, the boiler was heating up well. A few more bits of wood and it was ready. I stuffed the washing in and swirled it round to get it properly wet. Sometimes I have to do without soap powder because it's so dear. I put the iron lid on with a clang and went in. It was coming on to rain. I sat on my stool inside the doorway listening to the raindrops hissing on the boiler's hot cover. I was supposed to be thinking, but all I could feel was relief. After all, if Leckie had no precious antiques it meant there could be no motive for murder, right? And no motive for killing Leckie meant that Leckie's loyal old pal Lovejoy couldn't possibly be blamed for just sitting doing his washing in his safe old garden when he should have been chasing after Leckie's murderers on his own. Right?

'Right,' I said fervently, congratulating myself.

The rest of the morning was great. I milled about, happily sussing out antiques, reading between bits of washing. I cleaned up the cottage in case Sue came later, and put my decrepit mac on to hang my washing out in the rain. I eyed the dark skies hopefully. If it rained all day the stuff wouldn't dry before tomorrow evening at the latest, with luck. A reprieve from ironing.

Things seemed to be looking up for Lovejoy Antiques, Inc. A reprieve from ironing, and now safely absolved from chasing after Leckie's killers, and therefore immune from risk. I whistled happily as I locked the cottage. I'd celebrate by having nosh in Woody's café, and persuade Erica to let me pay in promises.

My crate made it proudly into town with only one thrombosis, and that was on the railway slope, which I don't count. I parked boldly in the town solicitors' yard because it was pouring.

The antiques Arcade is a glass-roofed alley between two sets of rickety shops. One end is open to wind and weather. The other's full of Woody's obnoxious caff. There's a dozen leaning tables and scattered chairs. Woody spends his life cooking nosh and losing half-smoked fags in the grease. His idea of nourishment's to start off with carbohydrate and protein and simply add congealed fat.

I entered, coughing and spluttering at the first smoggy breath of airborne cholesterol, and signalling for tea. It's the only thing not fried. To my surprise Tinker Dill was absent. That's very odd because, had I been able to see through the solid air between me and Woody's wall clock, it would have confirmed that it wasn't yet

51

opening time for the nation's taverns.

'Over here, Lovejoy.'

'How do, Sven.' I crossed and sat opposite him.

A few other dealers were in, already stoking up for the day's knavery. I gave them my electioneering wave to indicate affluence and ease. Antique dealers can detect poverty in a colleague quick as light, and everybody knows how contagious poverty is.

'And a pasty, Woody,' I yelled, to show them all.

'I got a stool, Lovejoy.' Sven said, grinning. 'Been waiting for you.'

'Date?'

'About 1720, maybe earlier.'

'Great,' I said evenly. The chances of Sven actually flashing a genuine stool that age are remote. 'Sitting on it?' I joked.

He made my heart turn over by saying, 'Yes,' and pulled this stool out from under himself. Lucky I wasn't half-way through my pasty or I'd have choked. Eyes swivelled as the others gazed across like a suspicious herd at grass.

It had everything, a luscious stool weighing heavy in the hand. I stood it reverently on Woody's plastic table.

'Do you mind, Lovejoy?' The waitress stood tapping her foot. 'Take that dirty little stool off our table.'

I gave her one of my special stares and took the tea from her in case of war. 'Not be a minute, Erica.'

'It's an important deal,' Sven boasted to her, ever the born optimist.

'Money, Lovejoy.' Erica tried to keep her voice down, but Sam Denton and his partner Jean overheard and chuckled. I tried not to go red. 'Woody *says,*' Erica told me desperately.

'Okay, love.' I made a show of delving in my pocket. 'What price do you put on it, Sven?' That was a distraction. While everybody hung on Sven's lunatic guess I pressed Erica's hand, giving her a mute glance of appeal. She knew I was broke again, and gave me a tight-lipped glare, but you could tell she'd square it with Woody again somehow. She slammed the pasty down and stalked off. I thought of yelling to keep the change, but decided better of it, and concentrated on the stool.

An ancient stool's practically always worth its weight in gold. A chair isn't, because stools are much rarer. Oh, they weren't once, but whereas chairs tended to be carefully preserved stools were just chucked on the fire. People simply replaced them. It's a modern trick to take a genuine eighteenth-century chair and cut it down to make a stool. The trouble was that my bell was silent. My antennae didn't give a single quiver. If Sven's stool was original and genuine I'd have been ringing like a cathedral at Christmas.

As it was, not a single chime. My heart sank. I felt underneath the stool and bent to peer. Sure enough it was covered beneath with two layers of hessian, the old give-away. And Sven was still grinning like a fool.

'The original hessian, too,' he said, nodding. He's no idea.

'It's a fraud, Sven.' I avoided his eyes as I whispered the terrible news. All this truth hurt me more than him, but I knew how he'd feel. I ran my thumb along the little rails of the stool and felt the telltale Roman numeral incised under the bar. The stool had started life as V, fifth of a set of chairs. A cut-down.

'We could do a special price,' he offered eagerly.

'No, thanks.' I can make fakes myself, and cheaper than anybody else.

The door clanged open and in breezed — well, stumbled — Tinker Dill. He homed in on me and Sven and flopped down.

'We buying that, Lovejoy?' he rasped, coughing and wheezing, nodding at the stool.

'Not today, Tinker. Where've you been?'

'Doing as I was told,' he said with feeling. He slurped my tea and filched my pasty. He meant I'd told him to suss out Jake Pelman and Fergus. 'Your pal Maslow's out shopping. I had to come the back way to miss him, the bleeder.' I grinned at this, then had a sudden thought. Now I felt let off the hook I could go out and rile the Old Bill as any rightfully indignant citizen would.

'Back in a minute. Get some grub, Tinker. On the slate.'

I left Tinker and Sven and shot out of the Arcade. There he was, sour and useless as ever, talking to his brother Tom near the post office. People were hurrying along the crowded pavements in the rain. Moll was talking prettily under a coloured umbrella. Pity her bloke was huge, and a copper. I trotted over at the traffic lights, sure I'd surprise him.

'You're supposed to wait till the cars stop.' Maslow had been watching me out of the corner of his beady little eye.

'Morning.' I gave a hearty smile, because his sort likes us gloomy. 'How's the case?'

He actually blushed. I mean it. Honestly, he looked down at his feet and shifted his weight. I had a sudden funny feeling things were going to go wrong. Peelers don't blush easy.

'Er, the case?' He sounded hesitant.

'Yes. The c-a-s-e.' I waited a bit. Like a fool I was still beaming. 'Leckie. Remember?'

He faced me at last, after a quick glance at Tom. 'It's closed, Lovejoy. And before you start — '

I couldn't understand for a minute. You can't close a case without catching the baddie, can you? Everybody knows that, even goons like Maslow.

'Did you catch them, then?' I was asking, still thick, when Moll broke in.

'Oh, how *can* you?' She stamped her foot with a splash, glaring from Tom to Maslow. They hadn't told her.

'Road accident,' Maslow said doggedly. 'It's closed.'

'But he was murdered,' I said. It still wouldn't sink in.

Moll gasped at the word and rounded on them both.

'There! I knew something was wrong when he came — '

'A road accident's a road accident, Lovejoy,' Maslow pronounced. 'Unless you saw something or have firm evidence . . .'

We all stopped. People were staying close to the shop front for dryness. Cars swished by on wet tyres. I looked about, clearing my throat. I could hardly see for the red mist in my vision. How I didn't clock him one I'll never know. I took two goes to speak.

'You've given up? Is that it, Maslow?' I managed finally. 'You've done your very, very best for Leckie?'

'I don't want any lip from you — ' He began a lecture about public co-operation.

If I owned up to seeing the killing Sue would be roped in. And witnesses, even in dear old England, get crisped by tearaways who feel that evidence is often undesirable. So me and Sue would 'accidentally' get done, same as Leckie, soon as I opened my mouth.

'How does it feel to be utterly useless, Maslow?' I said the words politely because my face was tight and my voice shook. Tom looked uncomfortable. Moll was being furious with them both, but pretty women are handicapped in a way.

'One more word out of you . . ' Maslow threatened. I watched a cluster of kids clatter past into a toyshop. Their dad was laughing, trying to keep up and fold his umbrella at the same time. Some hopes.

'It's all right,' I said kindly. The words were out before I could control them. 'I'll do it, Maslow. You just go home and put your feet up. Watch telly football or something.' I leant towards him, my voice just about keeping going. 'I'll see the bastards off. You rest.' And I turned and left them there.

I don't remember much about the next hour, except that I splashed about the town pavements and got wetter still looking in shop windows. There seemed to be so many people about. I kept having to say sorry for bumping into folk going in and out of shop doorways. Once a couple of girls nearly put my eye out with the prongs of their bloody umbrella. They spent a whole giggly minute apologizing. I said I was fine, and we parted friends.

When I came to I was outside the Arcade again, standing at the same traffic lights in the pouring rain and just looking across at the stalls under the glass roof opposite. Twice cars stopped to wave me across, but I wouldn't move. I realized I was on a traffic island half-way across the main road. People were looking. Tinker was bawling at me from near the Arcade. I went over in case he'd accidentally left some of my grub.

'You'll get yourself bleeding run over,' he grumbled as I approached. 'Then what?'

'You'd work for Elsie.' I try to give as good as I get, but I was feeling really down. He cackled, and pushed ahead of me into Woody's. Elsie's rumoured to make most of her antique deals in bed.

'Seen Elsie's thighs?' he was chuckling as we crossed over to where Moll was sitting. 'One of those would drive me in like a tent peg.'

'Charmingly put,' I said, staring. *Moll?*

'At *last!*' she squeaked, rising. Her face was pink. She'd been braving Woody's tea. 'Lovejoy! You're *soaked!* Now just sit right down here and we'll get some lovely hot food – '

'Eh?'

She pulled me into a chair and rushed at the counter. I heard her prattling away to Woody saying not too well done and things women say like that about grub. Tinker shrugged, all bashful.

'We've been talking,' he said. I saw he'd taken one of his mittens off, revealing a row of blackened digits and filthy bitten nails. I've never seen him eat without this horrible woollen mitten before. This was obviously an occasion. 'Talking about what?' I was thinking how I'm always ten moves behind these days.

'You. She keeps on.'

'What have you been telling her?' I grabbed his evil throat.

'Nowt.' He rubbed his neck. 'Chance'd be a fine thing. She's a gabby cow.'

'*Now!*' Moll flounced back and settled her elbows on the table in a conspirator's attitude. She whispered, frowning, 'Is this gentleman to be trusted, Lovejoy? Implicitly?'

I looked about, but she meant Tinker, so I nodded. She squealed jubilantly and clapped her hands.

'Marvellous!' she cried. 'Then we are . . . Three Musketeers! Isn't this deliciously exciting?'

'Er . . . what, exactly?'

'Why!' She gave me a blinding smile. 'You setting out to do battle with Leckie's murd – '

I clapped my hand over her mouth, frantic.

'Here, Lovejoy.' Tinker had that shifty look about him. 'it's not

55

like last time, is it? I don't want any bother.'

'How despicable!' Moll wrenched herself free from my hand to turn on Tinker. 'And you with so many medals! All that brave war experience – '

I gave Tinker one of my sardonics. He had the gall to simper. This is what a pretty bird does for a bloke, saps strength and sense. Look at Samson. Then look at Tinker. I decided on the spot I'd have no allies.

'Shut it,' I hissed, head bent forward. We were like a Dickens tableau. All we needed were striped jerseys and a candle in a bottle and we could have played the Old Vic. 'I don't need help, Missus. And no more noisy chat, for Christ's sake.'

She wasn't at all abashed. Just smiled sweetly and waited for Erica to come. Chips, meat pies, beans, peas, gravy. Tea. Even rolls and margarine. Erica's foot started tapping as Tinker whaled straight into his plateful. Mine steamed reproachfully untouched. I shrugged to Erica. She shrugged coldly back. I get mercy when I'm on my own. With another and showier bird like Moll Maslow sitting opposite I'd get none. I felt the sweat prickle on my shoulders from embarrassment. The rest of the crowd watched, pleased.

'Oh,' Moll said innocently after about a year or so. 'How *foolish* of me. Of *course.*' Her blue eyes stayed on mine as she flicked her handbag and brought out a note. I sensed Tinker's eyes swivel in to the money as Erica took it and flounced off. Talk began again. Moll smiled and patted her hair absently, eyes still holding mine ever so casually. Hello, I thought warily, what have we here?

'Er, I'll owe it,' I said in a croak. The aroma of the nosh was driving me mad.

'No need, Lovejoy.' Moll reached over hesitantly and touched my hand. 'Partners don't owe, do they?'

'Partners?'

'Yes.' No hesitation now. If anything I was being ordered. 'Anyhow,' she continued, 'I don't expect it will be the first expense we shall incur. Do you?' There was a pause while Tinker sloshed and noshed.

'What about Tom?' First things first.

'Tom's just leaving on a course for two weeks.' She split my roll and stirred my tea. 'By then we'll have settled the entire affair. I have adequate funds.'

I tried to reason out a quick way of using her money to keep me going without having to take Leckie's killers on, but her eyes kept getting in the way of my thinking. Women take advantage of people

'Eat up, Lovejoy.' She did that mysterious bit with a powder compact and glanced across, smiling. 'We have so *much* to do, haven't we?'

I avoided Tinker's gaze and started on my grub, trying not to wolf it. Moll watched me, still smiling. Women like to see appetites, any sort. I have this theory that appetites are the cause of most troubles, especially mine.

7

Entering another person's house is probably quite enjoyable, as long as you're not an antique dealer. You can sit and chat, eye the bird and chat her up and see how cleverly she's arranged the dahlias. For me it's not that easy.

First of all there's suspicion. It strikes straight to your cerebrum: *antiques might be here!* And when coffee's up you find yourself crawling all over the crockery looking for Spode or Rockingham ware. You can't for the life of you focus on anything else. Then there's the skulduggery bit. As soon as she's gone for more milk you hurtle round the room fingering chairs and mauling the sideboard to see if it's vintage. I don't really mean to pry. It's just the way we are, because antiques are everything. It's no wonder I can sense an antique through a brick wall.

Moll turned out to be one of those women who never stops talking — well, almost never. All the way to her house she prattled. I didn't bother to listen to the actual words, just kept an earhole open for the sense. She drove like a scatterbrain, pointing out the sights and occasionally waggling the wheel experimentally for nothing, presumably just to test the universe hurtling erratically past on the other side of the car windows.

'Why do you drive in third gear all the time?' I'd had to ask.

She tutted furiously. 'I *have* to,' she complained. 'So I can hang my handbag on the lever. There's just *nowhere* else. These *designers!*'

Silly me.'

But we made it to her home. I could tell she was mentally gauging my face for a sketch while she rushed about brewing up and deciding where I was to sit. Round the room she had other people's art work, which pleased me, though it was all costly modern stuff and therefore of no possible account. Her furniture was flouncy and feminine, the sort you know has been chosen by a high-spirited woman who usually smiles and will always be one

57

jump ahead. Bright colours, lots of windows with pot plants that didn't look trapped. By the time she came in with tea I'd resignedly sussed out the furniture and paintings and was all attention while she poured. We sat opposite, across a modern Chinese rosewood low table like chess players at a match. When I was flat broke I'd cut one down and made a Pembroke table. Another dealer bought it. He advertized it as 'possibly eighteenth-century' and made a mint (which is quite legal because those words also mean 'possibly *not*'). I was innocent in those days. It makes you wonder whether innocence and poverty go together.

'Here you are, Lovejoy.' Moll was patiently holding a cup and saucer out.

'Sorry.'

Being in another bloke's chair makes for difficulty, especially if his wife's bonny and vivacious like Moll. When he's in the CID and she's bent on some daft Robin Hood type of crusade you can't help feeling even more uncomfortable. All along I'd felt this was not my scene.

'Look, Mrs Maslow —'

'You will call me Moll.'

'Moll.' I was a second too long. It sounded uncomfortably like an order again. 'I'm not sure what it is you think we decided, er, but . . .'

'Biscuit?' She was smiling.

'Er, thanks.' I cleared my throat and began again, careful as I could. 'Look. I can't afford to rub your old man up the wrong way, Moll. And your brother-in-law's, er, known for putting the elbow on us antique dealers . . .'

'Go on.'

Her gaze was disconcerting, but I found new resolve from somewhere. 'What I mean is,' I said, more uneasy with every word, 'maybe we should drop the whole thing.'

'What whole thing?' She'd stopped smiling and that exaggerated innocence was back. Talking to women's like watching a kaleidoscope and trying to guess the next pattern.

'Er, well. Looking for Leckie's . . . er . . .'

'I take it you want to welsh on our arrangement.' She rose and crossed to a bureau. I watched her uncertainly. The file she fetched had an awful official look about it.

'Well, yes.'

'Why, Lovejoy?' She lit a cigarette and crossed her legs, suddenly so much calmer and a great deal less innocent. 'Fear?'

I swallowed, nodded. 'Yes.'

'What exactly happened to Leckie?' For all her new assurance her eyes avoided mine.

'Dunno.'

She leaned forward for the ashtray, a modern greenish agate. 'Yes you do, Lovejoy.' She opened the file. 'This is the county CID file.'

'File? On . . .?' The bloody thing had my name on.

'You.' She nodded, flipping the leaves casually. 'Want to read, Lovejoy? But of course you'll know everything about yourself, won't you?'

'Most of that's – '

Moll closed it and interrupted my indignation skilfully. 'Concocted? Misreported? Biased?'

'Yes. Especially if Maslow's reports are in there.'

'The trouble is, Lovejoy, that it's *there*. Recorded. All about you.'

I rose, angry at letting myself get put on this way. 'That does it. I'm off.'

'Not for a moment, please.'

She sounded so bloody sure of herself I suddenly lost my wool and stood over her blazing. I always finish up doing what everybody else wants.

'Listen here, lady. I admit it – I saw Leckie killed. Two blokes in a black car deliberately crashed him up.'

'I knew it – '

'Shut your teeth and listen for once in your posh smarmy life.' I was shaking with rage. 'I can just see you now, that day. What sort of welcome did you give Leckie? Go on, admit it. You were *bored*. Your cousin turns up, first time for maybe months – '

'How dare you –' She struggled to rise, her face pale.

I clocked her one. She fell back, hand on her face. I knew she was thinking: This can't be happening. Men don't clout women of my class. It's not done.

'Listen, you smug bitch.' I realized I was wagging my finger at her and folded it away, embarrassed. 'Leckie came here, and I'll bet it was all you could do to give him the time of day. He called at an "inconvenient moment" – isn't that what your kind says when they mean piss off?'

'I'll report you to –'

'Did he ask to stay?'

'I'm not going to continue this discussion –'

I shook her wildly till her hands flopped and her teeth clicked. Hearing her neck-bones rattle fetched me to my senses. I dropped her, frightened I'd done damage, but still wild.

'*Did he?*'

She was a mess now. Tears poured down her face.

'Yes.' She sniffed and did those dry hiccups.

I looked about the room.

'Where did he sit?' Maybe he'd slipped a message into the upholstery.

She huddled in the corner of her sofa, sobbing and jerking. Her eyes didn't meet mine any more.

'He didn't.' She could hardly speak for weeping. 'Please don't. You're right. He knocked at the door. It was practically dark. He'd put his car near the garage. The engine was still running.' She found a hankie.

'I'm waiting,' I said, 'partner.'

'Please.' She was heartbroken, but I'd had enough of all this fencing crap and forced her chin out of her hands, to make her look at me. 'Please, Lovejoy. He – he just said, "Any chance of a sundowner, old girl?" I . . . I was in the middle of a sketch and said could we leave it till another time.'

I let her go, trying not to recoil.

'Please don't look like that, Lovejoy.'

'You didn't even *let him in?*' Dear God, I thought. Dear frigging God. I turned away from the bitch, sick to my soul. It's not just me. Or me and Maslow. It's all of us.

'I'd promised the sketch for the morning –'

'Of course,' I said with vicious politeness. I couldn't help myself. 'An important jumble sale, no doubt?'

'Church charities,' she answered mechanically. 'He never said. Just shrugged and said fine. I suggested he come round next week instead. He said fine again.' That was Leckie, politely saying 'fine' and 'not at all', when condemned to death. I'd have battered my way in screaming for help.

'Did you see – ?'

'Nothing else. No car lights. The lane's visible from the door.'

'And then you shut the door on him?'

She wept again, face in her hands.

'We never had much in common. Cousins aren't always close. I only thought it odd afterwards, coming over without giving me a ring first.'

'You waved him off?'

'No. I wanted – '

' – to finish your sketch,' I capped nastily. 'And now you want me to get rid of your guilt. Well, do your own dirty work.'

I went to the front door. It had stopped raining. You could see four other houses, the village green at the end of the lane, a church spire. Not a busy place, but not the back of beyond, either. I tried to work it out. Moll had shut the door on Leckie. He'd put the crummy bureau in Tom's garage, hoping the watching followers would be misled. Some chance.

Moll was behind me. I felt her arm touch my arm but stepped out on to the little garden. I'd had enough.

'Please, Lovejoy.' She followed me desperately to the lane. 'I know you'll try to catch them on your own. You'll need help. I have money –'

I pushed her back into her garden and shut the low gate on her, suddenly exhausted by all these bastards. Some days there are just too many know-alls.

'Keep it, lady. Keep everything. Just leave me alone.'

'I'll drive you home –'

'I want to walk, or there'll be a bus.'

'Lovejoy.' Her voice made me pause and turn. 'If you do catch them, be careful.'

'Catch?' I spat sour phlegm on to the unpaved lane's stones. 'You've read my file, love. Who said anything about catch?'

'But you can't – ' She hung over the gate, aghast.

'What do your menfolk do when they *catch?*' I grated on, irritated beyond endurance. Two neighbours were out in the next garden, obviously in case Moll needed rescuing from this wild-eyed visiting scruff. 'Two years with remission, isn't it? Colour telly, central heating, good grub, and books on the good old tax-payer?'

I gave a grin and stepped back to face her. She put a hand apprehensively to her face. One neighbour exclaimed, 'I *say!*' I waved nonchalantly and called, 'It's all right, Councillor,' without glancing his way.

'That's . . . anarchy, Lovejoy.' She could only muster a whisper.

'Anarchy's when the Old Bill can't make the rules work, love. You can't blame me.'

I was several yards away when I heard her say in a bewildered voice. 'But people aren't *allowed*, Lovejoy.' The eternal cry of the innocent and the dispossessed. I didn't bother to turn back.

The old neighbour was still bristling busily as I passed. He didn't raise his hat to me, but standards of behaviour are falling everywhere. I've noticed that.

8

Sometimes you wake up ready to conquer the universe. You know that rare feeling: everything seems sunny and easy; women are spectacular, available, and money comes in; genuine antiques glow everywhere you drop your eyes. Other days can appear perfect, yet you wake like a sick refugee. The morning after I'd blacked Moll's eye was one of these; exquisite sunshine with that cool deep crystalline air you only get in East Anglia. I should have been happy as a lark, but I was in a worse state than China.

All night long I'd had nightmares. You know, the sort you can't even bear to go over again even though you're safe noshing breakfast. I'd woken drenched in sweat, with my mind in turmoil. The cottage had seemed full of reproof — but what the hell had I done? An innocent snog — well, almost innocent — in a country lane even with another bloke's missus isn't a capital crime, now, is it? Yet that had accidentally started it all.

I banged and crashed about the place frying breakfast, making myself madder because I only had bread left and I hate fried bread on its own. The milkman had stopped coming before the Jubilee, so I have to use that powdery stuff when I can afford it. The birds were tapping on the window. I suppose it's my fault for trying to train them away from massacring worms.

'Fried bread, lads. Sorry.' I chucked them some pieces. My robin came and defecated unceremoniously on the sleeve of my tatty dressing-gown. Obviously a critic as well as a songster. I told it angrily, 'If snogging with a bloke's wife was the worst we ever got up to, the world wouldn't be in such a bloody mess.' I pushed it off and slammed back inside in a temper.

Before I was half-way through this young woman with horn-rimmed specs was knocking on the door. Some days it's nothing but people.

'Good morning!' She was past me before I realized, wrinkling her nose at the sordid scene. 'Oh! Still not fully prepared to leap piping into the world, and it's almost nine!' Roguish smiles in the early morning are poisonous.

'Don't misquote Blake to me,' I growled. She had a clip-board.

'We are here on a health visit,' she carolled briskly, making it sound like I'd won a prize.

'We bloody well aren't — '

'Our doctor has put us down for health training.' She checked her neffie list. 'Our name's Lovejoy, isn't it? Two sessions weekly.'

I hate officials. 'Tell Doc Lancaster to sod off.'

She went all hurt. 'He's very concerned at the lack of fitness in his patients in this village,' she informed me soulfully.

I snatched her clip-board and scanned the names furiously. I was listed. Doc wasn't. 'He smokes, and drinks like a fish,' I reminded her. 'Why isn't he down?'

'Doctor,' she informed me distantly, 'has *decided*.' Her aloof tone announced that he was somehow above all this mortality business.

If I hadn't been so tired I'd have just given her the sailor's elbow. As it was I made a fatal mistake, though looking back, how could I have avoided any of the consequences? My mistake was to argue. Never argue with a bird. You start out right and finish up wrong.

'I don't want two sessions of anything.'

She was horrified. 'But you can't refuse! You're part of the test group.'

'Can't I?' I was on the phone in a flash, bullying my way past Doc's snotty receptionist by the simple expedient of pretending I was dying. The specky bird tried verbal disuasion, but since when has that ever succeeded? Doc was his usual poisonous chuckly self.

'Lovejoy,' I snapped. 'This bird you sent. Get her off my back.' She tut-tutted angrily behind me.

Doc tried to sound professional, but I could tell he was falling about laughing on the other end. 'I've scored you as Unfit,' he chuckled. 'We need four hundred of you, and suddenly I'm one short. Don't let us down.'

'Two short,' I corrected icily. 'I'm the second that got away.'

He went all smooth. 'Can't Miss Haverill persuade you?' He was smiling. 'She managed to inveigle several recalcitrants in Chase's control group − '

'*Eh?*' Suddenly I was awake. *Chase?*

'We send her to, er, persuade our male patients − '

'*Whose* control group?'

'Dr Chase. My late partner.' He paused, puzzled. 'We worked this clinical trial out before he died. Miss Haverill's my co-ordinator, though she's based at Six Elm Green. Did you know him?'

'Er, no.' I paused, thinking fast. 'Er, well, Doc.' I cleared my throat, smooth and casual. 'I've reconsidered. Seeing you've explained what an, er, important, er . . .'

'Clinical trial,' he prompted.

'Er, clinical trial it actually *is* . . .'

'What changed your mind?' he was asking suspiciously when I hung up.

I turned back to ask it, full of dread and already knowing the answer. They'd had four hundred active men for their tests. Now Doc was suddenly one short. I cleared my throat, grinning nervously.

'So I'm a replacement for, er, for . . . ?'

'Poor Mr Leckworth,' she said sadly. 'Such a good friend of Dr Chase. A tragic accident. But driving these days . . .'

Leckie. I'd known it the instant Doc spoke.

'A *friend?*'

'Yes. Quite casual. Only because Mrs Leckworth was Doctor's receptionist for a while.' I got the feeling things were out of control again. Leckie. Leckie's blonde wife Doc Chase's receptionist. Chase's stuff in the auction. Her and Fergie's lot. Leckie dead, the antiques smashed up. And . . . and . . .

'It's my duty to the nation to stand in for him, I suppose,' I said bravely. 'I'll join your, er, group . . .'

Miss Haverill was looking sceptical. I swept a muddle from a chair and said to sit down. She did, gingerly, as if the place was contaminated.

'What an interesting piece of, er, medical, er − ' I began, smiling through my stubble and wishing I'd shaved. Events were ganging up on me.

'Did Doctor explain what you'll have to do?'

'Er, no.' I covered the ruin of my divan bed with the coverlet. It folds into a smaller thing and pushes back against the wall.

'Wait!' she cried. 'The bed isn't made!'

'Eh?' I'd gone back to my foul nosh when I realized she'd unfolded the bed again and was ripping the bedclothes off, the maniac. I shrugged and let her get on with it. Whatever turns people on, I always say.

'You really *must* be more hygienic, Lovejoy!'

'About these, er, sessions . . .?' The quicker I got to hear more about Doc Chase the quicker I'd learn if he'd had any antiques which could be mistaken for his grotty old bureau. After all, Leckie had died for it.

'Two miles and exercises.'

Two miles away, I thought, my mouth full of fried bread. Not far. I could manage that, but I didn't like the sound of those exercises.

'Have you running shoes?' She was really quite attractive without her clip-board. I watched her making the bed, full of thought.

'Er, no. I can do exercises without.' In my innocence I was trying to be helpful.

She smiled. 'You'll need some old shoes for running. The path to Friday Wood's absolutely awful − '

'*Running?*' Friday Wood's at least a mile away. I was gripped by a sudden overwhelming fear. One mile to the wood plus one mile back equals two. She couldn't mean *run* two miles, could she? The lunatic. I haven't run anywhere since I was courting. 'Er − '

'You'll *love* it!' She paused, glowing with crusading fervour. 'The invigorating dawn air! The crush of fallen leaves underfoot!

Think how you'll benefit, Lovejoy. Your muscles will ripple and tingle with health as you sprint through the forests at sunrise.' She plumped the cushions.

'Sounds great,' I said miserably. 'Er, if I have a bad leg can I get a doctor's certificate – ?'

Miss Haverill smiled a brilliant but knowing smile and wagged a finger. 'Doctor said you'd ask that, Lovejoy.'

I laughed merrily. 'Only my little joke,' I said, thinking, the cunning old swine. Well, if I was in I was in, but I deserved my pound of flesh. 'You work for Dr Chase, Elizabeth?' Her initial was on the clip-board.

She reddened slightly. 'Elspeth, actually.' She finished the bed and started mechanically on the rest of the room, folding things and making piles. I'd never find a bloody thing. It takes days to get back to normal after they tidy me up.

I got her reminiscing about her old boss. She told me how keen he'd been on physique assessments as parameters of health indices predictions, whatever that means. I told her that was really great. He'd hit on this maniacal scheme to compare his patients with his partner's after different sorts of exercises. I was now one of their statistics.

'Wasn't Doc Chase the doctor with that interesting hobby?' I asked casually, going to wash up. 'I heard about it.'

'Oh, his old history.' She smiled, coming over to help me at the sink. 'He was always pottering about the countryside measuring mounds and things.'

'I'm interested in history.' This is absolutely true. I am. History's where antiques come from.

'You'd have got on well with him. Here, let me.' She swapped us over, me drying instead of washing. I keep meaning to get one of those stick mops. Hot water burns my fingers. I don't know how women do it. They can even drink hot coffee straight down, thermodynamic throats or something.

'Didn't he write some book about the place by, er, over by . . .?'

'Scratton.' She nodded, smiling. 'I used to pull his leg, say to him why didn't he just read his own book to learn about that silly old tunnel!'

My hands froze. She laughed, then tutted as a plate crashed and broke.

'Oh! Mind the pieces, Lovejoy, you butterfingers!'

I tried to smile at all this drollery but my heart was in a vice. I'd felt my stomach turn over when she'd said tunnel. No wonder I'd been postponing thinking about Leckie's message. Not that a deep dark tunnel's anything to be scared of. I mean to say. And I'm really not frightened of a long tunnel with water trickling down the bricks and the mountain creaking and settling all around you. I'm not, honestly. But I felt a sudden unreasoning violent rage against Leckie. Why the hell couldn't he have just given the heavies what they wanted for Christ's sake, and saved me from being more and more terrified? Getting himself killed like that suddenly seemed the height of inconsideration.

'Tunnel?' I asked in a light croak. I tried to grin but my face wouldn't work. My forehead was cold and damp.

'He even went down into it, so they say.' She was glancing about for a dustpan. She'd be lucky. I've plenty of dust but no dustpan. 'Mind you don't cut yourself on the bits. You've nothing on your feet.'

'I don't suppose he ever found much treasure trove.' I went and got a broom while my heart hammered and my brow dripped. I felt I was back in a tunnel's mouth near a bamboo bridge over a gorge for an odd minute. It's funny how your mind works.

'Oh, he found some old railway things. Gave them to the Elm Trees.' That's a museum near the Three Cups pub in town. I hadn't been for over a year. 'Lovejoy. Are you all right?' She was looking at me.

'Fine, fine,' I said heartily, staring her straight in the eye and beaming.

'You're not diabetic?' she asked hopefully. 'I *did* interrupt your breakfast . . .'

'Not today, thanks,' I joked.

She left about tennish, not without incident. I went to the front door to see her off. Sue, an expression of pleased anticipation on her face, was on the doorstep just about to knock. Her car was on the gravel. A red Ford stood in the lane, probably Elspeth's.

'Ah,' I said swiftly. 'Er, hello, er, Mrs Vaughan.'

'Oh. Good morning.' Sue's quick at these situations, like all women. 'I called about that antique . . . watch.'

'Very well. I'll pack it for you.' Actually Sue wouldn't know a Tompion timepiece from a sundial. 'Would you mind waiting, please? I'm just seeing, er, Miss Haverill off. She's my health visitor. She called about my exercises . . .'

'Oh, really?' Sue asked sweetly. From the look on her face I'd gilded the gingerbread. There was that fractional pause while she and Elspeth decided on mutual hatred as today's best social policy. 'Did you perform to her satisfaction?'

Elspeth decided to cut out. 'I'll telephone about your programme, Lovejoy.'

'Er, great.'

'Not *too* strenuous, I hope?' Sue cooed innocently.

I grinned farewell as Elspeth swung down the path, then dragged Sue in and rammed my fist threateningly under her nose.

'Cut out the icicles, Sue, or I'll tan your bum.'

'Promises, promises! I might do it all the more.' She gave me a light kiss, smiling properly now, and walked ahead into the living-room. I trailed after her. I try, but I've never been much good at telling people off. Sue rounded on her heel, fingers suddenly drumming on elbows. 'How tidily you've made your bed!'

'Er, my health visitor . . .' I tried lamely.

'And breakfast cleared away, too!' she gritted. 'Isn't the Health Service considerate these days!'

'Shut it. Doc Lancaster sent her.'

'A likely tale – '

'I'm glad you called, love. I've been wanting to ask you about the other night.' I went and got my shaver while Sue started rearranging the room on principle. 'Those two people, one tall and the other short.'

She stilled. 'The ones who caused . . . the accident?'

'Yes. Could one have been a woman?'

She thought hard, then nodded.

'Sure?' I pressed.

'*Could* have been. I'm uncertain.'

The door banged again, making me jump a mile. From the side window I could see Moll's car blocking the gate. My cottage is like Piccadilly sometimes.

'It's Mrs Maslow,' I said. 'Copper's wife.'

'What a lot of visitors you . . . entertain these days.'

She was getting ready for war again, but I hoofed her out, ready again to pretend I was seeing a buyer off. Sue neatly scuppered that act.

'Good morning!' she chirped, stepping past Moll at the door. 'I'm Miss Haverill, Lovejoy's health visitor. I've been deciding which exercises he's best at. He's really very vigorous – '

'Thank you.' I pushed her out on to the gravel.

'I'll phone about your programme, Lovejoy,' Sue called over her shoulder. And she meant it. 'Good morning.'

'Great. Good morning.'

'Good morning,' Moll said, looking doubtfully from me to Sue and back again. She had sun-glasses on.

'Good morning.'

All these good mornings should have made me feel quite calm, but that's what they say before a duel, isn't it?

I sat on my unfinished wall, thinking. It doesn't separate any particular bit of garden from anything, just a wall. But my best guesses come when I'm sitting on it.

Moll had only stayed a couple of minutes. Behind her sunglasses she had a real shiner, left eye. There was a graze under the lower lid. I went red when I saw it, but from her attitude we might have been simply renewing an old friendship.

'Er, shall I brew up?' I felt I had to offer something. I didn't tell her it was either that or fried bread.

'No thanks, Lovejoy.'

I didn't care much for that quiet voice.

'Are you all right?'

'Yes, thank you.' She wouldn't sit down.

When you've blacked a bird's eye you can't look straight at them like you normally do. I mean head on with your gaze evenly distributed, so many watts per eye as it were. You find your stare somehow concentrates itself into the injured eye while your mind squirms and you wait for the lawyers' eerie politeness to come cascading through the letterbox.

'Er, I suppose you called the Old Bill?'

'No.' Still quiet.

'Phoned your Tom instead?'

'That neither.'

We watched each other in silence. Any woman can achieve a look. Moll was dressed for spring, small white gloves and everything different colours but matching. I wished now I'd not belted her one.

'A summons?' One of our local magistrates is a right cow. She's got it in for me, through no fault of mine.

'No.'

I thought a bit. 'Look, Moll. I've not a groat — '

She shook her head impatiently. 'I'm not here to take it out on you,' she said at last. 'You were quite right to — to be angry, Lovejoy.

'*Eh*?'

'I deserved it.' She gazed dispassionately round at the cottage's insides, taking in the general level of wealth. I waited uneasily for my sentence. Birds can be very odd, especially where blokes are concerned. 'Leckie should be alive today, Lovejoy. And it's my fault.'

She pulled out an envelope. It crackled slightly, a beautiful and melodious sound. I felt dizzy. I always do when money raises its exquisite head.

'For your expenses, Lovejoy.'

I couldn't take my eyes off it. 'Expenses?'

'Yes.' She dropped it on the table. She watched me and I watched the envelope. 'I've read your file — ' She stopped me with a gesture when I drew breath. 'Let me finish. You're a violent man. Some of the things — '

'Not my fault,' I got in quickly, hating all this. Women are easier when they're mad at you.

'Of course not.' Moll gave me that level agreement which means just the opposite. 'I know you'll try to kill them, Lovejoy. You'll do it for Leckie, for you, for all of us. I know it. Take the money. It'll help.'

'Rubbish,' I said cagily. 'Anyway, you're a cop's wife.'

'It's not a trick, Lovejoy.' She half-smiled as I backed off. 'Don't worry. I'm not going to weep all over you, though I suppose I ought to. I've been very stupid. Just take it. I realize now I was only wanting to play cops and robbers.'

'No.' Saying it took a bit of nerve and a lot of idiocy.

She waited, thinking. 'I expected that.'

She walked about, looking and occasionally touching what passes for furniture. I suddenly wished I hadn't had to sell my last good piece, a small mutton-fat finger jade, early Ch'ien Lung. It was the only thing I'd had in living memory worth looking at. She'd have been really impressed if I'd had that to show her. As it was my cottage looks like a doss-house.

'Lovejoy. You first come to my place looking for some precious antiques Leckie had just bought.'

'I got them, but they're duff.'

'Duff?'

'Wrong. Not worth anything. Maybe they're not even the ones he started out with.'

'Very well.' She walked past me to the front door, pausing to pat her hair at the mirror. 'Find them, then. Find the real ones. That money's the commission.'

'It can't be,' I explained. 'Commission's — '

'Don't be obtuse, Lovejoy.' She opened the door herself. For once there was no woman on the doorstep. 'Find the — the unduff antiques. I'll buy them, or it. Whichever it turns out to be.'

Unduff, for gawd's sake.

'But how can you buy them, if we don't know what it is?'

'I collect unidentified objects,' she said serenely. 'I've just begun, today. And I'm employing you. Get on with it.' She clicked down to where the gravel begins.

'What if it's too dear?' I called after her, wondering what was going on.

'I'll make the price up to you somehow,' she said over her shoulder but not looking.

And that was that. Her car weaved its way back to the main road in second gear, the blackthorn hedges scraping her paint all the way. I stood, listening. Sure enough, it changed up to third by the chapel. Satisfied she now had her handbag dangling correctly from the gear lever, I went in to go over the evidence. I decided to look up obtuse in the dictionary. I'd get mad with her again if it turned out to be an insult.

In the bath I did some thinking. Not really cerebral stuff, but feeling my way outwards into the bloody mix-up. I'd honestly tried to keep out of it, hadn't I? But Maslow was going to do sod all, and there wasn't anybody else but me to keep faith with fairness in this mad tangled world. I'd have to do it — yet where the hell do you start?

Leckie's lovely blonde missus kept forcing her way into my mind, but why? All these events were all somehow connected. And the connection was through Leckie, now deceased by violence. I splashed my toes against the taps, though it always makes a mess over the side. Sue does her nut and moans about having to mop the floor.

So Leckie and Doc Chase were friends. My mind went: first Doc Chase dies (but when and how? Maybe I ought to ask). Then some of his rubbishy odds and ends are disposed of in a tatty local auction, Virgil's dump in Medham. They're always scouring the villages for stuff to sell on commission, so no mystery there. Then Leckie bids and wins it. Maybe his blonde wife learned somehow from Leckie that Chase's effects contained something precious. She then disclosed it to, say, Black Fergus or Jake Pelman or the jittery Nodge — or all three? Maybe they then tried to 'chop' (this is dealers' slang: to share profit and risk) with Leckie, and he refused. They then decide on hard aggro. Leckie's killed. They realize the stuff's still at Virgil's. They go back during the night hours, tell old George to get lost and break in. They rummage about and whistle Chase's stuff up, but did they find whatever was precious hidden in it? If I'd guessed right they hadn't found a bloody thing, judging from Nodge's nervous face and Jake Pelman's clumsy shadowing — always assuming they were the baddies.

I sighed and stood up, dripping water. The best thing about having a bath is getting out of it, except when Sue's in it too. It seemed I couldn't escape from Leckie's last request no matter how hard I tried. There seemed nothing for it. I decided to start by breaking a couple of fingers, one on Nodge and then one on old George. I whistled absently as I dried, pleased now that matters were out of my hands.

Start as you mean to go on, I always say.

9

Nodge is one of those antique dealers who are called 'caley' men in
our part of this lunatic game. Somebody once told me it started out
as ceilidh, Celtic for dingdong, a spree. Nodge goes along for
months nervous as a trout, never buying without agonies of
indecision and worried about selling. Then he'll buy everything in
sight, good and bad, spending like a drunken sailor and plunging
into debt.

Once every six months he ends up with a ton of pseudo-antiques
nobody in his right mind would look at twice. It's all hit or miss.
You'd be surprised which world-famous collectors — I include
museums — are run on the caley principle. Why people go along
like this, hoping that ignorance might in fact actually turn out to be
bliss in the end, nobody knows.

It took me an hour to find Tinker. He was in our local bookie's
with his mate Lemuel (not 'Lem', except at your peril). Lemuel's
an asthmatic and grubby old soldier who breathes like my car. He
gambles his — and possibly others' — social security money as long
as it lasts, then cadges the rest of the week. Social workers are
good to him, though. They bought him a wheelchair last Lady
Day. He sold it after an instantaneous and miraculous recovery
from his limp. He wears an old forage cap without badges.

The bookie's was just crowding up before the afternoon races. I
caught them both there in the planning stage.

'Nodge?' Tinker thought a second. He always offers to roll me a
corrupt cigarette on one of those little pocket machines.

'He comes in here sometimes, Lovejoy,' Lemuel wheezed. He
took the first fag off Tinker's assembly line.

'Nodge isn't in town yet.' Tinker's verdict.

'How long will he be?' You can ask Tinker things like this. He
always knows.

'Not long. Ten minutes. In here.'

'I'll wait.'

They lit up, spluttering and wheezing on the ends of their
respective Tinker-made monstrosities. Tinker's fags are better-
looking after being smoked than when they start off. I watched,
marvelling. Never had so many lungs managed so little

While Tinker and Lemuel unerringly sussed out today's losers I gazed round at the maelstrom. Our town's gambling fraternity is an assorted bunch. I don't often come in except for the Derby and the Grand National, maybe the St Leger. There are housewives, layabouts, neatly dressed blokes fresh from selling insurance confident hard-faced ladies with Jags left running at the kerb, the whole gamut. They all seem to smoke. My eyes run after a few minutes. I listened, bored to death, seeing those mysterious numbers being chalked up on the boards. Lemuel, advised by Tinker, was filling in papers with a pencil stub. It was a real drag. So one horse runs faster than another. Who cares? And yet water-colours of Georgian and early William IV racehorses, not to mention the Victorian, are soaring in value. The prints as well, so be on the look-out. Always go for fame: Eclipse, Hermit, Hyperion, even as late as Airborne. For heaven's sake, though, make sure the print you buy is *named* (horse, owner, the race and jockey if possible). The rule is: the more factual detail the better. If you merely want to invest and you don't care about real antiques much, go for the best such paintings or prints you can buy at a good dealer's. Anything up to and including even the Brown Jack era should reap rewards. When buying originals, demand certificates of provenance − that is, what the painting's been up to since it left the artist's lilywhites. Don't worry so much about provenance if it's a print, because they're not being forged yet. I mean so far. It won't be long.

Nodge came in hunched and forlorn. He was startled to see me among the muttering, obsessed crowd. I was across in a flash, pulling him in and smiling. I didn't let go.

'Over here.'

Tinker and Lemuel were huddled in a corner. There aren't any tables or chairs in these dumps, only mounds of fag-ends and possibly a shelf to write on. Tinker gave me a bleary glance then carefully took no notice. I could say what I like. He's on my side. Lemuel's not, but he's not daft.

'Nodge,' I said in an affable undertone. 'You heard Leckie got done?'

'I heard.'

I smiled at him. 'I think it was Fergie, Jake Pelman and you.'

'Me?' His yelp made a few heads turn for a second. 'Me?' he hissed, white.

'Any two of the three of you.'

'I wasn't even in the bleeding car, Lovejoy.'

'What car, Nodge?' I saw the penny drop. We were muttering in the corner like punters, buffeted by preoccupied people pushing all around.

'Er − it was a car accident, wasn't it?'

72

'Don't try covering up, Nodge.'

'Let me go, Lovejoy.' He was desperate now, lips trembling and sweaty. A punter tried elbowing past to reach the betting slips on the shelf, but Tinker got in the way with studied absent-mindedness. The punter swore and moved off. Tinker never even looked my way. A good lad.

'You did Virgil's warehouse, right?'

Nodge's eyes widened. It warned me he was going to try it on so I snapped his finger. His attempted rush for the door halted before it was begun. He squawked and doubled up.

'Here, you lot.' The bouncer started out from behind his false grille. I have him one of my looks through the smoke and he hesitated. 'Less of that. We want no trouble.'

'Just going.' I called, smiling over the heads. The bouncer dithered.

'*Christ.*' Nodge was nearly fainting. There's nothing so painful as a broken digit. It matters which digit, of course.

'Yes or no, Nodge?' I helped him into the vestibule and stood between him and the street door.

'They'll kill me.'

'You did the warehouse?'

'Yeah.'

'What were you looking for?' I helped him a little. 'Come on, Nodge. I know all about Doc Chase.'

That let him off the hook of conscience, such as it was. 'They weren't sure what. Summat hidden in his things. Fergus said it would tell us where the stuff was hidden in Scratton.'

'Come on.' I indicated the door.

'I'd better go out on my own, Lovejoy – '

'No, Nodge,' I said contentedly. 'I want you in trouble with Jake and Fergie.'

'Please, Lovejoy – '

I nodded to Tinker and Lemuel and we barged slowly towards the door in a mob. 'Out, Nodge,' I told him. We left Tinker and Lemuel in the smoke and babble. I pushed Nodge out on to the pavement but kept hold. We had to be seen together. The smog of the market square seemed fresh as milk.

Jake Pelman was across the way, coming forward among the stalls. He saw us and stared.

'Jake's always out shopping these days,' I said pleasantly to Nodge. He groaned, more from seeing Jake than his finger.

'You bastard, Lovejoy. They'll do for me.'

'We can but hope, lad. See you.' I stepped away, still smiling for Jake's sake and waving casually to Nodge. 'It's a deal, Nodge,' I said loudly, nodding.

73

'Jake!' Nodge shouted urgently, beckoning.

I felt rather than saw them come together among the shoppers. Nodge would have to do some quick explaining or go the way of all flesh. Jake would assume we'd done a private deal. Nodge was for it. I went whistling towards the pub. Happiness makes you peckish.

I called in at the Three Cups for a drink and a pasty, happy that things had started moving. I'd learned not only who'd killed Leckie, but that they were no nearer finding the valuable item than I was.

Jean was in the saloon bar. I was glad. When one thing cheers you up lots of other things join in the jollity, don't they? I've often noticed that. Here was Leckie's mystery practically solving itself, me with a wodge of gelt in my pocket and Jean buying me a drink. She had a rare piece of 'toy' porcelain from the Girl-in-a-Swing Factory — look for *tiny* figurines with streaky brown hair, minuscule mottoes with atrocious spelling, and you're half-way there.

I perched on a stool, elbows on the bar and gazed at the lovely piece. Sit down when you meet a genuine antique. I do. Don't rush. It wants friendship. It needs company. Hang about for a few minutes and listen to its viewpoint, because it's got civil rights just like you. Take your time and acquaint yourself with its exquisite truth. Just as women are the living instruments of the sacrament of love, so are antiques their counterpart, only a little more inanimate at first sight. I sometimes wonder if antiques are really a vigil between different women. Or maybe vice versa. Anyhow, you get the idea.

To get the price down I told Jean it wasn't genuine, but she could see how breathless and quivering I was, and only laughed.

'Yeah, yeah.' She doesn't actually know much, so we had a good chat. I told her how Charlie Gouyn had slammed out of Lawrence Street full of Huguenot temper in 1749, leaving his partner Nicholas Sprimont in the lurch, and started up the Girl-in-a-Swing Factory. We don't know its proper name. We dealers actually call it that nowadays from a little piece in the Victoria and Albert. The funny thing is that Gouyn was a superb silversmith, yet often put gold mounts on his tiny scent-bottles, figurines or chain-seals. My own trick is to see if the lassies' dresses (usually whitish with a red rose pattern) are lined with deep rose or yellow, and see if the base has a rose on patterned leaves. You can't really go wrong because they're so exquisite. Jean's delicious piece was three luscious ladies leaning against a tree stump. Charlie Gouyn's buxom wenches often do that. I wonder about the symbolism sometimes. I bought it off her there and then with the expenses money Moll had given me. Well, I'd tell Moll I used a lot of petrol.

By the time I left town on the Medham road I was chirpy as a cricket and singing that Tallis madrigal which changes key a million times in the first bar. I was in good voice. When a crisis comes to the crunch I'm full of this alert feeling. I think it's a sort of realization that honesty's the best policy.

Something like that.

The damaged doors were repaired. New frosted glass glittered in the windows. Old George and Wilkinson were busy supervising the unloading of some stuff in the cobbled yard. A few people milled about, an early viewer and a dealer or two. I put my crate facing down the yard's slope in case of possible engine non-cooperation and strolled inside.

'Out of it, Lovejoy,' Wilkie called bossily, arms a-dangle.

'Get stuffed, Wilkie.'

I was up the ramp and inside as the vannies sniggered. Wilkie came after me. I shook him off. There was only the office girl Brenda there, and she was behind the glass partition near the posh entrance. For once she seemed to be engaged in work.

'I said, out.'

'Wilkie,' I said in my business voice. He shuffled a bit at that. 'What did you do with the escritoire?'

He shrugged. 'It got smashed up. You saw it.'

'Where are the bits?'

'Chucked out at the back. We'll burn it.'

I got him to show me the heap. They'd piled it among other broken bits against the yard wall out of the way of the traders' cars. There are some old sheds for storing stuff they can't sell. The escritoire still looked a cheap Edwardian copy smashed up, yet something was niggling me. The wood was honestly fairly new when looked at closely. The Bramah lock was obviously nicked from an old piece and screwed into this feeble reproduction furniture to make it seem older. It had been only recently done judging from the scratches, and inexpertly done at that. This is a common trick to make a relatively modern piece of furniture seem old. It shouldn't deceive an infant. The lock was hardly worth taking, because lock-and-key collectors are rare and the items are many.

I let Wilkie go and stayed in the warehouse yard an hour, scrutinizing every splinter and handling it all inch by inch.

No good. I rose at last, stiff as hell, and wandered out to watch them loading. After a few minutes I gave George the bent eye. He came over after a glance at Wilkie, who nodded at him once. Wilkie must have warned him I was around and being critical. I took him to see the heap.

'Nobody to see us or hear us, George,' I began. He looked about. I shook my head warningly.

'Look here, Lovejoy . . .'

'You're an old geezer, George. And you know me, tough and nasty with it. Old geezers fall and break legs, right?' We both analysed the situation. Charitably I gave him an extra minute.

'I don't know − '

' − Nuffink?' I capped cheerfully for him. 'But you do, George.'

'Don't touch me, Lovejoy. I'll shout out.' If he hadn't helped to kill Leckie I'd have felt quite sorry for him, a shaky old sweat scraping a meagre living. The way I felt, though, I wouldn't piss on him in hell to cool him down. He takes a few quid to tip dealers off when good items are coming in for auction. That's all he's good for. And it got Leckie crashed.

'What's it to be, George?' I gripped his arm. He winced and finally nodded. 'Nodge did the place over, right? He told me.'

'Then what're you asking me for? It's bleeding killing me − '

'Who else?'

'Him with the fancy whistle.' Whistle-and-flute, suit. Only Jake wears fancy bright green gear.

'Jake. And Fergie?'

'No.'

It had the ring of extorted truth. I let go. Nodge and Jake had known Old George dossed in the warehouse when there was stuff passing through. That meant any day before or after an auction. They'd probably just knocked on the door and barged in past him. A few threats probably shut him up.

'Here, Lovejoy,' he quavered. 'Don't tell them it was me grassed, eh?'

'Cross my heart, George.' And, I prayed kindly, God help you, because that's the first thing I would do.

The funny feeling was there still as I watched him shuffle off down the yard to the corner where the vans were standing. I turned the shattered wood pieces over with my foot. It was simply modernish wood, poor quality with horrible varnish and wrong staining. So what was there to worry about? And why was I dithering like this? I decided to get back to town at the finish. Maybe I should go over to the late Dr Chase's surgery and suss it out.

I was actually in my crate fumbling for my keys when the light came on and I froze. *Keys.* Keys have locks. Locks are in escritoires. But who on earth takes a genuine Bramah lock *recently* from a genuine piece of antique furniture and plonks it in a piece of trashy reproduction furniture? I dropped my keys and hurtled back up the yard. A dealer called, grinning, 'What's the hurry, Lovejoy?' the burke. The lock was still there, still screwed on its piece of backing wood among the rubbish. I'd been right. It had only recently been put on. You can always tell from the screw lines and the lock edges, especially if it's been done by somebody who has never done it before. And it looked a botch job, done by somebody with no skill but a lot of determination. Somebody maybe like Dr Chase?

The crowd by the loading ramp was still watching the new items coming in for auction. I went inside the warehouse. Wilkie was talking to Brenda in her illuminated glass cell. He quickly looked away from me. On my hands and knees I crawled about the floor, feeling along each board as I went. I crisscrossed the site where the escritoire had stood. Every yard I got a new splinter but the weight of the Bramah lock in my pocket goaded me. The key was in a corner, a cylindrical rod on a fixed ring.

The key probably didn't matter, though, only the lock. I just had to have both because there were endless possibilities. I slotted the key in. It fitted. Tired now, I went out to my crate the back way.

Wilkie called, 'Here, Lovejoy. Did you pinch anything . . .?' but only when he knew I'd not bother to turn back.

I ignored his shout, smiling to myself. Aren't people odd? We work like dogs to trick ourselves. Maybe we all know we don't admire the real bits of our own personalities. I'll bet I'm the only person on earth who's really honest about myself, honest and fair minded.

It took a real effort to switch the engine on. I knew most of the story now. Who killed Leckie was obvious – Jake, Nodge and/or Blackie. Possibly Mrs Leckie egged them on. Motive: greed. For what? Well, that would be revealed once I got the lock home and took it to bits.

My chirpiness had gone. I didn't sing a note this time as I clattered along the main village street towards the exit road.

I'd better explain at this stage how I killed him. It's clear in my mind still, and nothing trains your mind to be retentive like antiques. Of course, some antique dealers have better memories than others. Patrick, for example. He can even tell you if a single Staffordshire figure had been seen in the district during the past ten years. And Tinker's like that with auctions. I once asked him about a silver-topped walking-stick, plain as a pikestaff and monogrammed 1881 in Cheltenham. Somebody had auctioned it locally six years ago. I only had the vaguest recollection. If it had been an eighteenth-century cane swordstick with a gold-mounted

77

ivory or porcelain figurine handle — worth a year's wages — well, anybody can remember gems like that. But this particular stick even nowadays would only bring in a week's wages. They're still common. Tinker just wrinkled his gnarled face and said, 'Top-angled, straited, monogram not edged, ebony with horn-based tip? Thirty-quid, Easter auction six years back. Elsie. She sold it to Brad. He's still got it.' Margaret's good too, but keeps careful files and clippings on everything she sees, same as me. It's good observation. So I remember killing him in some detail.

I told you I was subdued driving homewards from Virgil's that day. There was trouble ahead, but Fergie and Jake seemed not too much of a threat, not as threats go these days. Nodge would be no bother. My only worry was if Fergus fetched a couple of London lads up to put the elbow on me. Or if he got the Item before I did and reaped all the benefit.

You might be wondering why I instinctively believed in the Doc Chase story, discovering a vital and precious 'find'. On the face of it, an elderly quack isn't much of a Hawkeyes when blundering round East Anglia's scenery. But this old island creaks under the weight of its history. Within literally a ten-mile radius of my crummy thatched cottage there are thirty buried temples, over a hundred pre-Christian burial mounds of tributary kings, numerous sunken treasure ships in the estuaries and graveyards of famous Roman legions. And, in the same area, two hundred important 'finds' of rare and precious valuable antiques have been made this year alone — none by Lovejoy Antiques, Inc, worse luck.

As I said, minds are funny things. When you hear of a find, you tend only to think of the great bronze head of Claudius being fished up intact from our riverbed. Your mind lingers on the treasure troves found in the craziest places, like the Ardquin Treasure in that bloody fishpond or the Winterslow Trove in that chalk pit. Like that gravedigger business in that churchyard, now famous as the Hickleton Hoard. But you don't have to go digging for antiques. After all, that Vlaminck daub 'by an unknown artist' was merely hanging on the wall. People saw it every day for ages. Yet once it was identified Sotheby's sold it for a fortune.

What I mean is, it's only natural in these circumstances to believe old Chase had come across a valuable find, something worth killing for. And if you think people won't kill for antiques my tip is stay innocent. But I was on about how I killed him.

Our roads in East Anglia are only two kinds. One's the newly built dash-track several maniacs wide. The other's the ancient and narrow switchback blundering between hedges and round sudden unnecessary blind corners. Both are as daft. Like many motorists, including drivers of the long distance double-trailer wagons, I keep off the new roads because they're a waste of all the places in between.

Leaving Virgil's I took the small side road which, signposts promise, will eventually head vaguely in the direction of Norwich should you live that long. I didn't mind because I had to have time to think. Once I got back to the town the other dealers would be sussing me out as usual and antiques would take over.

Presumably the Bramah lock would tell me somehow where the old doctor had found the Item. Or maybe where he'd hidden it. Perhaps, I thought excitedly, it was even hidden inside the lock. If it was . . .

My reverie was interrupted by a sharp nudge. The crate gave a sudden jump. My neck nearly dislocated as the car jerked forward. I have to look round because I have no proper mirrors. An enormous black humped car was practically stuck to my tail. It looked horribly familiar. I quickly tried to use that glance to see who was driving but the sun was coming from behind. It nosed forward and belted my feeble old crate, whiplashing my neck dangerously. I remember yelping with fear and swearing. The bend in the road allowed me to struggle my motor on line again, but the huge black car came alongside and pushed me sideways.

'Get over! Get over!' I shouted. I tried accelerating, but it had me for speed and was there again, coming on my right side and slewing my stern round again. My crate only just kept going.

'Sodding murderer!' I screamed, foot down. I'd never heard the cylinders so loud. I tried desperately thinking where we were. The nearest village was about five miles. I could only remember a farmhouse a couple of miles ahead, and even that stands back from the road behind hedges. They'd chosen well. A long, narrow, tortuous and undulating road, with no witnesses.

I tried leaving my brakes off going down the next hill, but my nerves gave out. The old banger can't take the stress of sudden turns any more and I could see the sharp oblique climb up the other side of the slope. We were rushing downhill towards the small stone bridge at the bottom. I was going as fast as I could.

He took me again at the turn. The massive sinister black bulge came on the inside and was forcing my stern across the road as we tore down to the bridge. It was all happening so bloody quick and sudden. I got free this time by risking everything, letting my brakes free and stamping on the throttle. Better to get crisped trying to escape than meekly submit by driving carefully. The extra speed and the bend saved me for a brief instant.

The stone bridge is an ancient medieval span they built with recesses for people keeping out of the way of horse-drawn carts. The humped roadway was too narrow for the big saloon and it braked suddenly, revving high with a boom. I made a lunatic ninety-degree screech and clattered on up the hill.

My old crate was gasping now, climbing the macadam between the thick hawthorn hedges with diminishing speed. Every third beat was missing, and something was whining steadily between my back wheels. It wasn't used to all this. I swear it was as terrified as I was. The black car came thundering close and with a crash belted me again. My head nearly flew off my shoulders. It took a few seconds for my vision to clear.

Then, in respite, my crate gave that giveaway juddering sound, warning me. Something big was coming the opposite way. It always makes my little motor shake. Maybe one of the juggernauts, I prayed, with a bloody great trailer. They're always in a hurry and come on fast, confident in their smooth air brakes and high-seated power. Frantically I smashed into second gear, sacrificing a few yards for better control. My engine caught up again and sounded healthy for several beats as the bronchitic cylinders strained easier.

The saloon hammered me again but I'd guessed their timing and corrected early enough for once. I realized I was alternately screaming with terror and babbling abuse. They were going to do me like they did Leckie. I'd end up crushed in a ditch, battered and emptied of life.

The narrow climb had forty yards to go when I took the sudden decision. They wouldn't kill me. Not Lovejoy Antiques, Inc. If anybody had to go it would be them, the evil bastards. I went stone cold. My foot lifted once then forced itself down hard. At first I'd determined to go as slowly as I dared on the hill, hoping to save time while frantically praying for somebody to come along to be a safe witness. Now it was time for killing.

The road banked left at the top. I could see it easily. Hedges stood close to the left verge but on the right there was a small grassy space with a few trees. Any juggernaut hurtling our way, suddenly coming across an obstruction, would instinctively straighten for a few yards in a desperate attempt to avoid a crash by using the meagre verge, then try to correct for the rest of the curve and continue its downward rush – and all in an instant. Even the best driver would jack-knife his two linked wagons. I'd seen it happen.

Please God, I prayed, as the crest loomed. A sudden crashing blow from behind came again. I felt the crate's floor judder with the rumbling approach of the unseen vehicle. The black car's engine notched up half an octave getting ready for the kill. They'd changed gear for even more power. So they were going to take me on the inside at the top, force me to slide to the right and leave me only the tree-crowded space to drive into. All because I hadn't the power to cut clear. If the tree trunks didn't get me I'd slam into the high bank beyond. The best I could hope for was having to stop and be at their mercy.

The juddering told me the oncoming juggernaut was almost on us. The booming saloon rammed against my tail with another crash. My engine cut, recovered, howled once, and just as suddenly steadied. Glass tinkled as a side window went. And abruptly I was at the crest. The black shape swelled darkly on my inside. I saw it out of the corner of my eye.

I wrenched the wheel to the right and stamped on the brakes, wishing to God I'd had the money to get them mended properly. I remember yelling one final insult at the bastards. I heard the saloon's engine mute. My tyres slithered, gripped, squealed as the crate slid across the narrow road sideways on towards the crowded trees. The trunks thickened horribly towards me. And a beautiful immense juggernaut came hissing on to the hill, its radiator tall as a church surmounted by windows like a liner's bridge. All in a millisec I banged the throttle pedal down, whining with fright. The juggernaut saw me across its path and bucked. Its engine shrilled. For one second I thought it wouldn't see the space, but its impetus was just too colossal. Its front heaved to my right. The sky darkened above me as the gigantic vehicle poised fractionally at the top. Then it jack-knifed. The trailing half clattered loudly into the leading part and swung across towards me, shuddering crazily. I hadn't the power to get clear. It caught my offside rear wheel. Glass exploded and spattered my neck and scalp like a million needles. I saw twigs and grass. My windscreen went and the steering-wheel crashed against my chest. The world suddenly seemed full of noises and fire and rubbery stenches. I heard somebody screaming and another voice saying Dear God, Dear God, over and over. All the hedgerows on earth seemed to be full of flames. Then the sky was streaming blood, but at least things were steady and trying to stay still.

My vision cleared about fifteen minutes later. I inspected the mad scene from a lady's lap a few yards from the crest of the hill. She was dabbing my forehead with a scented hankie and kept telling me how long it was since the accident and that I was going to be all right. Her frock was powder-blue. For a mad moment I thought I was in Paradise, because all I could see at first were five strands of baroque pearls, alternate white and rose. Strung thus they shrieked of Italy before this century. The woman moved. She told me she was on her way to a play rehearsal when they saw the crash. Her husband had phoned for ambulances and police from the farmhouse I mentioned, and now was trying to help to get the poor man out of his car. It was burning, hopeless.

'I hope nobody's hurt,' I said, for the record.

'Lie still, dear. Don't you worry.' She kept dabbing at me.

'A car tried to overtake on the wrong side . . .' I let my voice dwindle wearily. It didn't take much acting.

'Lie still. Everything's all right.'

We stayed like this for some time. I saw the police arrive, with Maslow coming in the second wave. Spectators gradually accumulated. Ambulances came and went. I refused to go in one, and struggled erect after a team of tired emergency people tinkered with me a bit. They covered one of my eyes up and turbanned my head. The Bramah lock had been driven into my side. A young quack put six bloody stitches in, but I got the lock back. They padded me up and wound strapping round my middle.

I got the lady's name and address before they continued to the rehearsal. Her lap deserved better than a half-conscious bloke in it, and her Italian pearl necklace was gold-clasped. I waved them off, wobbling somewhat.

Maslow took a statement from me, a constable doing the heavy paper labour. I reported faithfully how this car had simply tried to overtake on the wrong side, to my astonishment.

'A juggernaut came round the bend just then,' I explained. 'That's all I remember.'

'Look at me, Lovejoy.' Maslow's voice cold as a frog.

'I'm trying,' I said. 'With my one good eye. Will I still be able to play the piano?'

'If I thought . . .'

'Good heavens!' I sounded really quite good, properly horrified. 'You're surely not suggesting − '

He flapped a hand wearily. 'Go home, Lovejoy.'

'Wait.'

I went to look at my crate. It was a hell of a mess, but maybe rescuable. On the other side of the road the juggernaut stood, its driver still dictating trembling answers to a woman copper, poor bloke. The black saloon was still burning. A fire engine was there, a few helmeted firemen standing about. There wasn't much more for them to do now. I felt Maslow join me.

'Reported stolen,' he said morosely. I didn't look at him.

'From anybody in particular?'

'Chap called Fergus, London. An antique dealer.'

'How terrible.' I shook my head sadly, then had a theatrical after-thought. 'Oh, Inspector. Who was driving?'

'Your friend Nodge.'

I gazed back at him then with my one eye steady as a laser. 'Tut fucking tut,' I said evenly. 'The things people do.'

I stepped closer to the smouldering motor and its unspeakable inner mass. 'God rest, Nodge.' I'd broken more than his finger, as it turned out, but what else could I have done? It hadn't been my fault, not really.

They got a police car to run me home. On the way I asked the copper to stop a minute. We pulled in. I reeled out and vomited spectacularly in the hedge. I retched and retched. The peeler asked if I was all right. After a few minutes I wiped my mouth on a handful of grass and got back in.

'You'll be fine,' the lad said kindly. 'It's just reaction.'

'Thanks,' I said back.

But fear isn't got rid of as easily as that. I should know.

10

The spectacular sunrise surprised me. A mist covered our valley so densely I could have walked across to Lexton on it. Trees close to my cottage projected through it like small mountains. It was a gentle, unassuming and blissful picture. Then the sun bounced up quite suddenly. The valley mist showed red. Gold tinted the world's edges. I'd never seen such a sight. And in this lovely daylight I was black and blue. My face was bloated. The skin bulged green and purple. I was sore as hell. I could hardly stand up from the wall where I'd been sitting most of the night. But I was alive, solid and breathing and beating. Even aching was pleasant.

Last night before going the bobby had asked if I needed help. I'd said I was great. They'd come back today. They always do. Good old Fergus must have lent Nodge his car then reported his car stolen to keep himself in the clear. Maybe they'd made some telephone arrangement before Nodge was sent off to do me. I didn't blame myself for not sleeping much, because the Girl-in-a-Swing piece was ground to powder in my jacket pocket. I'd only found out when I tried to get undressed. I won't admit whether or not I wept at odd times behind my darkened cottage thinking of Nodge, or maybe the porcelain. Once anything's gone it's gone for good, but the passing is too much to take sometimes. I mean, in one go, as it were.

Once I'd got the sun properly up I went in and got in a blazing temper trying to brew up. I needed help. Things were starting to move and I had to move with them. But who to ask? Tinker's not on the phone, which narrowed the choice. He'd be caylied until opening time anyway. Sue's tough husband probably wouldn't prove co-operative if I tried to borrow her for a few days, selfish sod. Helen only wakes slow – pretty, but slow. Margaret was up in the Smoke for her weekly spending spree on the Belly, Portobello Road street market. I can't really rely on Jill, Jean or Lily like I can the rest, so they were out of it. And Miss Haverill would have me sprinting to Friday Wood and back when I couldn't raise a trot. I couldn't even think that far.

Painfully I dialled Moll. She lifted third ring.

'Lovejoy here,' I told her, trying to speak through split oedematous lips.

'Oh, Lovejoy!' she cried. 'I've just heard about your accident from – '

I cut in. 'Busy?'

'No. I was just about to ring you.'

'Get your coat on and come over.'

'This instant. Don't move.'

'I promise. Oh,' I added. 'One thing. Bring some grub, partner. I'm starving.'

She paused, then said of course, partner, politely.

I set to on the Bramah lock in my shed. You're sure to see a genuine one if you go to any antique shop, but don't write them off just because lock-and-key collectors are pretty rare folk. The Bramah lock is a delightful piece of wondrous engineering in lovely warm brass. Its precision and delicacy are exhilarating. They are the only honestly important antiques *you can still get for nothing*. Junk shops round here still chuck them out, like this one at Virgil's, but the time will come . . .

Joseph Bramah was a Yorkie, and a genius at that. His legendary lock patent is dated 1784. Nowadays we can only imagine what a sensation his new design caused in Georgian London. A real furore. He thought up some radial sliders, with the key pin pushing in against a spring. In his description he claims it is infallible, but even the addition of a metal "curtain" inside it failed to protect it against the breathtaking (and quite legitimate) lockpicking skills of that quiet American A.C. Hobbs. Knightsbridge was in uproar for half a century in lockpicking contests, as locksmiths battled night and day to keep one step ahead of burglars and people who claimed they could pick any old lock any time. Groups of gentlemen assembled to referee claims. There were even lawsuits. Public competitions were arranged, with multitudes gasping and applauding every flick of the wrist.

In those early days locksmithing was centred in Willenhall. People still call the place 'Humpshire' because the Staffordshire men were practically deformed from filing locks on the bench. They walked the streets with their hands frozen around an imaginary file and their shoulders hunched. Nowadays the manufacturing is spread around a bit, especially since young Linus Yale gave up portrait painting and set about explaining how good his dad's lock design really was.

The Bramah lock's simplicity is so stylish you tend to forget that Joe's innovation was the first major step forward since the locks of Ancient Egypt.

I made myself stop admiring the masterpiece and get myself going. I got the key in. It turned with a succulent click. No sign of anything hidden, though. They key emerged with traces of carbon which smudged my fingertip. Somebody, presumably Chase, had seen to it that the lock was properly cared for. No stupid dollops of oil to harden with the passing years, but careful gusts of powdered graphite blown into the lock aperture once every ten years.

Even though the escritoire itself was gone I had to summon all my nerve to damage the wood sliver on which the lock was fixed. I finally fixed the wood in a vice and lifted the lock's brass plate off after a struggle. It took half an hour to get it away undamaged. I'd have done it quicker but for my one eye and getting the shakes from the bruising. The plate came away. I was quivering with eagerness. I'd put a folded car blanket underneath the vice to catch the precious clue I knew would undoubtedly be concealed behind the lock. Gingerly I lifted the plate away. A small disc fell on to the blanket. That was all.

I peered at the back of the plate with a lens and along the wooden recess. Nothing. Disappointed, I found the coin and examined it slowly. Even there any hopes were dashed. It wasn't gold, or even silver. It wasn't even a Roman copper denarius. Not even a coin. I took it to the shed door and peered at it in direct daylight. It was a measly train pass, a grotty Victorian common-as-muck passenger chit. You can find even the rarest ones for a few quid. They're often in what we call the tuppeny tray, that little box you see set outside junk-shops, filled with duff buttons, jettons, tokens and neffie modern foreign coins. An interesting collecting field if you like that sort of thing, but even a hundred of these cheap little tokens won't make your fortune. It was blank on one side. The other bore the words 'The Rt Worthy Jno Case – No 1 – Mt St Mary Rlwy Grand Opening.' Not even a date, either. Mount St Mary is not far. I knew for a fact there was no railway there. It was probably just some sentimental child's play by old Doc Chase, him concealing his ancestor's train pass and playing secrets. Some people do this sort of thing for a giggle. Or maybe another decoy? If so, it had worked.

'Big deal,' I told the little disc in disgust.

I'd just finished tidying the shed as Moll bowled in. You can imagine the scene we had, Moll doing her nut at the state I was in and me saying oh leave off for gawd's sake. She unloaded a ton of stuff and made us breakfast. I'm always amazed at how little grub women eat. Beats me how they keep going. Anyhow, we became more or less friends. By the time she'd washed up and I'd put the things away we'd stopped jumping a mile whenever the other spoke. I told her about the accident and kept very few details back.

'Was Nodge trying to . . .?' She had two attempts at it.

'We'll never know,' I said gravely. I couldn't forget she was a peeler's wife.

'You poor man.' Her eyes filled. 'And he was your friend.'

'Well, er, yes.' I was uncomfortable. She kept on about this for some time, saying things like the tragic ironies with which life abounds and all that, and drawing unrealistic parallels from her own family's humdrum experiences. I said, isn't life astounding.

About elevenish, Miss Haverill phoned in. I was due at Chase's surgery for the first exercise pattern in the health scheme at noon. I told her I would toe the line.

Moll was aghast. 'You can't possibly do exercises – '

But I was already locking up, and told her it was where the next clues were coming from. She nodded determinedly then, and helped me with my jacket. In the interests of morale I didn't dare admit what a useless trail I'd found so far.

'Six Elm Green,' I said. 'Then Scratton. Where the tunnel is.'

As Moll drove us over to Six Elm Green I couldn't help glancing at her. It wasn't just the knees going up and down in that alluring way as she managed the pedals. She definitely had something, an extra erg of attraction. Of course all women have it, but in some it can't be avoided. They glow with a chemotactic radiation. You can't keep your eyes off. I suppose being admired must get on their wick much of the time. She caught my one-eyed awareness and decided to fix me good and proper.

'Who is Mrs Markham, Lovejoy?'

That was Janie. 'Er, a . . . a sort of cousin.'

'And Lydia?'

'Oh. She's, er, another cousin.' I cleared my throat. 'Used to visit me now and again.'

'Lisa?' Her tone was very critical. 'Another cousin, I suppose?'

'Er . . . yes.' I said brightly. She bit her lip. Her face was starting to colour up.

You can go off people. She must have found their names in my file. Trust women to be bitter about other women, even when a relationship's innocent. Well, almost innocent. The peelers should be catching tearaways, instead of keeping tabs on innocent law-abiding members of the public like me. She pulled us into a lay-by. An overtaking lorry honked joyously, predicting a snogging session. If only they knew.

'Listen to me, Lovejoy.' She had one of those chiffon scarves. It only needed a Georgian cameo brooch to be dazzling. 'I've read your file from cover to cover. Your record is one of utter degradation. Your behaviour is loose, completely improper.'

I wasn't having that. 'The police never check properly – '

'Let me finish.' She was furious at me, but why? I hadn't done anything. 'These episodes of . . . of carnal practices, and these terrible so-called accidents which keep happening. And always you're involved.'

'It's antiques,' I explained.

'It's *you!* One woman after another. And the deaths – '

I took her hand gently and let her rhyme on for a bit before I interrupted.

'Moll, love. It's antiques. It's not me, not ever.' She clearly didn't believe me so I tried to explain. 'All we ever want on earth, any of us, is love. There's nothing else worth breathing for. Antiques *are* love, but in a material form. They're just inert matter carved or shaped with love. That's why they're valuable to everyone. We see the love in them. Wanting them so badly is only natural. Get it?'

'But Nodge's death. It follows the pattern you create – '

I wasn't having that either. 'Nodge only lusted after Chase's precious item, same as the rest of us.' I shrugged. 'He wasn't careful enough, that's all.'

She wouldn't be mollified. 'What I started to say,' she announced primly, 'is that you're not to presume on our . . . relationship, such as it is. Our partnership is entirely . . . entirely . . . '

'Judicial?'

'Judicial.' She caught at the word with relief. 'A judicial working arrangement.'

'Agreed.' We shook hands soberly. She got us out on to the road again. We carried on, chatting of the possible meaning of the tin disc and the Bramah lock. We both stared studiously ahead, me not seeing Moll's knees out of the corner of my eye and her not seeing me not looking.

The trouble is you see more when you're deliberately not looking. Ever noticed that?

Dr Chase's surgery stands among neat houses and bungalows. The village is a scattered affair with an ancient church and three pubs. It's not as big as ours, maybe a thousand people served by two small grocery shops. The surgery's just a converted house, with no place to park. All I ever see in Six Elm Green is little lawns.

The house lies back from the pavement. Beyond the line of dwellings is a row of gardens. Then the dreadful countryside starts, rolling fields, woods, streams, trees. Really horrible, not an antique shop anywhere. I hate the bloody stuff.

And there was Miss Haverill, keen as mustard for us all to run round it. She was still chained to her clip-board. If only she'd wear a ton more make-up, I couldn't help thinking. Five assorted blokes stood about in their idea of athletic garb, all red faces and white hairy knees. They looked a sight.

'Lovejoy! What a terrible mess!' Elspeth came rushing at me as soon as I stepped out of Moll's car.

I glanced sardonically at her track team. 'I'm the best you've got, love.'

'But you can't run in your condition!' she squeaked, horrified. I thought bitterly, I can hardly bloody *walk*.

'I had to come,' I said nobly. 'You stressed how important it is.'

'How very . . . fine of you, Lovejoy.' She went all misty. I limped a bit more, obviously biting on the bullet.

'Oh. You've met Mrs Maslow? Miss Haverill.'

Elspeth said hello, but Moll looked puzzled. Oh, hell. I'd forgotten Sue's little game. I'd have to think up some tale for later. I pressed matters on hastily.

'I've some stitches and dressings needing attention, if Nurse Patmore's free.'

'Very well.' Elspeth looked harassed. 'An accident, I suppose? Do go through, please. I'll start my group off and be with you in a moment.'

I saw a familiar face and grinned. 'How do, Bernard.' I gave him a wink. Bern's a machinist in a local factory. He glowered threateningly, a terrifying figure of bulbous middle age in his thin podgy vest and flappy running shorts. Like two tents tied together wrong.

'You supposed to be in our group, Lovejoy?'

'Yes, lads.' I beamed encouragingly. 'Good luck. Can't make it today, I'm afraid.'

One or two made cracks back at me, grinning. Bernard looked miserable as sin. I had to laugh. He was probably having to waste his day off doing this maniac stunt. His idea of fun's sitting on the railway bridge across the valley photographing signals and talking with the level-crossing gatekeeper.

'Are you ready?' Elspeth cried, horn-rims poised in her hand. 'Now remember. No *undue* exertion. Are we all agreed?' She got a few dejected mumbles.

'Only *due* exertion, Bern,' I reminded him cheerfully. Then I had a sudden thought and stepped across. They were lined up doing nervous practice flexings. 'Here, Bern. Know anybody who collects passenger passes?'

'For railways? Me. Got one?'

'Mount St Mary.' I didn't need to explain there's no such railway.

He shook his head doubtfully. 'None struck that I know of. It never opened, not after the disaster.' I didn't like the sound of that. I thought I knew Mount St Mary well. There just isn't a railway. 'Got it with you? I'd like to see it.'

Elspeth was glaring and tutting. They had to be off.

'I'll wait,' I told him. 'How long will you be?'

'They'll be back in thirty minutes,' said Elspeth, all keen still. She naturally would be. She didn't have to go.

'We'll be back next Thursday,' Bern grinned, and trotted off with the rest. Elspeth clicked a watch and made notes.

'Need England Tremble,' I quoted loudly after them, receiving a chorus of abuse.

The next hour I had Nurse Patmore all to myself. And vice versa. She ripped the dressings off my stitches and put new ones on. She tore the bandages off my head and covered me in yellow fluid. My two eyes had a bad time working out distances for some time.

I was bullied and thoroughly chastised. She went on and on about careless driving, though I tried telling her it wasn't my fault. She had me on one of those gruesome steel tables with tubes and tins everywhere. Makes you think of Frankenstein. 'You're supposed to be full of sympathy,' I moaned.

'No I'm not, Lovejoy,' she slammed back, doing things with hideous instruments. 'I'm here to patch you up so you can go and do it again, stupid man.'

'I'll complain about your manner to Dr Lancaster,' I said sternly. 'That'll sort you out.'

'Do,' she said sweetly. 'Shall I dial for you? He'll be *so* interested to hear you've had a crash. Keep still.'

I glared at her. If only my eyes would agree on where she was. 'Er, not just yet.' Doc's berserk on accident prevention. And I'd messed up his physique pantomime by making his first group one short.

'He'll see your clinical card this afternoon, Lovejoy,' she persisted triumphantly. Women love rubbing it in. 'He'll go mental.

89

I'd keep keep out of his way if I were you.'

Until then I'd had visions of dropping in on him for a light chat about Doc Chase's hobby. I decided she was right.

On the other hand Nurse Patmore must have known almost as much as the old chap. It was worth the risk. 'How did Doc Chase die, Pat?' I tried a casual air.

'Nurse Patmore while on duty, if you please.' She clashed tins together. I always want to look what they're doing to me but I'm too scared. 'A stroke, poor man. He didn't linger.'

'Elspeth said he was interested in history.'

'Miss Haverill has no business disclosing Doctor's private affairs.'

I ducked these arrows. 'Didn't he write a book?'

'Yes.' She started reminiscing. 'He was a lovely old man. Very keen on exercise. Every single day off he'd cycle to Scratton, then back to Mount St Mary for an hour's fishing by the river. Always the same spot. We miss him.'

She prattled on a bit more, then let me go. I was bulky round my middle from dressings. Moll was outside on a garden seat watching her heroes totter back across the fields. They looked knackered. Elspeth was with her, jubilant.

'Aren't they perfectly *splendid,* Lovejoy?' she cried.

'Great,' I said as they straggled in. I've seen better retreats.

Bern was in no fit state to discuss Victorian passes and tokens. In fact I doubted if he'd last the day. They sprawled on the grass, huge bellies heaving with every gasp.

'I'll call round, Bern,' I called. 'I'm off.'

He managed to raise an arm but couldn't speak.

'Scratton, Moll.' I got in the car and reached for her maps in the glove compartment. 'Then Mount St Mary.'

She sat beside me a moment, then glanced back at Elspeth. 'What was all that, Lovejoy?' Her fingers were drumming on the steering wheel. 'I thought I'd already met Miss Haverill at your cottage. It was a different woman altogether.'

'Ah,' I said. I'd forgotten to think up a story. 'Ah, well, you see, it's like this. By a strange coincidence there are these two health visitors with identical names . . .'

By the time we were in Scratton village I could tell Moll hadn't believed a word. I was in the dog-house again. That's the trouble with women. They always think you're lying when you're actually trying hard to tell them only what's good for them, put things in the best light. It must be terrible to be like that, suspicious as hell all day long. I'm glad I'm not that way. Innocence makes you a better person.

11

This tunnel.

Ever seriously thought what a crime a tunnel must be? It's not just a horizontal hole. To the mountain it must be a deadly insult, vicious as a knife thrust. And let's face it — the motive's greed. Gain. Money. You gang up and dig a hole for good old gelt, not for art or adventure or somewhere to live, not any more. Modern Man digs for shekels and nothing else. That's how far civilization's got. Cavemen knew better.

And even before Leckie blew those charges that day, doing my job, I'd felt this way. If you were a hill you wouldn't want anybody strolling about your insides. It's not natural. That's why I stared from the deep railway culvert from among the dog daisies, and didn't go in.

'Maybe there's a train coming,' I told Moll airily. 'Best to be careful.'

'It looks disused.' Moll pointed at the train lines. 'There are weeds everywhere.'

'It isn't. I gave a light laugh, casual and off-hand. 'I, er, telephoned from the surgery. The railway people said it's still used.'

Moll glanced at me. 'Are you all right, Lovejoy?'

That's all stupid women ever say to me. 'Right as rain,' I snapped.

We were peering from the side of the cutting. I slid down to the granite chippings from bravado and stood on a sleeper. My heart was thumping. I felt my hands go cold and thrust them in my pockets. My shoulders went damp.

I knew the Scratton tunnel wasn't used these five years. It looked it, too, with elderberry and hawthorns already enroaching on the tunnel's mouth. I shuddered. Moll saw me and linked her arm through mine. It's an evil thought. No sooner does Man abandon anything than seeds blow along and settle in cracks and the greenery snakes in to strangle every sign that Man's enterprise ever existed. You could see a dark smudge against the tunnel's parapet. Steam trains had run through it for well over a century, each adding slightly to the grime, year after year. Now derelict.

'Do we walk through?' Moll asked. 'Isn't that what we came for?'

I shrugged, abandoning all pretence that an express was due any second among the undergrowth. 'No need, really.' But I was desperate to see if there was any sign of Chase's activities in there. 'Well, er, maybe.'

'Look, Lovejoy,' Moll said suddenly, far too brightly. 'I wonder if you'd do something? Could you drive the car round to the other side? First left, I think. I'll go through and have a quick search.'

'You've no torch,' I said feebly.

'I always carry a pencil light.' She rummaged in her handbag. 'For finding keyholes when it's dark.'

'That's not fair, though.' Feebler.

'I don't want you falling down in there.' Moll showed me her little torch was working. 'Nurse would come after me.'

'Well, if you insist . . .'

Sometimes I think I'm pathetic. I watched her trek along the lines and vanish down a tunnel. I climbed slowly to the top of the embankment. The car seemed friendly, safe. Funny how you get these anthropomorphisms.

I was waiting for her when she came out at the far side. She was slightly breathless and indignant.

'There are *creatures* in there, Lovejoy!'

'What kind?' My voice must have sounded strangled.

'Oh. Only scuttly ones, little things. Bats, I suppose. The squeaky sort.'

Her natural sciences were on a par with mine.

'No sign of any digging? No bricks loose?'

'I didn't see any. Nothing recent, anyhow.'

That was Scratton tunnel. A disused old railway structure with no signs of tampering. So why did Doc Chase come all this way so often to look at a tunnel, and do nothing?

Moll did her face with lipstick and all that. I drove the car the three miles or so to Mount St Mary. The motor seemed to stop outside the Three Tiles of its own accord. Even now I don't know if it was a mistake, but I told Moll about Leckie and the time he blew the bridge. She kept her gaze on me as I drove.

'Why didn't you say you were frightened?' she asked as we got out in the pub's coachyard. 'It's nothing to be ashamed of.'

That irked me. 'Who said I'm frightened?' I demanded. 'What's there to be scared of in a rotten old tunnel?'

'Sorry, Lovejoy.' She caught the keys I threw her.

'I'm just careful,' I said, in a huff. 'Careful's not frightened.'

'Sorry, dear.' We went into the pub, marching frostily side by side. 'I didn't actually mean frightened,' she said, 'I really meant careful.'

The usual midday rural mob was in, a score of workers tanking up for the afternoon's assault on the land. I ordered for us and started my patter instantly with an agile geriatric in hobnails.

'Bet it doesn't seem the same round here without old Doc Chase fishing, eh?' I said, grimacing ruefully. I jerked my head towards the road. The curve follows the bend of the river. Sane friends and spouses watch their loved ones from beside the bar's fire during fishing contests in winter.

'Who?' He looked blank. A couple of others pricked up their ears.

'Doc Chase. My old pal,' I lied easily. 'Always seemed to be fishing when I drove through.'

'He means the Champ,' an old geezer cackled. They fell about at that, even the barman laughing.

'We called him that, God rest him,' I was told.

'Was he that great?'

That was the signal for convulsive hilarity. The old gaffer practically had apoplexy and spilled his pint. Moll had to bang his back to get him breathing again. He wiped his eyes.

'Lord love ye, young feller,' he gasped. (They really talk like this. I'm not putting you on.) 'Never caught a fish all the time we seed him at it.'

'Aye,' another chipped in. 'Forgot the frigging worm, often as not.'

'Never remembered his maggots!'

They rolled on the aisles while I tried hard to grin.

'Forgetful old bugger,' the first old cock rasped. 'Knew no better than to sit among those nettles on the wrong side!' I had his glass topped up while we laughed at Doc Chase's hopelessly bad angling technique.

We chatted some more before leaving. I learned that Chase's favourite place was on the opposite bank. 'The same spot,' Nurse Patmore had told me. I gave Moll the eye. We drank up and were waved off.

Moll drove. A few hundred yards homeward I told her to stop. We were on the upward slope, where the road turns away from the river to run towards our distant town.

This river has three bends. The first lies between barley fields, and straightens before the Mount itself is reached. The third is further inland, beyond the actual village, and consists of a gentle curve with woods crowding densely along both banks. It was the second that interested me.

It is double. The river courses across the small plain where the village houses cluster. There is the inevitable gaggle of thatched roofs, the flintstone church with its impressive spire, and the ornate Early English stone bridge. It all speaks of the wealth of the mediaeval wool trade and commerce channelled by the dour

Christian zeal of those days. The Three Tiles pub is at the crossroads near the bridge, lying snugly on the outside bank of the curve. Doc Chase's favourite fishing spot was almost directly opposite the tavern. I could see birds flashing into the sandy patch.

'Sand martins.' Moll pointed. 'Maybe he liked to watch them.'

'Maybe,' I said. But you can see them better from the other bank. If you sit on the same side of the river as the sandy mounds you have your back to them all the time.

The Mount stands on the pub side of the river. It's tall, as East Anglian hills go, but nobody else would think so, except perhaps a Dutchman. From where we stood, though, it seemed spectacularly large, maybe because there are no other hills thereabouts. A house or two shows on the inland side of its lower slopes. On this side, however, there is only a dense low scrub of broom and grass with humps of small hillocky bushes here and there. People put the odd sheep out on it sometimes but that's about all.

A cloud darkened the sky as we stared at it. The sunshine was slowly caressed from the Mount's face in a gradual sweep. I couldn't help thinking what a bloody place to stare at for day after day, month after month, as Chase must have done from his vantage point across the river. Had he fished from the tavern bank he'd have had plenty to look at – the village, the road, the downstream flow of the river and the lovely old church. As it was, he'd only faced the empty hill.

'I hope they didn't pull his leg too much in the tavern,' Moll said, smiling. 'He must have been the world's worst fisherman.'

'So he must,' I said. It makes you think. Too bad, in fact. Even a hopeless angler will catch something sooner or later.

I got her to pull in as soon as we saw a phone box. I pretended my arm was stiff so she came pressing in with me and did the dialling. She was a bit mistrustful, but it was very pleasant.

'Hello, Pat darling!'

'Get off the line, Lovejoy,' Nurse Patmore snapped. 'Medical calls only.'

'About Dr Chase,' I said. 'Tell me how many fish he caught on his days off. On average.'

'Well, it was a bit of a joke with us, actually.' She sounded on the defensive. 'He wasn't very lucky.'

'You mean none,' I said.

'It's not a very good river.' She was smiling. Isn't loyalty wonderful? 'I think he had rather a soft spot for the fish. He used to say "Lucky again!" meaning they'd all got away.' She paused. 'Why are you asking all this, Lovejoy?'

'Thank you,' I told her. 'Keep taking the tablets.'

Moll and I drove back to the cottage. She told me my hands were quite cold when we got there and our fingers accidentally touched. I blamed her motor, said it was full of draughts.

12

Moll left at about eight that evening, but I have to tell you about something that happened after she'd gone. It was unexpected. I'd not planned for anything so frank, which only shows how stupid I can be most of the time. The trouble is that when you start finding things out and events finally go your way you start assuming that you're driving the bus. In fact you might only be a passenger on the wretched thing.

Moll got ready to go. We were in one of our epidemics of politeness. She kept asking if I'd got her phone number in case I wanted anything and I kept checking it was written down right.

'You're all alone here,' she explained. 'You can't shout out for help if anything happens.'

'It's quite safe,' I assured her, like an idiot.

'Do lock your door, won't you?'

That nettled me. 'I'll be all right. I'm not scared.'

'I know,' she said swiftly. 'Of course you're not. But I'm worried your crash was deliberate.'

She thought Jake and Fergus sounded bad people just from their names. That's just typical of the sort of illogical allies I usually get. Efficiency's always on the side of the wrong people. I finally waved her off, dishing out profuse thanks for a day's help.

The story pieced neatly together. Neat, but disturbing. An old village quack, interested in local history most of his life, stumbles across a valuable rare find. It's near Mount St Mary. Aware that maybe others would not only become interested but could nick his precious Item before he could get his own clutching hands on it, he starts some evasive tactics. He zooms over to the Scratton tunnel to mislead followers. Then he goes to Mount St Mary where he sits working out where his Item is buried, or maybe just merely keeping an eye on it. Being a kindly old geezer, he hates the idea of hooking fish for nothing so he pretends to be the universe's most forgetful and useless angler, to everybody's merriment.

You couldn't help but admire him. He remained true to his collector's instincts and stuck to his act. It worked. He deceived everybody, including Black Fergus and his crew. Nodge had said that whatever was hidden in the auctioned items would explain where in Scratton the precious thing was hidden. Nodge had said Scratton, not Mount St Mary. So they must have followed him yet still been misled by Doc Chase's feint. The clever old sod. Nothing in the tunnel at all, thank God.

But I knew something they didn't. The little disc-shaped railway pass did not refer to the Scratton tunnel at all. Moll had examined it and found nothing. So the disc was a pass for a non-existent line to Mount St Mary. Doc Chase had hidden it to prevent his gem of worthless information falling into the wrong hands. Being wise he'd concealed it behind a Bramah lock in a cheap old piece of crummy furniture, knowing no true collector would miss that. Maybe he'd actually told Leckie about it. Either way, Leckie had successfully bid for the stuff.

I took out the pass and examined it again. It looked the same, and I was no wiser. Yet there was something making me uneasy. You get these feelings.

For the next hour I pondered the problem, trying to look up auction catalogues and filing notes away. I stared at maps of the area. It was hopeless. I finished up having a glass of cider and doing nothing. I was on the wall in the garden, ruminating, about nine with dusk coming on. That was how they caught me.

I heard the car stop in the lane. A door slammed. I never thought it would be Fergus and Jake. I especially never thought they would have two tearaways with them. They came crunching up the gravel. Fergus was beaming.

'Convalescing, Lovejoy?'

'I'm better.' I hadn't the sense to run in and slam the door.

'You don't look it.' He puffed up and plonked himself down beside me. 'Nasty accident, I heard.'

'Nasty.'

'Nodge bought it,' he said sadly. His grin never left him. Jake and the goons stood silently by, listening. Their eyes were on me.

'Shame,' I said.

'You did it, didn't you, Lovejoy?'

I looked about, realizing I was caught. 'If you say so Fergie.'

'Save yourself, Lovejoy.' His persistent bloody cheerfulness was sickening. 'Give me Chase's thing.'

'Thing?' I decided to be dim.

'Wilkie told us how you went back for some wood. Give it us.'

I'd have to have a word with Wilkie. 'I don't know what you mean, Fergie.'

'Do him,' Jake said.

One of the goons kicked my leg, right against my shin. I yelped and stood up to hop. That brought the end goon between me and the one who kicked me. I cracked my cider glass on the wall and scagged his face open, all in a single sweep of an arm.

'*Jesus!*' The goon stepped back, dabbing his face and looking at his bloodstained hands in horror.

'Mind your new suit, Jake,' I told him. It was maroon, today's fashionable colour. I held the shattered glass lightly by the handle.

'Lads, lads,' Fergus reproved, sorrowfully shaking his head. The bastard was still sitting down. 'This is no way to behave.'

'They the best you can do, Fergie?' I tried my best to sound scornful but I felt shaky. 'Where I come from they'd starve.'

Jake and the healthy goon were separating, watching me. They had knuckledusters on now. Even if I set off running I'd not get far.

Then, mercifully, Moll's car pulled in.

'Hello, Moll,' I yelled, drenched in a sudden sweat of relief.

'Get rid of her, Lovejoy.' Fergus gave his bleeding nerk the bent eye. He stepped back, hands and handkerchiefs to his face.

'No. She's a copper's wife.'

'Hello, Lovejoy.' Moll saw the blood and my broken mug. 'I came back to . . .' She glanced at Fergus, me, the two men. Jake was softly giving instructions to the undamaged goon.

'It's time for tea, love,' I said brightly.

'Go away, lady.' Fergus rose and nodded to Jake. 'Put a match to it, Jake.'

'Eh?' The goon had a petrol tin. The bastards were going to fire my cottage. He was moving towards my open doorway.

Jake gave an unlikely yelp of glee. 'We'll warm your beer, Lovejoy.'

I was stepping forward with my puny glass to do the best I could when Moll sorted it all out.

'Stop that!' Her voice cut through the dusk like a ray. We all stopped where we were, more surprised than anything. 'I shall phone the constable.'

'Leave off, lady.' Fergus chuckled. 'I've a dozen witnesses who'll say we're miles away.'

'Very well, then. If that's your attitude.' Moll rummaged in her handbag. Believe it or not she handed me a small purse and then a powder compact while she searched feverishly. I stood there holding them, feeling a right lemon. We all waited from curiosity, wondering what the hell she was going to bring out.

'Get on with it, Jake,' Fergus was just saying, when we learned what Moll had brought.

The goon with the petrol tin was starting forward as Moll finally gave a satisfied murmur. She pulled out a blued Smith and Webley. There was a sharp sound like silk tearing. One of my windows crashed and my eyes were momentarily blinded by the explosion. The nerk howled with fright and Fergus swore.

'There!' Moll said breathlessly. She was holding this howitzer out as if offering somebody desert. 'There now. You must stop,' she instructed, 'or take the consequences. I won't have this kind of behaviour.'

'Christ.' Jake was stuck. The goon with the petrol put it down and nervously backed away from it. I knew how he felt.

'Now, lady,' Fergus said. He was less cocky now.

'Please stand still.' She was hardly the fastest draw in the West, but it's wise to do as you are told when being pointed at.

He was moving forward at her, beaming, when she hit him. The ripping sound and the flash set us diving for cover. Moll pulled the trigger three times, swinging wildly. I was screaming for her to stop. I heard this crack and a dull thud but didn't think at the time. Moll stilled. Jake and the injured goon were lying down. The healthy nerk had scarpered, leaving his petrol tin. I could hear him crashing gears trying to reverse the car in the lane. Fergus was on the ground. It looked like his leg. He was shouting for Moll to stop.

'Give it here, love.' I took the pistol.

'It's Tom's,' she explained.

Even police aren't allowed to keep guns at home. I knew that. I decided to report Tom Maslow when all this was over. He's no right evading the law.

'Off you go, Fergie,' I said cheerfully.

'She fucking well shot me.' He moaned and rolled over to get up. He really was bleeding badly.

'Sue her.'

'I'm so sorry,' Moll told me penitently. 'I only meant to make them nervous.'

'You did that all right. You frightened us all to death.' I waggled the weapon uneasily at the three. I'm as useless with these murderous things as Moll. Now, if it had been a lovely Mortimer dueller of Regency days, or a delectable flintlock holster pistol by Sandwell or James Freeman of London, with that luscious browning and perfect balance . . .

We stood there while Jake Pelman and his uninjured tearaway carried Fergus to their car.

'Take your petrol, lads,' I called.

Jake came back for it, keeping his eyes on us. For some reason he seemed angry with me.

'There'll be another time, Lovejoy,' he said.

'Wait a minute, Jake.' I went over and booted him on the shins, right and left. He yelled and hobbled about. 'Off home, now.' I grinned and saw him safely down the path.

'You wait, Lovejoy.' Fergus was sprawled across the back seat.

The others were crammed in the front, one goon holding his face together still. 'One day your tame tart won't be here to hide behind, lad.'

I stuck my head in the open window and we looked eye to eye for a minute.

'What's the antique, Fergie?' I asked him straight out.

'Dunno. And neither do you, Lovejoy.'

'True.'

He gritted his teeth because I tapped his shot leg hard with the pistol barrel. 'The minute you step outside your gate, Lovejoy, we'll be here.' He managed a beam, a rudiment of his usual expression. 'And we'll take Chase's clue off you like toffee off a brat.'

'I'd make it easy for you, Fergus,' I said. 'But I can't forget you killed Leckie.'

The thought made me clout his leg in earnest. He screamed so loudly I reflexly started back. The combination of that scream and this terrible persistent grin was horrifying. I stood there while the motor rode up the slope. Moll came and stood beside me. We listened to the sound. A pause at the chapel, a rev-up on to the main road. Turn right, then descend a few notes as they set off out of the village into town.

The sound faded. I looked about. It was quite dusky now. I saw that Moll had happened to park her car inside the garden half-way up the gravel path, almost as if somebody intended to stay. We walked slowly to the cottage.

'Did I do right?'

'More than that, love.'

'Are you pleased I came back?'

'Delighted.'

We paused in the doorway.

'I just wondered about your being safe,' she explained.

'Good judgement,' I said. 'That's what it was.'

'I'd leave you Tom's pistol,' she said carefully. 'Except it's his licence, you see. So I can't let it out of my possession.'

'I see,' I said.

'But I suppose . . .'

'Yes?'

'Have you a spare room? If I were to stay, just overnight perhaps, until you get on your feet properly again . . .'

'Then we could keep the gun here,' I concluded brightly.

'Well, yes. It would be . . . legal, then, wouldn't it?'

'Why, so it would.' I switched the hall light on.

'I'll just get my things from the car. I usually have a suitcase with me.' She hesitated. 'Are you sure this will be all right?'

'Certain,' I assured her gravely. 'Anyhow, my granny always said to share.'

13

Next morning Moll answered the phone twice before I could get to it. Both times the other end rang off before speaking.

'Can't think what's got into people,' Moll announced sweetly.

'Er, I'd better answer.' I was thinking of Val, Helen, or Elspeth Haverill with some fresh Olympic programme and, last but by no means least, good old Sue.

Apart from this tiff we adjusted fairly well. I reclined grandly on my unfolding divan because of 'my condition', as Moll called it, like I was seven months gone. Naturally we went through a stage of typically English hesitancy, worrying sick about using our knives and forks properly, no elbows on the table and being desperately silent on the loo. In spite of it all we finished up quite well attuned. I was narked at her flashing to the phone first, but what can you do?

I sent her to the Corporal's on East Hill about nine.

'I have to pay for services rendered,' I explained. 'To you.'

'There's no need — '

'Do as you're told. Got some money?'

'Some. I have my cheque-book. Will that do?'

'Almost certainly,' I answered, straight-faced, thinking, the poor innocent.

'What are we going to buy?'

'You,' I corrected. '*You* are going to buy for yourself a small collection of treen.'

'What's treen? Is it a kind of antique?' She got all interested. 'I do hope so. I'm fascinated.'

I pushed her into a chair. 'Sit and listen.'

'I once bought a teapot with a decorated spout. They said it was ever so valuable.'

I put my fingers in my ears to keep out this rubbish. People will keep on talking gibberish. She shut up, and I started to explain. There are fashions in antiques. If you want a tip about profit it's this: try to *anticipate* the next fashions, and you'll be well away. I'll give you some guidance. Firstly, unless you are loaded, go for fairly recent first editions. They aren't real antiques, but dealers pretend they are for sordid gain. Secondly I'd go for Victorian jewellery of the semi-precious kind — sombre jet brooches, garnets and so on. Thirdly I'd go for 'fringe' household items that are seriously underpriced: pewter, polescreens, soapstone ornaments, decorative glass table bells, that sort of thing. And treen. Treen is dealers' slang for any wooden kitchen-ware. You can still, believe it or not, find even the rarest genuine Tudor treen for a few quid. Any old town has a stock of it. I defy any collector with half an eye for antiques to fail to find it, and cheap. You buy it in junk shops, or even these travelling antique fairs which abound everywhere at weekends these days.

The commonest treen is the old family bread-board, with or without knife slots and decoration to match. That and little peppermills, salt-boxes (made for hanging by the fireside to keep the deliquescent impure salt mixtures dried out), platters, decorative butter moulds and carved cheese paddles, wooden cups, scissor-shaped glove-stretchers, anything from lovely sycamore cooking mortars to ingenious wooden washing tallies for checking that the serfs were hard at it. If you don't believe me, try it. I did a favour once for Taffy, a local dealer I owed for a lovely illuminated parchment manuscript Book of Devotional Hours. He was getting after me for the price and I hadn't managed to bring myself to sell it. He was broke and had a buyer. I staved him off by borrowing a hundred quid and taking him round about twenty antique shops in two days. It knackered us both, but he finished up believing me. We bought a luscious little Welsh oak herb chest, an Elizabethan spice grinder, three seventeenth-century lemon squeezers, a basting stick inscribed 1647, gingerbread boards galore, and six square platters with handles and salt 'sinkings' (smoothly hollowed recesses). We got a lot more for the same money, but I'll lose the thread if I go on. Taffy sold the lot as a 'collection' of historic treen at an auction by the following week. He made plenty and shut up whining for his gelt. It's still that easy.

'Get it?' I concluded.

Moll was wide-eyed. 'But what if I buy the wrong things?'

I described the layout of Corporal's crummy dump on East Hill. He isn't bad as antique dealers go. Rough-mannered and a bit greedy, but quite fair on those rare occasions when he's not sloshed on pale ale. He believes he is a major world authority on Norwich School and Dutch oil paintings, though Christie's are rumoured not to have lost any sleep over this claim. Corporal's thick as a plank.

'Can't I just ask Mr Corporal for them?' Moll was saying.

I closed my eyes. Women like Moll give me a headache. 'It isn't done that way, love.'

'Why not?'

'He'll know what you've come for. And he'll increase his price. See?'

She was instantly indignant. 'How very unfair!'

'True, true,' I said with deep feeling. 'But look for the money code. That'll tell you if he's hiked the mark-up.'

Women are good listeners when you mention money, and Moll for once listened intently. We have no 'fixed' prices in the world of antiques. Whether we're dealing for the fabulous Eureka Gem or a mundane Edwardian inkwell *there is no fixed price* except the one the dealer himself puts on. Always remember that. So every dealer above the junk-shop level invents his own code, or uses somebody else's. Even famous firms do it. You simply take any word or words totalling ten (or possibly nine) letters, and they become the numbers from 1 to 9 plus 0.

'Am I allowed to look at each sticker?' Moll asked.

'Look?' I tapped the air vehemently. 'You must crawl all over the bloody things.'

'But the code – '

'Every dealer's code's easy to break, simply because no letter can ever recur. Get it? By asking the price of about three items you can deduce the code in practically every shop you come to.' She looked blank so I made it easy. 'Corporal uses *Come and Buy*,' I told her. 'Copied from a famous firm in St James's.' I didn't tell her which one, because I'm sure Spink's of London would prefer to remain anonymous. Continental dealers have their own codes but most of the ones I know use *Goldschmit*, like Münzen & Medaillen secretly used to in Basel.

'How many do I have to buy?'

'As many as you can without an overdraft.'

'Really?' I could tell she was becoming excited at the thought of a spending spree.

She was gone in a few more minutes. I gave her a wave and streaked to the phone. There was no chance of raising Tinker this early, so I rang Margaret. She was just opening her place in the Arcade. I made her promise to catch Tinker as he reeled past towards breakfast at opening time, and get him to phone in for instructions. In case she missed him among the shoppers I rang Woody's and told Erica the same thing. She was all set for telling me off but I put the receiver down because women always get necessity in the wrong order. Finally I rang Bern's and told his missus I'd be calling round in his dinner hour. Rosie said one o'clock, but earlier if I wanted veal and two veg.

Moll returned so late I was sure we would miss Bern. I was in something of a temper, worried what nasty facts about my railway pass Bern was going to cough up. I told her off, but she was too flushed and excited to notice.

'Don't be angry, Lovejoy!' she cried, rushing in while I said where the hell have you been. 'I've had a lovely time. Done exactly as you said!'

'Hurry up.'

'One second.'

I waited, fuming, in the car while she hurtled crashing about the cottage. Bathroom going, her case under the divan, a door slamming, and out she zoomed. I had to drive because she was breathlessly eating bread and honey. She forgot to set the burglar alarm — all antique dealers have burglar alarms — and had to dash back while I turned the car round.

'Where is it?'

'The treen? Coming this afternoon,' she applauded herself with delight. 'You'll be thrilled!'

That seemed odd, but I said nothing. I didn't see why she couldn't have fetched it. The phone started up as I got in gear, but then it always does. I ignored it.

'Did Tinker catch you?' He'd eventually phoned in, sounding bleary. I'd sent him to find Moll and stay with her in case Corporal got delusions of grandeur at the sight of a genuine customer.

'Yes, Lovejoy. He's a perfect dear, isn't he?'

'Er, yes . . .' Nobody's called Tinker that before. 'Putting up with so much from his assistants, and being paid so little.' She slipped her arm through mine, but only friendly. 'I do wish he had an easier life, poor soul. Having to go off and do the shopping for his old Mum. Aren't some people marvellous?' She prattled on about how Tinker, that noble pillar of virtue, also cared for an old and feeble comrade-in-arms named Lemuel, whose terrible leg condition had caused the Minister of Health mercilessly to write him off, leaving him unprotected in a changing world. 'Poor Lemuel,' she said, practically tearful. 'He waited so patiently while Tinker advised me. Such a bad limp.'

A terrible suspicion was forming. 'You didn't give him any money, Moll?'

'Of *course*. He hadn't a penny. I gave him the money for his dinner, and a taxi to see his sister's child in Lexton. The poor mite's ill with a terrible disease they can't — '

I sighed wearily. One day I really will cripple Lemuel. 'Love,' I told her. 'Lemuel's fit as a flea. And his sister's lad is our local champion swimmer. Lemuel's a dirty old devil who gambles and boozes every farthing he can cadge. He does odd jobs for Tinker, who's as bad.'

'How dare you, Lovejoy!' She pulled her arm away. 'Typical,

just typical!'

I drove doggedly on. 'And Tinker's old Mum's an evil old cow worse than he is. They're the worst scroungers in the whole of East Anglia, love.'

'You're horrid, Lovejoy. They're two lovely old men who need *care*.' I gave up arguing. She raved at me then, as I drove out on the Wormham road north out of our village. She kept it up for bloody miles, going on about cynicism and selfishness. I even learned a new word, gravamen. She said the gravamen of our differences were so enormous as to make us irreconcilable. I didn't like the sound of gravamen, whatever it was.

I just shut up and held the wheel. Anyway, I had plenty to think of. While Moll was out I'd gone over the Ordnance Survey map of the Mount St Mary and Scratton areas, inch by painstaking inch. In fact, that's partly why I'd got her out of the way. There was no tunnel, not even a viaduct, in or on or even near the Mount St Mary hillside. And the river bridges are so narrow, being medieval, that even I wasn't scared of them.

But all morning I'd fretted uneasily. Maybe that's why I had shelved the idea of seeing Bern or some other local historian for so long, subconsciously knowing there was something unpleasant and even frightening at the end of it. And, as it turned out, there was.

We came to Wormham's erratic main street. Moll was still going on. 'How could you be so — '

'Shut it, Moll.'

' — positively callous and unfeeling — '

'*Shut it.*' She took a sidelong look at my face and shut up. I pulled into this small estate of uniform semi-detached houses and stopped us opposite the eighth house. A garden sign read '*The Junction*'. Good old Bern. 'We're here,' I told her.

My palms were damp. If Bern told me there really was a frigging tunnel under that frigging hill then I for one wasn't going down into its horrible deep slimy cobwebby blackness for all the tea in China. And, I thought with feeling, there's a hell of a lot of tea in China.

'Lovejoy,' Moll said as I started to get out. 'I think you should rest for a few days — '

I reached back in and got a handful of her blouse at the neck. 'One more word from you,' I said. 'Just one more word.'

'Yes, Lovejoy,' she said after a pause.

Bern was at the door, smiling. 'Thought you were never coming, Lovejoy. We've finished nosh.'

'Sorry, Bern.' I walked up the little garden path, Moll trailing. 'I have help these days. Always makes me late.'

I heard Moll snort and draw breath to make some retort, then wisely say nothing.

Train enthusiasts go in gaggles, like geese. If you find one wandering lone he's lost. There's another characteristic: no matter how amateur they are, they are very, very expert. It's true of the entire breed. I know one chap who can tell you the whole yearly timetable of the Maltese railways, and there hasn't been a railway there for decades. See what I mean? So I wasn't surprised to find Bern had another historian with him.

'I got Gordon along,' Bern told me as the young blond lad rose and said hello. 'He's our local branch-line expert.' That's another thing. You learn to expect all ages of expert. This lad was about fifteen, thin and tall as a house, as they all seem to be these days. I think it's school dinners.

'How do.' I explained Moll to them both, and we settled round the table. Rosie cleared the meal away with the practised alacrity of a wife escaping from a hobby.

Gordon and Bern began fetching maps and books. I watched uneasily. It seemed a big pile of fact for what I was hoping would be a legend. I contributed my disc, to Bert's excitement.

They did their mysterious bit with magnifying glasses and catalogues. Rosie hurried a table-lamp in, pretending to share in the thrills. I waited for the verdict.

'I never believed they'd struck one,' Bern concluded, marvelling.

'Me, neither,' from Gordon.

'Who's they?' I asked nervously.

'The railway company.'

'*Which* railway company?' I persisted. I wanted negatives, not vague replies that suggested there were horrible positives just around the corner.

Bern deferred to Gordon with a nod. 'This railway company tried to build a branch line through here,' the lad said earnestly. 'From town, on up the valley. One arm out through Scratton going inland. The other through Wormham to Mount St Mary.'

'They wanted to run it coastwards,' Bern put in, still goggling at the disc with a glass in his eye.

I said, 'But the old railway station here in Wormham's – '

' – the end of the line,' Gordon finished for me, reaching to show me its course on a 1930 Ordnance Survey map. 'Of course it was.'

'So it never actually ran to Mount St Mary?' There was no dotted line going north from Wormham station, thank God.

'No.'

I sighed with relief and rose smiling but trying to look disappointed. 'Well, that's that,' I said cheerfully.

'Is that all you want to know, Lovejoy?' The lad was obviously downcast.

'I've taken an extra hour off,' Bern complained.

'Good of you, Bern,' I countered happily. 'But another time. Come on, love.'

Gordon was puzzled, as well as sad he was going to lose his audience. As I started for the door he turned to Bern and said accusingly, 'You told me he'd want to know all about the Mount's railway disaster.'

I stopped. Moll bumped into me. 'Disaster?' My voice seemed miles away. Bern had mentioned a disaster when we'd met at Elspeth's medical centre.

'Why, yes. At Mount St Mary.'

I felt my hands chill with sudden cold. Surely you can't have a railway disaster without a railway, can you? 'You said it never reached there.'

'It didn't.' He held up a book which seemed familiar. *'Because* of the disaster.' It was a copy of Chase's book with the town library's gilded stamp on its spine.

I cleared my throat. 'Er, what happened?'

'The tunnel,' he said.

'Tunnel,' I repeated faintly. 'In Mount St Mary?'

Bern chuckled, the lunatic. 'Well it couldn't be on *top,* could it?'

I didn't smile. My eyes were riveted on Gordon.

'It was awful,' Gordon said. 'The tunnel caved in.'

Tunnel, I thought, keeping tight control. The deep dark tunnel. It caved in. Dark and deep and it caved in.

I felt Moll's hand clamp hard on my arm. She propelled me to a chair. Gordon's enthusiastic voice and Bern's cosy little front room receded into a mist as all cares vanished.

'There now.' Rosie was bullying us all, but mostly me. 'That's what comes of going back to work too soon after an accident.'

'He insisted.' Moll was defending herself, not me.

'You don't need to tell me, my dear.' Rosie had the table cleared of Bern and Gordon's clobber, which showed how narked she was. 'Men are born stupid and stay so.'

She had a bowl of water and some towels.

Bern's concerned face came close. 'Are you all right, Lovejoy?' I wish people would stop saying that.

'You almost keeled right over.' Gordon sounded quite pleased.

Moll was holding me, her hands cool on my forehead. 'I'd better get him home.'

Rosie wasn't going to be thwarted. 'Drink this herb tea, Lovejoy.'

I drank a ghoulish mess of unspeakable green liquid. It stripped my mucosa down to my boots. I thought I'd finished with all this when my granny went.

'He needs some thick gruel,' Rosie pronounced.

'Jesus, Rosie!' from me in a whine.

'Don't argue, Lovejoy. He does.'

I hate the way women talk all around you, as if you either aren't there or are imbecilic.

'And,' Rosie battled on, glaring at Bern and Gordon, 'if you ask me, he needs less of your ridiculous stories about people being buried alive and screaming for help – '

'You're perfectly correct,' Moll cut in swiftly, yanking me to my feet. She practically hauled me to the door.

Gordon and Bern, both now properly in Rosie's bad books for reasons beyond me, followed us meekly to the car. Gordon reached in and put a brown folder on the back seat.

'That's my stuff on it,' he said, worried. 'You can give it to Bern when you've done.'

'Thanks, Gordon. Sorry about that, folks.'

'Get better soon, Lovejoy,' Bern said, giving a thumbs-up. 'Pop over when you want – '

'Not for at least a week, Bern,' Moll said firmly. 'He's to rest.'

'But look, Moll . . .' I started. She gunned the engine.

'People who are too stubborn,' Rosie said with satisfaction, 'have to be *told*.' She was still rabbiting on at them when we drove off. And one look at Moll's face told me I was in trouble with her as well. That's women. Just when they should be sympathetic they get mad as hell.

I decided to break the ice with some merry chatter. 'Sorry, Moll,' I said brightly. 'I – '

'Shut it.' She snapped it out just like me, so I did.

It was probably just as well we didn't speak on the way home. I never know what women mean half the bloody time anyhow.

In my garden a vannie called Doug was sitting on the grass. Tinker was there. They were part-way through a crate of brown ale, bottles everywhere. Two other vannies were smoking and swilling. A right party. They'd parked two vans on my gravel.

'What's going on?' I was all ready for a dust-up.

'Wotcher, Lovejoy.' Tinker gave me a wave.

'It's my treens,' Moll exclaimed, pleased.

'Treen,' I corrected mechanically. 'Collective noun.'

'You'll be so thrilled, darling.'

I hesitated at that 'darling', but as long as our tiff was forgotten I'd bear it.

'It's all here, Moll.' Tinker handed me a brown ale. He took Doug's bottle off him, wiped it on his filthy sleeve and gave it to Moll. His idea of gallantry.

'Oh,' she said faintly, taking it like something ticking. 'How kind.'

'Cheers.'

We all said cheers and drank, some more enthusiastically than others. My eyes were on the two covered vans.

'Right, lads.' I questioned Tinker with a nod. 'What's the game?'

He looked at me, puzzled. 'Should I have taken it to Val's?'

'I told you, Lovejoy,' Moll said. 'My treen.'

I stepped across and flicked the canvas aside. It was crammed with antiques from floor to ceiling. I'd never seen so many antiques on the road all at once. I thought, Moll hasn't bought two lorryloads in one morning, that's for sure. She came beside me, smiling eagerly and pointing.

'That was from Corporal. And that from Big Frank. And Jenny Bateman on North Hill sold us that table — '

'Wait,' I told her. I went to the other van. It was packed, too.

It was definitely one of those days. I took her to one side while the blokes loafed and swilled on the grass.

'You *bought* all this, Moll?'

'Yes.' She searched my face. 'You said.'

'*All* of it?'

'You told me, Lovejoy. Until I ran out of cheques.'

I closed my eyes and leant on the van's nearside.

'You know how much this lot'll cost?'

'Oh yes.' She rummaged in her handbag and brought out the stubby remains of a cheque-book. I nearly fainted again. 'I've kept a list.'

'You'll be paying till you're ninety, love.'

She laughed at that. 'Oh, Lovejoy. Don't worry. I'm really quite wealthy. Now. What are we going to do with it?'

An ache was splitting my forehead. 'It's yours, Moll.'

I explained I'd wanted her to make a profit. 'The expenses money you gave me, well, I spent on a porcelain. The accident smashed it. So I really owed it you back.'

She stared at me, her eyes filling.

'Oh, Lovejoy. How absolutely sweet. I thought it was for your ordinary business.'

As if my ordinary business came in lorryloads, I thought sardonically. There was nothing for it. Taking it all to Val's cran would set tongues — and worse — wagging. So it had to be here. I unlocked the door and waved to Tinker. He came up, sensing some uncertainty.

108

'It's all right, isn't it, Lovejoy?'

'Sure, Tinker.'

He shrugged. 'She said you'd given her two hours to buy all the wooden antiques in town. Here.' He plucked at my sleeve and whispered. 'Where the hell did we get the gelt?'

'That's taken care of,' I said.

'Thank gawd for that.' He took my bottle absently and emptied it down his throat. 'Did we get everything on your list?'

'Oh.' I made my reply in a studied voice. 'I think so. I'll have to check.'

'Great.' He whistled to the vannies. 'Shell it inside, lads.'

The vannies rose and did their stuff, all three eyeing Moll with unconcealed lust as they carried the things in. Tinker supervised, sitting contentedly on the beer crate. I got hold of Moll.

'What list?' I demanded softly.

She giggled. I'd never seen anybody so pleased with herself. 'I got confused about the codes and forgot the passwords. I pretended I was your partner. So they would bring the prices down.'

I wouldn't let go. '*What* list?'

'I had an old shopping list. I made them think you'd given me a list. We went into twelve shops. I knew they might cheat me, but all the dealers seemed very careful when I mentioned you.'

I'd never heard of anything like this in my life. And a bloody novice at that.

'Why the furniture? Treen's small kitchen stuff.'

She said brightly, 'But it's *wood*, Lovejoy. You said wood.'

And then I forgave her everything. Because a vannie carried past into the cottage a brilliant scintillating pre-Empire carver chair of genuine Sheraton design. I gasped. It was from Jason's place in the Arcade.

'That was very expensive,' Moll chatted happily. 'The stupid man took *such* a long time making up his mind to sell. I really had to act quite cross . . .'

The vannies unloaded piece after piece. She must have gone through town like a vacuum cleaner. There were walking sticks, minute stamp boxes, carved Bible rests, tobacco jars, pipes and racks galore, letter cases, drinking-glass cups, Pembroke tables, Sven's crummy fake stool, Chinese screens and lacquered trays, a serpentine silver-table with a pierced gallery (a sort of raised rim) unbelievably intact and at least eighteenth-century mahogany, wall plaques, polescreens, a sixteenth-century egg-tempera religious painting on a wood panel, a Canterbury . . . They were finished in an hour. Moll asked me how much to give them. Tinker told her that traditionally it's two pints each. She said how much is that, please? We waved them off a few minutes later.

'Let's go and look at it all, darling.'

Oho, I thought. Darling's back. She was delighted. I went inside gingerly. There was hardly room left to swing a cat. We'd be lucky to find the sink.

'Wasn't it fortunate, Tinker knowing the price of two pints?' she said.

'A real fluke,' I agreed gravely.

We'd hardly started making a genuine list when Maslow's bulk filled the doorway. You can imagine how I felt.

I won't go into details about his suspicions, or what he said. His reason for calling was to ask where I'd suddenly got enough money to drain our town of antiques, and so quickly after Nodge died at my hands. Just shows what a nasty-minded bloke he is.

Worse, he was not pleased finding Moll in my cottage. I guessed that his sinister little eyes would be sure to spot indications of her residence. He took Moll outside. I didn't interfere. They talked in the garden for nearly an hour while I got on with the job.

Eventually I heard his car go. Moll came in and paused on the threshold. I waited, not looking up but pretending to be examining a dumb-waiter. (Tip: these started about 1750 and genuine early ones *must* have three trays. If the bottom one is fretworked it will be invariably three-ply wood.) I spun it out, waiting for her to say she was going home and start packing. Then I heard her fill a kettle in the kitchen alcove. I relaxed and carried on.

'We'd better have a meal, Lovejoy,' she said in a quiet voice. 'I rather think it's been one of those days.'

14

We went to sleep that night thinking different things but in the same sort of way. I'd said yet again I wanted no bother with Tom. Moll pointed out there's strength in numbers. I said, fine, but would the Maslow brood see our relationship in those practical terms? Moll asked innocently what kind of relationship did I have in mind exactly, which made us both go quiet. Women are always one move ahead.

She told me the next morning I'd talked a lot in my sleep. Twice I'd seemed to be having nightmares. I answered lightly it was probably something I ate. She said sharply it was nothing of the kind.

The whole valley of the Bures river was layered in mist. It was still early, before seven. A watery sun managed to throw straight slivers of shadows through the erect elms and beeches of the northern end. Some cowbells tinkled nearby. Now and again a splash came from the river. The birds seemed late today, for some reason. Probably all gathered at my cottage shrieking their silly heads off for their cheese. Well, they could wait. Moll and I had driven as far as the village church and doubled back on the unpopulated bank. The mist filled the river hollow between its rims of trees so we could only vaguely see the roofs opposite, not the houses themselves. One car started up. Otherwise the only noise was Moll and me walking the bankside in the long grass.

We headed downstream. The river has low patches of reeds and some overhangs of trees and bushes. Here and there anglers had spread reeds to fish from. A big swan rose once nearby, frightening us as it held its wings and hissed. Moll said it had a nest on some low muddy recess next to the river. I used to think swans were placid.

I spotted the tavern first. We got ourselves orientated, lining up opposite the chimneys which poked from the mist and working out where the patch of nettles and that small sand hill would be. We found Chase's fishing spot with no trouble.

Moll had fetched a flask and some nosh. I sat dangling my bare feet in the water reading Gordon's file. Moll said we should keep an eye out for the shape of the hill as it became visible when the mist cleared. 'First impressions are always best,' she instructed.

I drew breath to say, oho, are they, but didn't. Gordon's file held some diagrams of a tunnel, section by section. They were labelled 'Scratton/Mount St Mary.' His own notes on lined paper in a round schoolboyish hand filled about eight pages. Then there was this newspaper cutting.

In 1847 the railway boom was on. Steam power had come to propel the Industrial Revolution as vigorously as watermill power had brought the world hurtling out of the Dark Ages a millennium previously. And even dozy East Anglia was caught up in the great drive to communicate and join in the motion. Any centre of population or industry had to have a railway. Profits at first promised to be enormous. The only thing needed was a pair of iron rails and a few wooden sleepers. And men.

The newspaper cutting was of the grand opening ceremony of the Mount St Mary tunnel. They had dug it out before the railway progressed this far. Even the Romans did this, having construction units begin viaducts or aqueducts in bits along their length rather than simply having the road or canal extend from its growing tip as a twig does. The tunnel was completed ahead of time. A ceremony was planned at which two engineers would crank a small decorated bogie northwards. On it, seated in elegant style, would be one of our esteemed local councillors in his regalia. Jonathan Chase, no less. As the town's mayor-elect he would wear the ancient seal and important chain of office and be the first official traveller through the tunnel. To symbolize the occasion, some artistic enthusiast hit on the idea of levelling contributuions from the railway companies and having this dignitary carry an appropriate gift to the small hamlet of Mount St Mary. So this is what they did, on a terrible rainy day. I read on while Moll sketched the river bank.

A band played. Crowds attended for the festive occasion. Morris dancers danced. Schools were unleashed. Speeches were made about the prosperity to come, about joining the great onward concourse of Mankind and suchlike jazz. Then the decorated carriage rolled up, pumped by two workmen, and Chase's ancestor stepped up to claim his mobile throne to enormous acclaim and the waving of streamers. The band played 'See the Conquering Hero Comes', and (I hated this bit) the little iron carriage trundled into the long tunnel.

It had rained for days. The river was higher than it had ever been in recorded memory. Farmers were grumbling about harvests. The brave tunnellers had had to cope with landslips, soaks, springing waters. Several times extra shoring was needed. The local clays were given to unpredictable shifts when the water-table rose, and four men died in the bricking alone. One had died of drowning when the tunnel was about half-way and was being driven through the course of an old lined well. It had been easily blocked and covered in, of course, but it served as yet another bad omen. The newspaper report said labourers had spoken for weeks about the running slurries which had necessitated sleepers being relaid several times during the finishing phase. Another ominous hint of coming tragedy was a monstrous crack which had appeared the Saturday before the ceremony.

Anybody but the Victorians would have chucked it in. But this much-maligned race was made of sterner stuff. Dangers existed to be faced down. Tragedy was there simply to be endured. Whether from a horde of charging fiends or a mountain cracking over you, the Victorian's task was merely to do one's duty, preferably with a casual smile playing around one's lips and a touch to the hat in farewell. You'll have guessed it's not my scene.

The year before, 1846, was the Great Railway Panic when 272 Acts zipped through Parliament and the iron horses really hit the road. Everybody on earth seemed to be inventing patented gadgets to do with railways, from Footwarmers For Ladies in Railway Coaches While Travelling to winches for raising counterweighted engines up inclines. A company whose tunnel opened late or − worse − not at all was utterly doomed in the scramble. And those stoic Victorians knew Duty when they saw it. Example had to be given to the lower social orders. Courage was the main necessity of life. Inevitably the omens were written off. Mankind was omnipotent, after all. There was no question of postponement, in some namby-pamby manner. God so clearly was an Englishman, especially if you sorted other upstart contenders out first.

So the iron carriage rumbled fatefully into the hill. The tunnel walls dripped. The echoes beat and reverberated. The two workmen's steady breathing was the only other sound. Behind, the band's playing faded. The cheering was cut off. Up ahead the hoop of daylight showed where the assembled crowds were waiting. Chase probably kept his gaze on the distant light. Maybe he mouthed the words of his forthcoming speech.

People afterwards estimated the carriage was at about the midpoint of the tunnel when the hill slipped. Just slipped. Maybe it was the weight of hillside waters held from drainage by the clay subsoil. Maybe some fault in building. Or maybe the bands and the crowds set up a growing flux of sound waves which established a tremor in the tunnel. But the hill slid sideways, slowly and with a fearsome whooing sound which quietened the spectators and the music.

The people ran, clutching children and heading away from the sight of trees and mounds of earth slithering down towards the river below. A small group was trapped and almost asphyxiated. Bandsmen dug with bare hands and clawed them free of the muddy deluge. Not a life was lost; except that deep in the earth three men were entombed.

Teams of workmen attacked the hill within minutes.

Strings of paniered horses were fetched. The men worked with that berserk fury rescuers always find, spurred on by feeble tapping signals from deep inside the Mount. The trouble seemed to be that nobody knew precisely which way the mountain had slipped. The tapping sounds emerged at a vent-hole, a cylindrical aperture tunnellers drive upwards to give themselves air while digging deeper into a hillside. Mercifully the vent-holes had not been covered in before the ceremony, but the landslip had either deformed them or severed them across. Rescuers hacking their way in along these vent-holes were obstructed by solid walls of dark clay. They had no means of guessing how long the new geological fault was.

A day passed. Then the now indescribable figure of the Right Honourable Jonathan Chase was seen clambering up the hillside towards the clusters of rescuers. He was identified as the dignitary only after being washed, and he was demented. Half out of his mind, he babbled how it was his duty to try to climb the nearest vent-hole and lead the rescuers in. He remembered starting struggling up some vent-hole but got lost. Everywhere there seemed solid clay and seas of mud. Twice he found himself drowning when the mud level rose sharply. He could remember nothing further until suddenly he was rolling downhill in the open air and two waiting children had screamed at the macabre sight.

Teams tried to backtrack for three days, led by the desperate Chase. They opened up all seven vent-holes and started tunnelling through the clay obstructing each one, though no clear place was detected where Chase could have escaped from. The conclusion was that the land had made several further surreptitious slips in the meantime. There was no clue to the route he took and he, poor man, was too overwrought to remember.

'Coffee?'

I jumped a mile at Moll's words. My feet were wrinkled from being immersed in the river too long. The Mount was just coming through the mist above us.

'Thanks.'

'Interesting?'

'You can read it after.'

The tunnel simply was no more. Eventually, after the inquest, the terrain around Mount St Mary was regarded as unsuitable for tunnelling. A different coastwards route would be sought at a later date, and that was that. The tunnel mouths were covered in, and traces of the disaster vanished with age.

Sipping Moll's hot coffee, I went back to the beginning. Chase had been presented with a cased gift for the Mount St Mary officials. The cutting stated that it was a 'munificent mechanical device' manufactured with 'consummate artistry' by George Adams and Francis Higgins. The company had contributed a sum equal to one full day's wage for every labouring man employed on the tunnel. The object, the reporter said, was a mechanical contrivance 'moving in all its parts and being of precious metal much admired'. As a 'humorous counterpoint', he narrated, certain workmen had donated with much improvised ceremonial a railway passenger's 'permissive token or pass' to Jonathan Chase. The listening spectators had been considerably amused by this levity. Chase took it in good part, announcing he was thereby legitimately entitled to travel as the very first passenger.

I took out the disc. The account explained the 'No 1' and the existence of a pass for a non-existent railway.

We watched the hillside emerge across the river into the pale morning sun. Moll took the clipping and started to read.

She asked questions here and there, but all I could think of was George W. Adams, maker of silver spoons. He worked from 1840 onwards in partnership with a wealthy lady called Mary Chawner. Francis Higgins was more famous. He was always at international exhibitions. You have to go a long way before you find more beautiful floral decorative cutlery than his. How odd that two spoonmakers were asked to make a 'mechanical contrivance', in precious metal. Maybe they were closer to the booming centre of industry and more familiar with engines. My eyes were fixed on the hill. The thought of a unique creation in silver lying preserved in pristine condition in there was breathtaking. It was miraculous. And made by two of the most fashionable silversmiths in an age of silversmithing brilliance. Preserved in a presentation casket in all its perfect loveliness. And priceless, almost.

Now, I'm no railway enthusiast. And modellers like Bert and Gordon really give me a bit of a pain when they're on about their subject. But even the most humdrum of clockwork models brings heady prices at famous London auctions nowadays. It's an area of neo-antiques you can't ignore, not any more. My mouth watered, but my heart screamed fear from my boots. Somebody had to go into the hill to find the contrivance. Deep inside.

'More coffee, Lovejoy?'

I jumped again. 'I wish you'd stop that,' I snapped irritably.

'Sorry, dear. Penny for your thoughts.'

'How many men does it take to build a tunnel, by hand?'

'Won't Gordon know?'

I already knew roughly the price of silver, but only for mid-1850s when it stuck at 61 pence an ounce, say five old shillings. At a rough guess a labourer got twice this a week. So translated into ounces of silver one man got equivalant to maybe a third of an ounce of silver a day. How wonderful it must have been when money was real. And how strange. I made a quick calculation. Ten labourers meant the Contrivance was three ounces. If they employed a hundred men it weighed thirty ounces. On the other hand, if they meant all the men on their bit of the nation's railways . . . I realized I was moaning softly and tried to turn it into a cough.

'Lovejoy. We must tell the police.' Moll had finished the article. She spoke full of determination. We were both sitting dangling our bare feet in the water now.

'Eh?'

'About the tunnel in there.'

'What have the police to do with it? The newspaper's nearly a century and a half old.'

'Well,' she said breathlessly, 'it's what police are for. Keeping order. That sort of thing.'

'No, love.'

'Tom says the police give us a code to live by.'

There's only one way to stop this kind of crap, so I said, 'Like they did for Leckie?'

She said nothing else. We sat side by side in silence, staring at the hillside. The big swan came and looked us over angrily from time to time. As if anybody would want to pinch any of its little grey ducks.

I think Moll knew then that we were going to try to find the way into the hill. How else to get back at Fergus and Jake? Getting the Contrivance when they wanted it was the only means I had of striking at them. And I'd laugh in their faces when I sold it for a fortune. It would be known as the Lovejoy Contrivance. Or maybe the Lovejoy Trove? The Lovejoy Treasure? *At Claridge's Reception today, in the presence of the Keeper of the Royal Museums, London Society paid glowing tribute to Lovejoy's bravery and ingenuity. The Coroner, in handing over a cheque, stated* –

'Can't we hire a potholer to dig it up for us?' Moll demanded.

'No. Whoever finds it first gets its full market value.' I shrugged. 'That's got to be me.'

'Us, darling.'

Oh, well. 'Us, then,' I said after a pause.

There was no point in putting it off. The mist had cleared. The hill stood mild and benign above the small hamlet. It was so bloody pastoral and innocent.

'Come on, love,' I said. We dried each other's feet on a towel and set off for the bridge.

15

You can *smell* precious antiques. I swear it. All that day as Moll and I climbed the hillside I could feel that lovely sexy exquisite Contrivance beneath us, inside the living breast of the Mount. I felt its glowing strength radiate up through the rock and the hill's bones into my chest. There it set up a chiming and a clanging lovelier to me than any peal of cathedral bells. Antiques are life. They are everything.

Allow me a digression, folks.

There are more stolen antiques than there are straight ones. And there are more lying buried, waiting to be found, than both those put together. I can show you the precise spot in a sandbank off our coast here — you can stand on it at low tide — where it is known for certain that scores of ships lie sunken in the sands. Their cargoes were merely valuable centuries ago, but now they're beyond utterance. There's no word beyond priceless, is there?

The trouble is we all want these precious things. So we buy what's available. And think a moment: what *is* available, to be exact? Well, stuff for sale, as in antique shops or auctions, and stuff we dig up ourselves. And that's all.

The main difference is that stuff we dig up — should we be so lucky — is free. And nothing else in this life ever is, nothing else at all. Think, therefore, how wonderful it would be actually to dig up a ship like the Viking King's tomb in Sutton Hoo, and claim the lot. Naturally, it goes into the national museums, but you get the gelt and the prestige.

But hold hard. Before you rush out with bucket and spade, ponder how much *more* wonderful it would be not to do any digging at all, yet *still* finish up owning real genuine priceless (or even pricey will do) antiques. This equation has preoccupied Mankind since Adam dressed. It has been solved by two kinds of people. They are the crooks, and the rich unscrupulous collectors.

In countries with a wealth of archaelogical remains — Italy, Greece, Turkey, the Latin Americas, India, Egypt, Iraq, *et cetera* — there's a thriving criminality. There are diggers who locate, say, a tomb and dig up the stuff to sell. They're called *tombaroli* in Italy, *tymborychoi* in ancient Macedonia, and 'scavvies' around here. The trick is to loot genuine antiques from their place of rest and sell to the highest bidder who'll keep his mouth shut. Don't tell me it's illegal and dangerous — it's been that since Emperor Vespasian passed his famous law against it. But people still do it. And it doesn't have to be an ancient building such as a Celtic ring-grave or a buried temple. Nowadays the biggest boom in this kind of illegal knavery is 'industrial archaeology'. This daft term means prototype engines, whole buildings, clothes, models working and otherwise, engineering drawings, architectural mock-ups, patent copies, navvies' diaries, sociological records, expense books, legal records, instruments, medical devices, commercial samples, and hundreds of kinds of artifacts. If you don't believe me, look at the latest price catalogue from your local auction. You'll find somebody just paid a sum equal to your entire year's wages for some little clockwork sundry, and maybe ten times that for a big one.

Theft therefore raises its ugly head. Nowadays people will steal

117

rushlight holders from outside your house. Your old street gas-lamps. Your elderly car. Your fascinating old garden gate with those quaint old hinges, and Grandad's old watch and his pince-nez while he dozes at the seaside. Theft, and forgery. The only risk is getting caught.

A legitimately lost antique, though, is different. It's quite legal to find it. And that's exactly what is so exciting. And that's what was exciting me now. Somewhere in the hill was *my* precious discovery.

Normally I'm not very patient. You can imagine how I was on that bloody hillside. I was almost frantic, hurrying to and fro over the ground and scratching myself to blazes on the gorse. Moll kept on stopping for a rest but I got her up each time. We quartered the ground and walked in waggles, six paces one side and six the other. I knew the contours, very roughly. The hill is a sort of skew-shaped mound, with the river cutting its way round the steeper slope and a road following it until the houses begin almost as soon as the bend is complete. A Roman road runs straight as a die northwards through there, maybe two miles off. But even from the very top there seemed to be no sign of the ventholes. The notes Gordon gave me said seven. It didn't seem enough to draw air in for a gang of men slogging away knee deep in mud. Maybe they had some kind of wind engine to funnel air down on to the labouring teams.

There was a line of gorse bushes running obliquely across the steeper face of the hill. The growth was interrupted by a small hollow, after which the line began again further down. We sat in the dip and had another glug of Moll's brew.

'I'm tired, Lovejoy.' And she looked it.

'So am I,' I said mercilessly. You can't go stopping for a doze when you're so near, can you? 'The problem as I see it is old Chase.'

All we knew about Doc Chase was that he stuck to a routine on his day off. Zip to Scratton's archaic tunnel for a few minutes, then down to the river. There, pretending to fish, he would sit on the opposite bank *which meant he was facing this way*. I scrambled to the downhill margin of the dip and looked out. You could just see the swan's big flat nest. The sand hill was in clear view but the gorse bushes near me partly obscured Doc's fishing spot.

I slid down and explained to Moll. She was unimpressed. 'What's so marvellous? If you sit opposite a hill of *course* you can see it,' she said heartlessly, 'you can't miss it.'

'But it explains why he sat *there*, Moll.'

She shrugged. 'An angler needs a river or he can't fish.'

'He only *pretended* to.'

'Lovejoy,' she said with maddening reason, 'if the old man

118

wanted to find what's inside this hill, why didn't he come up and search like we're doing?'

Women are exasperating. 'He was old. Maybe he knew he was close to a stroke.'

'Then he should have been more sensible,' Moll said calmly. 'Leckie would have helped him.'

'Maybe he tried to tell Leckie, through Leckie's wife?'

'I never liked Julia. Mean little eyes. More coffee?'

We rested for a few more minutes, then started on the summit and worked downwards, heading towards the southern slope. It took a long time but I reached the end of my area before Moll did, and whistled to her. She looked up and waved. I pointed to show I was coming up. That was another quarter of an hour. We met on the lip of our hollow. I looked around to see where the cigarette smoke was coming from.

'Found anything, Lovejoy?'

Jake Pelman and his nerk were lounging in the dip. They had Moll's hamper open.

'Caught you,' I said lightly.

'You didn't leave us much,' he complained, grinning.

'Next time you'll get less, Jake.'

Moll was furious. 'How dare you! You've eaten the salmon!' she blazed. 'Lovejoy, I had some lovely salmon — '

The nerk kept his eyes on me. They rose as Moll and I came down slowly. I'd quickly scanned the rest of the hillside. They seemed to be all the enemy there was. For the moment. I had to hold Moll back. She was all for taking a swing at them.

'You'll get yourselves in trouble,' I told Jake.

'That's what Fergus sent us to say, Lovejoy.' Jake blew fag smoke at us. 'Trouble. You're in it.' He nudged his goon to share the joke. 'Somebody's just paged a certain CID man. Passed word his wife's shagging Lovejoy in the long grass.'

'You — ' Moll started for Jake but I yanked her still.

'I'll ask you again, Lovejoy.' I'd never seen Jake smile properly before. 'Found anything?'

'No,' I admitted candidly. 'But I know what I'm looking for.'

I hit the goon with a stone. I'd picked it up on the edge of the hollow on the pretence of helping Moll down. His teeth splintered and he staggered on his heels. Splashes of red radiated over his countenance and blood drooled down his chin. He fell back with a gratifying thump, dazed. Jake was instantly ten feet off. He had one of those knives. I just had to laugh. He looked like a staid amateur dramatics showing of a Parisian apache.

'Put it away, Jake,' I told him, still amused. 'You'll frighten the life out of me.'

He stayed where he was, eyeing me warily while his mate groaned. 'Fergie's getting mad, Lovejoy.'

'Message received, Jake.' I still held my stone. The nerk was spitting and feeling his teeth.

Jake gave his pal a nod. They made their way out of the dip. For a second they stood looking down at us both. I could tell what they were thinking, and smiled nastily.

'You dare,' I chided, all friendly.

They glanced at each other and went. We gave them a few minutes to get clear, collected our stuff and then cut through the zigzag line of gorse bushes towards the Three Tiles. As we walked through the cobbled yard Fergus merrily raised a glass to us from the window. He was still beaming.

That night Moll phone Tom from my cottage while I went out and sat on my unfinished wall, thinking. It was a long conversation.

And that night, too, a crowd of blokes disrupted the usual gaiety of the pub in town where Val's husband George works. They injured George and the two other barmen, but not too much. There was a good old-fashioned rumble. Several customers were hurt. By all accounts the public bar and the taproom were left in an absolute shambles. And all the windows in Val's house were broken, front and back. Not one other house in the street was touched. Margaret phoned me to tell me all this about midnight. Tinker had just got the news to her. Maybe he had been trying to get through when Moll and Tom were speaking. I asked if Val was hurt. Margaret said no, just frightened. Inspector Maslow was there now, and asking questions. I wonder he doesn't get a job and go to work like everybody else.

Moll drowsily asked what's the matter when I got back to bed.

'Nothing,' I told her. 'Go to sleep.'

16

The next few days were hard work. I combed the library for maps of the Mount. I plagued the history department in a local college. I kept on at the Folklore Club, which meets every Sunday in the Hole-in-the-Wall, our oldest pub for miles. I even got on to the University, but finally wrote them off. I finished up knowing more about the geology of our district than anybody I know. And I was no wiser.

Of course, what was narking me was that I knew precisely what the precious Item was. It was almost certainly a working model of the first engine due to come along the new railway line. And I knew precisely what it was made of because silversmiths work in silver, right? And even who made it. And I knew where it was — somewhere inside one of East Anglia's very few definite hills. When you say it quick it sounds easy. If you know where and what and that it's free . . . The galling thing was getting my claws on it.

Gordon and Bern came over to the cottage twice. I had to keep up the pretence of developing an interest in their hobby. It's very difficult, especially when a train to me is just a long box on wheels. And *real* antiques only start from 1836, backwards of course. Which means that railways and their gadgetry should properly be called modern, apart from the short run from 1813 when first William Hedley courageously replaced a pit pony by a travelling thing called a steaming engine in Wylam Colliery.

Still, I pretended enthusiasm as much as I could, and tried not to nod off or yawn too obviously. I kept trying to get us round to the structure of that horrible tunnel. They kept trying to tell me where I could travel on our few remaining steam trains. There was another problem. If Jake his nerks were watching out for my movements I'd not be doing Bern and young Gordon any favours by associating with them. Jake's thick, but with application and a bit of luck even he might work out about two and two being four.

The gorgeous Nurse Patmore took my stitches out the following Friday. Moll dropped me off at the surgery while she went shopping for us. Pat hurt me like hell, but told me with breezy determination that it didn't hurt at all and that I'd soon be as bad as new again. I called her heartless. Elspeth poked her clip-board in then and asked if Lovejoy was able to run yet. Pat ignored my frantic eyebrow signals. She said, smiling with sadistic glee, that I could run tomorrow, exercises as well.

One of Elspeth Haverill's teams was already lumbering across the countryside. I sat with her on a form waiting for any chance survivors to return. During my unstitching I'd pumped Pat for more information, until she got worried. They both knew I was asking too much, too often, but I wouldn't say why.

A local historian like Chase would naturally be fascinated by his ancestor Jonathan Chase's gruesome experience on that terrible day. Maybe tales had been passed down through the family. But the old doctor's trick of hiding his little railway pass, and his determinedly hopeless fishing, told me a great deal about the man. He was a thinker, a clever and quiet man. He wasn't the sort to go babbling to Mrs Leckworth, his clerical assistant. There was some obvious clue here, a clue as big as a barn. And I couldn't see the bloody thing for looking. I got to work, skilfully nudging Elspeth's attention off her list of atherosclerotics.

'Is that somebody?' I pointed, smiling and eager.

'Not yet.' Elspeth had a stopwatch. It was, I noticed with disgust, modern, accurate, and dull as ditchwater. 'Say five more minutes.'

'I'm looking forward to joining in,' I lied cheerfully.

She was pleased. 'I'm so glad you've come round to our way of thinking, Lovejoy. Such a *benefit.*'

'Were you working with old Chase when Mrs Leckworth was here?' It was too sudden a switch. Elspeth shot me through with a glance.

'No.' She said it primly, with dislike. 'And I'm quite glad.'

'Isn't, er, wasn't she very nice?' I was all innocence, peering towards the distant wood for her runners.

'She didn't have a very good reputation. Nurse Patmore found her bossy and . . . unprofessional.' Elspeth's eyes were on her lists, but her mind wasn't. 'Look, Lovejoy. I'm not stupid. Don't treat me as if I am.'

'Eh?'

She doodled idly on her paper. 'I *know* you're not really interested in our health scheme. I can feel it.' I tried to start an indignant denial but she got in first. 'There's something wrong, isn't there? To do with Doctor and Mr Leckworth. I sensed it in your cottage.'

I gave in, shrugged. 'Maybe, love.'

She turned her eyes full on me. 'Is Moll a police-woman?'

It was a horrible thought. See how devious women's minds are, deep down? That possibility hadn't even crossed my mind. I swallowed uneasily. Dear God. Moll a peeler. And in my divan, earlier and earlier every dusk.

'No. I hope not.'

A tubby runner trundled flabbily into view from the edge of the wood. Another tottered feebly after him. We watched without speaking for a second.

'You're in trouble with the police, aren't you, Lovejoy?'

So many people kept asking me this I was beginning to wonder. I made a face. 'Dunno.'

She put her hand on my arm. 'Inspector Maslow came here yesterday. He asked a lot about you. We aren't supposed to tell you. He said . . . he said criminal charges were pending.'

And Nurse Patmore hadn't so much as said a word to tip me off. The cow. I felt like asking for my stitches back.

'That's Maslow all over, Elspeth. Don't worry.'

'Is what you're doing . . . *good,* Lovejoy?'

The stragglers were all out of the wood now, the leader a few hundred yards off. She would have to start scribbling soon.

'How the hell do I answer that?'

'Well, would Dr Chase approve?'

I thought hard. He had gone to a lot of trouble to switch the Bramah lock. But why not simply *tell* Leckie about the principal clue, which was that simple little tin disc? Unless Leckie knew already, and Doc's decision to switch the Bramah lock was for somebody else.

'What happened to the rest of his furniture?' I asked her this as the sweating runners came reeling up, knackered.

'Given to the children's home in town.'

'And those three things? The old bag, the book, the escritoire?'

'I sent them to the local auction. He was most particular. Made Nurse Patmore and myself promise.' She smiled. 'Said it was part of some game.'

'Game?' The six men had flopped on the grass now, legs in the air like dead flies.

'The divvie game, he called it. I think he meant – '

'*He said that?*'

'Why, yes.'

Elspeth got started on the exhausted men. She got the back markers strapped into a transparent set of gear like a frogman's and set them breathing into a bag full of tubes. I watched nervously while she made the poor bastards pedal like the clappers on fixed bicycles. They looked in a state of collapse. If that's health, I thought, give me 'flu any time. Within minutes the men were calling over to Elspeth, demanding to be released. I kept out of the way while she checked them off. They went inside the house one by one to change.

Doc Chase had known that some divvie would sooner or later tune in to this Bramah lock, wherever it lay, and wonder what it concealed. It was a fail-safe, in case they got Leckie.

'Still here, Lovejoy?' Nurse Patmore, looking ominously at Elspeth and propping her bike against the wall.

'Er, waiting for Moll.'

'She's in her car out front.'

We said cheerios too cautiously for old friends, and I shouted to Elspeth to get a new hourglass for tomorrow's record-breaking run and I'd show the lot of them.

I got in beside Moll. 'Town, love,' I told her. 'Here, one thing. Are you a bobby?'

'No.' She looked a bit puzzled but let it go. She took us off, definitely peaky. 'I've had a message, Lovejoy. Tom's coming back for the weekend. I think I'd better . . .'

'Right,' I said, feeling rotten. 'Look. Can you lend me enough to get my car mended?' Sooner or later I'd make a start on our antique furniture and that treen.

'Send me the bill.' She added quickly, 'By post would be best.'

'Thanks,' I said. 'Er, I'll owe it you. All right?'

'If you insist.' She only said that after we'd gone another mile. I couldn't tell if she was mad at me again or not.

I said nothing else till we reached the High Street and she put me down outside the library. She said she would leave a meal ready and a load of groceries indoors, and to look out for Jake and his horrid assistants. I said I would. She already had a key to collect her things. I watched her motor off into the traffic. Funny how you can feel alone in a crowded street. I waited for her to wave, but she reached third gear for her handbag's sake and simply carried on going.

Because of my brief Elspeth-Nurse-Patmore-stitches-Moll drama at Six Elm Green, I was late for the auction. There was very little to interest me, but you can never tell. You can't ever trust a catalogue. You have to see for yourself.

By the time I made it down East Hill the cafés were bulging. Dealers' vans were neatly blocking the main sea road out of town. Pubs were fuming and slurping, pie-shops were roaring. This end of town was humming with life and interest. By the time I clinked open the glass doors and slid into the mob Tinker was mad as hell. Not a face turned from the auctioneer, but they all sensed a new rival had just walked in.

'Where the bleeding hell you been, Lovejoy?'

'Why's it Jive?'

Jive's the apprentice auctioneer, a pimply mirthless youth who gets all the rotten jobs. He was struggling to make sense of the bids. The lads were mucking him about, waving and pointing to each other to confuse an inexperienced auctioneer. If enough of you do it he'll knock valuable items down for a song, just from frustrated bewilderment. It's called 'flagging' in the trade, but it's only worth doing if you've a lot of friends in, otherwise you take a fearsome risk.

'Gaffer's ill.'

Lemuel was seated on a chaise-longue sucking on a dripping meat pie and picking losers again. It was the most horrible sight I've ever seen. Tinker saw me recoil and nudged me.

'Lemuel's found out so don't knock him.'

'Eh?'

'Black Fergus and Jake. They've got two blokes to nobble you.'

'Two?' I thought I'd got rid of one.

'Two. They're Brummie lads.'

I went cold. I should explain there's a sort of hierarchy of goons. There's always a lot of aggro where you get antiques and often goons are hired to see somebody off or to straighten a dealer up. But there are goons and goons. You can talk your way out of trouble with hard lads from Blackpool, and I assure you it is well worth the vocal effort. Brighton shells up a very rag-taggle mob — noisy, thick as planks, lots of wind and water. London's goons are so direct it's painful. Their idea of 'correction', as it's often termed, is to arrive like Fred Karno's army and simply flail about. Mancunians stay at home, so outside Manchester you are quite safe. Same with Newcastle. But Tinker's mention of two Birmingham nerks made my flesh crawl. They are real aggro men who'll marmalize anybody for a few quid.

I said, 'Keep calm, Tinker,' though my throat constricted. 'Are they the ones who did Val's gaff?'

'People say so.'

'Mine next, I suppose. How is she?'

'Val? Gone to her auntie's.'

'Thank God for that.'

We stood in the packed hall watching the bidding. Jive was quavering away, hopeless. Some dealers were grinning. The relatively few honest customers were unaware of anything amiss. They are easily spotted, having come to the auction merely for one item, rarely two. Antique dealers give these innocent genuine bidders a funny nickname: 'women'. For every wally and barker there's maybe one 'woman', in most auctions.

'Seen Helen?'

'No.' Tinker thought a moment, tuning his mental radar. 'She'll be at Patrick's place in a few minutes.'

Unlikely, but I knew better than to argue. I scanned the items on display. There was a dull mixture of Victorian furniture. One unidentified Norwich School oil was alluring, though it needed a lot of care. And there was a delectable silver cruet set by the two Fenton brothers of Sheffield. I could see Big Frank from Suffolk ogling it. Jean was in, and Madge. Brad was at the tea bar chatting up the lady. He would be waiting for a small percussion pepperbox pistol, low down in the lot numbers. Alfred's bowler hat was prominent down by the locked porcelain cabinet. He felt my gaze, looked across between the sea of shoulders, and raised comical eyebrows. He's a right one for remembering how cheap everything was before the Great War. I grinned and nodded. Sven was drifting about purposelessly. I had mixed feelings about Sven. He seemed cheerful, but I couldn't quite forget how servile he had looked that day in the White Hart with Fergus and Jake. Margaret was going over some pewter, so I slid through the mob and tackled her about Nodge's Bustelli.

'I got it,' she said, after helloing and quizzing me about my decrepit health. 'Lucky. Seeing,' she added quietly, 'seeing Nodge died so soon after.'

'Wasn't it just!' I shook my head sadly.

'Your lady friend's back at the cottage basting the duck, I suppose?'

'Shut it, love. Have you a buyer?'

'I think so. If it falls through, can I use Tinker to find one?'

'Mmmm. Look, love.' I pulled her away from the pewters. 'How safe is Bill Hassall?' She looked uncomfortable. I had to help because women are usually reticent about the other women who run around, especially when it's a man asking. 'I mean about his missus and Leckie.'

'I don't think he knew.'

'Is he anything to do with Jake Pelman? Fergus?' She gave me an immediate headshake, but hesitated after I added, 'Anything between Julia Leckworth and Bill Hassall, for instance?'

'No,' she said finally. 'But they say Julia's daft on Fergus. They're together now.'

'Thanks.'

I nodded to Tinker and pushed my way to the door. Those few minutes Tinker had predicted were up. Helen would be at Patrick's.

And she was, having a cigarette and going over some early Bilston enamels. Patrick screamed at me down the Arcade as soon as I came in view.

'Lovejoy! You perfect poppet!' He struck a theatrical pose of welcome in his doorway. He was wearing a maroon and orange caftan. 'Come in, dearie! Home,' he misquoted grandly in his shrillest voice, 'home is the sailor, home from the sea!'

'How do.' I always go red when he does this act. I could see Helen smiling inside his main display room. These places are only small, one room and an alcove. Helen had managed to find a tall stool again, her favourite pose to show off her shiny curved legs.

Patrick dragged me in. There were four or five customers looking about. He pushed them rudely aside and whispered to me, 'Don't notice Helen's impossible hairstyle, Lovejoy! Just *bear* it!' I went redder, because Patrick's penetrating whispers are made to be heard. Helen only laughed. It's odd, really, because if anybody else criticizes her she goes mad.

'Hello, Lovejoy.'

'Wotcher, love.'

126

'The brave young man!' Patrick swept aside a customer and did a grand gesture. 'So narrowly plucked from the jaws of death!' He meant the car accident.

The customers were as embarrassed as me. Lily came in from the alcove. She seemed pleased to see me and said how marvellous it was I'd managed to buy so many antiques. She said she liked Moll.

'She's perfectly sweet, Lovejoy,' Patrick agreed silkily. 'And when she *learns* about those off-the-peg pleated skirts with those *crippling* decorated belts from Haythorn's she'll be sweeter still. *Do* tell her.'

'Er, well.' I'd only come to see Helen.

'Helen's full of the joys of spring, Lovejoy.' Patrick sat on a chair to do his eyes. 'She's talked non-stop about you. Watch out. She'll go for your ankles.'

I took advantage of Patrick's preoccupation to pull Helen into the alcove. She guessed I was not so concerned about the lovely Bilston enamels this time.

'What is it, Lovejoy? You look desperate.'

'I am. Is there *anything* you haven't told me?'

'No, love. Except how much I dislike coppers' wives. She's too pretty-pretty sweet-little-Alice by far.'

'It's over.'

'That's good.'

'Nothing about Leckie?' I pressed her. 'Nothing he might have said?'

She flicked her cigarette. I told her not to smoke, because Patrick had coins, watercolours and a display of copper medallions but Helen never takes much notice of what I say.

'Why ask, Lovejoy?' She put down the Bilston carefully. 'You knew Leckie better than anybody. Do you seriously think he would send you a useless message?' She pursed her lips and told me that wasn't her idea of Leckie. 'He was cool as a cucumber when he scribbled it. He paused a bit, even smiled.' Her eyes were damp. 'The fault's in you, Lovejoy. Whatever it is you're looking for you probably already have in your pocket.'

'But this message didn't say much — '

'It will be enough.' She leant across and bussed me lightly on the face. 'Lovejoy. I don't know what's going on, why the CID are everywhere asking about you. Why everybody you know seems to be dying in road accidents. But don't let Leckie have done it for nothing.'

Before I knew it I'd flung myself into the Arcade in a blazing temper. Patrick shrilled some cutting remark after me, but I didn't pause until I was through the back street and into the old pub yard.

Some buskers were playing away there for the pedestrians. I stalked through the crowd, got a pint and sat at a table. The bloody cheek of it. I must have been white with rage.

Helen could have saved Leckie, the grumbling useless bitch. Yet all she did was carry a message, too late to do any good. Couldn't be bothered to lift a finger. Simply criticizes me the minute I want some help. That's the trouble with women. Full of useless bloody advice while they do absolutely sod all. Everybody knows that. I marched in for another glass, fuming.

By closing time I was sloshed. I got a taxi from the stand outside the corn-market and got myself driven back to the cottage. It took practically my last groat.

I paid him off and staggered up the gravel path. I remember even now how quiet the garden was, how the afternoon seemed one for dozing through. Soporific, I think the word is. I started singing, but what I don't know. I must have taken a year to unlock the door.

For an instant I thought it was Moll who had followed me in. When I looked around the woman was standing there, blonde and fetching. I gaped and tried to keep upright.

'We've never really met, Lovejoy,' she said. 'May I come in?'

'You're Julia,' I said foolishly. It was Leckie's wife.

She walked past me and went inside. I shrugged, followed her in and closed the door.

17

I'm not so proud of that Friday night that I want to tell everything that went on, even if I remembered blow by blow, which I don't. Julia seemed to expect it, so I fetched out my reserve bottle of dubious sherry. We talked about Leckie. She seemed really rather sad, genuinely so. I was sure she wasn't putting it on. I remember consoling her. We had some more sherry. I decided we ought to have a party to cheer ourselves up. She vanished, came back with more bottles.

By dusk we were in the garden. It came on to rain which drove us indoors. I insisted on making her some grub and shared a meal some friendly elves had kindly left out for me. I vaguely remember singing her a song, and her watching me but not joining in. After that it gets vaguely woozy. I told her about me and Leckie in the army, the bridge of bamboo and that bloody tunnel. At least, I think I did. I can recollect doing something with matchsticks on the table to show how illogical it is to be scared of tunnels falling on you when they are built on mathematical principles. In my hazy memory of this particular night Julia doesn't say much, just seems to be watching steadily. Then dusk fell and I had to put the lights on. I fell over a few things and I can remember laughing like a lunatic at not being able to get up. Then I tried to demonstrate how a savage karate chop would decapitate any Brummie goon that lurched in. Things seemed so funny. I laughed and laughed.

I woke next morning with the light still on. Julia was gone. The room showed that a lot of activity had taken place. My divan bed, for instance, was a shambles. There was no note. I had a splitting headache. It took me an hour to put the bedclothes out on the line to air. The grass was still wet, but the rain had stopped. I brewed up and sat miserably in the cool air, wondering how much I had told her. It's no good thinking I'm a crude vulgar layabout. I admit it. Julia and I had gone at each other like animals.

What worried me was a map, spread across the foot of the bed when I woke. I should have been more careful. It was the Ordnance Survey map of the Mount St Mary area. Worse still, I couldn't find the little railway pass. Maybe I had dropped it somewhere in town, though. Had Julia, I wondered, said *why* she'd called round in the first place? If so, I couldn't remember. I felt miserably that I ought to assume the worst. Maybe Julia simply knew I'd be easy, came and did her stuff and learned everything I knew about Leckie's and Chase's plan to recover the precious silver Contrivance, and simply find out from me whereabouts it was. I could have kicked myself. I had been ahead of Jake and Fergus in the race, and chucked all my advantage away for a mess of pottage, so to speak. That's the trouble with will-power. Everybody else's is so much better quality.

I showered and cleaned up. I shaved ferociously. I even swept the cottage out, as penance. I fed the birds and washed the windows aggressively. I washed crockery, re-made the bed and folded it away. By noon I'd recovered, with some aspirin. I was still mad at myself, but some determination had crept back into my actions.

The pasties I hotted up for dinner were iron hard. Normally I sling them out, but this time I ground my way through them inch by inch in atonement. I had a cold bath after that. Two pints of tea, and I was ready to face my responsibilities.

From now on I had to assume two things. First, that I'd told Julia all I knew, and that Fergus knew as much as I did. All it meant was that I was now in a flaming hurry, whereas before I'd been ambling along like a fool just hoping things would solve themselves. Second, I had to assume that Helen had been right, that I was mentally shirking truths *that I already knew*. I'd have to face up to it all. If she was right about my self-trickery, I could easily guess why I was evading the issue. I was probably scared of the tunnel I might find deep inside that hill. It was high time I went over all the events leading up to this morning, especially those concerning Leckie. I might make up part of the leeway I'd just lost.

I walked up to the post hut and borrowed Rose's local contour maps from her door. She'd be as mad as hell, but it was time other folk besides myself made a few sacrifices. I went back and sat on my wall. Listing all the things you know about a person isn't all that easy. Try it. You tend to miss things out simply *because* you know them so well. Despite my reluctance, I forced myself to go over every single detail of our relationship, from the moment Leckie took my first parade to the instant I saw him hurtle against the tree in that thunderstorm. There seemed nothing there, so I forced my mind on into the events of his death, right up to finding Jake and his nerk in that hollow on Mount St Mary in the severed line of gorse. I forced myself to go over what Gordon and Bert told me.

It took me three hours. By then I was bushed. I broke for a brew-up, knowing I was coming closer and closer. By four o'clock I was focused clearly and resolutely on the niggly bit that had rankled for so long. I'd found it. It was one of the things Margaret had said that day I phoned her from calling at Virgil's in Medham. She'd said Leckie was a collector of religious relics. I hadn't known that. I remembered how surprised I was.

I got the map out. A small circle was inscribed on a contour line. It would be just about where the hollow is on the Mount. My spine tingled. On the larger scale map there it was again, inscribed as well. My chin was suddenly stinging with sweat and my elbow flexures became sticky. And abruptly I knew it. I said, 'God Almighty.' The birds took no notice but the robin on my arm looked shocked for a minute. The well. The tunnel had pierced an old well.

Now I knew how Leckie and Doc Chase had come together, how Leckie knew of Chase's quest. I knew why Leckie considered himself the legitimate discoverer once Chase had passed on. I knew how old Jonathan Chase, that brave Victorian dignitary, had got out of the hill. And I knew exactly why he and the rescue workers hadn't managed to get back despite the desperate labour of several hundreds of them. I knew why Doc Chase sat for hours just staring at a hillside instead of wandering about on it. And why he went to Scratton to look briefly at a dull old tunnel before going 'fishing'. *And I knew that the tunnel deep inside Mount St Mary could be reached.*

But worst of all, I knew the way in. My teeth were chattering as I set the robin down and brushed the remaining bits off the paving with a broom. I'd have to go. Elspeth came in her car about then to take me to her training programme. I'd forgotten she was coming, but I went with her for company's sake. You can imagine the state I was in afterwards; bad enough before.

We had supper in a pub that evening. She told me which drinks and grub had least calories. I said, great, and borrowed from her because I happened to be a bit short at the time.

I was up at the ungodly hour of five o'clock. I'd tried the night before to phone Tinker at the White Hart, but failed. No mates, no car, no money and no bird. In spite of it all I got my bike pumped up and was burning the road up north-west to Scratton before dawn.

There's an advantage in a bicycle. It's silent. It can be fairly fast. It can be concealed in a way a motor cannot. And it doesn't need a motorway. I was certain nobody could see me as I mounted my trusty steed and freewheeled down to the watersplash. I crossed the river and pedalled laboriously up the other slope of the valley. The surgery at Six Elm Green was silent, and the village still kipping like a top.

From there I cut right, along a footpath leading due north. It runs between fields and through copses towards Scratton. I was surprised what a lot of cows were about. I thought they'd still be in bed. Only once I met some chap, a farm labourer leading a horse the size of an abbey. It frightened me to death, but he only said, 'Good luck, chum.' Probably thought I was out searching for birds.

On a bike I could avoid even the side roads. Where the absence of footpaths forced me towards the metalled Mount St Mary road I got off and walked on the fieldwards side of hedges, my plimsolls wet with dew. By the time I came in view of the Mount I was aching from all the unaccustomed exercise. I'd taken longer than I really wanted and the day was full up. The hillside stood clearly outlined. Funny, but it appeared somehow less anonymous than previously, more personal, as if it was getting to know these crummy people who kept coming to poke at its scrubby surface.

A car or two ran south towards our town, saloons. Jake's great heap was nowhere in sight. Surely a Brummie wouldn't be stationed on the hillside? They are notorious townies, even worse than me. I got to the edge of the line of dense gorse bushes and walked along it, pushing my bike with difficulty along the uneven slope. I don't suppose I did it very well, but I had this idea of using the gorse line as a screen from people down on the valley road.

It was seven-thirty when I reached the hollow where Moll and I had picnicked. Full of misgiving, I laid the bike down, covered it as best I could, and slid slowly down into the recess. It was the place all right. Its margins, tilted to accommodate the hill's slope, were rounded. What interested me most was that about half-way down, the sides gave a sudden levelling, as if somebody had tried to create a sort of ledge all the way round. The hollow bore a scattering of hawthorns and sloes, not very many, yet more than the rest of the hill had. No stones were visible.

At home I'd found a protractor, a cheap bit of plastic marked in degrees. I'd lashed a ruler and a pencil to it along fixed radii, using the Ordnance Survey map as a guide. If I pointed the ruler at the distant church spire, the pub below should fall exactly on the pencil's line, sixty-eight degrees of difference. I climbed out and stood by the nearest gorse bush. Spot on. The church line and the pub line intersected exactly where I stood. I put my home-made gadget into the bike's bag and sat down to look at the hollow, the hollow which I now knew marked the ancient well.

I don't want to make it sound enormous, because it's nothing like that. It can't be more than eighty feet across, and is only maybe twenty-five feet from the bottom of the bowl to the margin where it splits the line of gorse. The thought that Moll and I had lain there and actually noshed a picnic made me feel uneasy. We'd played about on the covered top of a bloody great hole leading down, down, down into the heart of a living hill.

I got my bike up after looking carefully at the road in the valley. No. And no innocent fishermen across the river peering at me with binoculars. I slithered down the hill, bouncing my bike's wheels for all they were worth, until I made the place where the gorse line began again. A freewheel bumpily down to the St Mary footpath and I reached the pub in a few more minutes.

There were a few more cars about. Nothing sinister. A cart pulled by a nag, a brewer's dray unloading at the Three Tiles. I pedalled airily across the bridge and got to Doc Chase's sandy fishing patch without being mangled by maniacal swans. It was hopeless trying to conceal myself there. I sat and watched the hillside just as the old man had done for so long.

The hill looked innocent again, utterly bland. Yet I shivered as I inspected its surface again. The Right Honourable Jonathan Chase had climbed from the tunnel to safety, not, as had been assumed, along one of the seven vent-holes which had been spaced out along the tunnel's course. *He had climbed up the ancient well.*

Then, by mistake, he'd told the people he'd escaped from one of the regular vent-holes. The tragedy was that any workman would have been able to tell the difference between the ancient brick-work of a medieval well and that which formed the inner facing of a tunneller's vent-hole. But an august dignitary probably wouldn't. In the horror of that muddy darkness he'd climbed blindly, struggling to feel space, any space, as the mud and slime had closed about him.

'Ooooh.' My moan frightened myself and a couple of little black ducks. They skittered flapping across the river. The dad swan came hissing along to see what the hell.

I shook myself free of the collywobbles and gave a last glance at the hillside. Jonathan Chase had struggled out, tumbled down the hill. Naturally, in the confusion and the rainstorm the rescuers had assumed he had come up through one of the apertures they *knew* connected to the tunnel. So they had floundered about, trying to open the vent-holes. Nobody had thought of the ancient well. Or had they believed it effectively closed off?

For absolute certain the little decorated carriage with its precious cargo would still be there, precisely where the railway tunnel intersected the course of the well. I had to get in. Presumably the deep, covered half of the well was still covered up by the tunnel's flooring. I hoped to God it was. I didn't fancy breaking into a tunnel only to go tumbling through a hole in its floor into a mile-deep derelict well.

I pedalled home to the cottage. As far as solving the problem went, I had reached approximately where the old doctor had before he died, though maybe he hadn't guessed about the well. It was then that it hit me.

I had to stop by the roadside with the shock. Of *course* the old quack knew about the well. And so did Leckie. Relics. Religious history, Leckie's specialist subject.

There's nothing so religious as a well, is there?

Jerry from the garage delivered my old crate soon after I got back. He was amused.

'Give you ten quid for it, Lovejoy,' he quipped. 'For the string alone.'

'Get knotted, Jerry.'

'Seriously,' he joked. 'Melt it down and sell the glue.'

'Jealous.' I signed the chit with a flourish. The price on the bottom made me swallow. Moll was going to have a lot of explaining for Tom. I hoped.

As soon as Jerry's estate van had gone I locked up and hurtled into town.

Our library now shuts on Saturday afternoons, this being the only time most people can get to it. It's part of our life-style nowadays, establishing social services skilfully beyond anyone's reach. This time I just streaked in before they could shut the door.

'All out, please. We're closing now, Lovejoy.'

Miss Vanston tried to block my path. I walked past into the reference section.

'Not be a minute, Marlene.'

She hates being called Marlene. 'Mr Scotchman! Mr Scotchman!'

She ran off for the librarian in a flurry while I dug out Attwater's book on Saints and a couple of local histories. They tried to prise me out twice until I lost my temper and pointed a finger, smiling one of my special smiles, at Scotchman; without a word. After that they left me alone, but Marlene banged the books about as they restocked. There was only her and the uniformed watchman left by the time I'd found what I wanted.

In Speed's map of the area the well was marked 'St Osyth's Well'. That was good enough for me. The little coastal resort town of St Osyth is where Leckie lived. What more natural than him taking an interest in the reliquaries and place-names associated with his own village? I stood up and stretched, weary as hell. After all, I'd been on the go since an early hour. And, thinking of Julia, the previous day had been tiring as well. Marlene was still slamming piles of books about as I left. She's a shapely thirtyish. She believes in Good Works, like not letting the public touch her books except as humble supplicants.

'See you, Marlene.' I clicked out through the turnstile. 'Think of me in bed.'

She ran a hand exasperatedly through her hair. 'Lovejoy. Why do you . . . why do you take no *notice* of anybody?'

What an extraordinary question. I stared at her. I take notice of other people all the bloody time. 'It's other people make me bad, love,' I said with conviction. 'Like you. I start out holy every single morning.'

I went out into the brightening day.

18

Yonks ago the chances of holiness were largely confined to eccentric nuts, warriors (of the right sort) and royalty. It's no surprise to learn that St Osyth was not only a raving beauty, but also sexy queen to Sighere, king of hereabouts in the seventh century. Eventually she decided to go straight, and founded a nunnery at the tiny coastal village of Chich. After some sea rovers massacred the lot we beatified her as a martyr and Chich village became St Osyth. The place where she built her convent's still there. Leckie's windmill is only a stone's throw.

You might think it sacrilegious, but there's a thriving trade in religious relics. Not as frank as in the Middle Ages, when the faithful would slice a finger off a dead − and even a dying − saint for luck. I believe our approach is a lot healthier. The trouble is finding *genuine* relics. Some are well authenticated. Others, like those paintings of the Blessed Virgin allegedly done by St Luke the Evangelist, are a bit dicey or even outright frauds. Yet Leckie only *studied*. Margaret didn't say he *collected* − did she? I was sure she was right. Tinker or maybe Lemuel would have sussed that out before long, or maybe I'd have learned of it through auctions.

So Leckie, interestingly examining St Osyth's Well in the course of his hobby, encountered Dr Chase. Maybe they'd got talking. Perhaps they'd agree to try for the discovery together. Things were falling into place.

Crossing the main London road, going out towards the village, I became aware of Jake Pelman. He was driving a natty little Japanese car. He gave me a sour nod, smiling. I didn't like that. It isn't often Jake cracks his ugly face. I gaped at all the cars that passed after that. Nobody looking like two Brummies full of aggro, thank God.

I stopped to use the phone at the village shop. Elspeth was in the surgery, presumably lashing a huddle of sweating slaves to a distant drumbeat.

'Lovejoy!' she exclaimed. 'I'm so pleased you rang! I tried to wake you this morning as I passed but you were so soundly asleep − '

'Look, love,' I interrupted. 'One thing. About Doc Chase.'

Her voice suddenly went all smooth and professional. 'Yes, sir,' she cooed. 'I'll arrange another appointment. Just one second while I shut the door . . .' She came back a little breathlessly. I guessed Nurse Patmore had popped her head in. 'Go on, Lovejoy.'

'*When* did Doc go, er, fishing?'

'I told you,' she replied, puzzled. 'Every day he possibly could.'

'No, love. I mean *when*. Morning? Afternoon?'

'Oh, always as early as he could. Early morning.'

'Did he ever say why?'

'Something to do with the light, I think. I vaguely remember he

135

said something about the light once.'

'Elspeth,' I said. 'If I come out of this alive, you can have me for a whole week. I promise.'

I rang off before she could draw breath. The last link was in the chain.

The clever old man. He wasn't working out how to get into the hillside. He hadn't been puzzling over a mystery at all. Because to him there just wasn't any mystery. He'd known everything all along, that the entrance to the tunnel was through St Osyth's Well. You can see the small hollow easiest in the morning light, so you could tell if it had been tampered with. By late afternoon it is in shadow. It was all that simple.

He'd not been searching for anything. He'd just been keeping watch. He was a guardian.

The rest of the day I planned with obsessional detail. If my onslaught on the tunnel was going to fail it wouldn't be because I'd forgotten some obvious and essential tool. I determined to take everything but the kitchen sink. And I'd take that, too, if I thought it would improve my chances.

That afternoon I thought of ringing people to explain my plan of action, at least roughly where I would be, but gave up. Tinker would be as petrified as me. Lemuel's known usefulness is a flat zero. Patrick would only have hysterics. All the others would try to beat me to it.

Helen and Margaret would dissuade me as much as possible. Moll had abandoned ship. Pat would tell Maslow. Sue was housebound, and in view of her suspicions about me and every other woman in the known universe she'd more probably chuck me down the bloody well than help. I was on my own.

It's easy to be brave on an afternoon with the post-girl calling and bright daylight everywhere. People came and went along the lane. One or two waved. I waved back. All innocence and peace.

By four I had a heap of things on my divan. It was still difficult getting about the interior of the cottage. Moll's treen and furniture kept catching my knees. I'm no mountaineer, but I assumed the job would call for some climbing. I fetched in my clothesline to add to the pile. It looked strong, and felt in good nick. I have a few tools and I picked the best. My hammer's pretty worn but looks tough. I included that, and got as many eight-inch nails as I could find. I use those when I'm making heavy picture frames, and managed ten of them. I tied them up with string and put them in a polythene bag.

Torch. I wish I was the sort of bloke that worries about batteries and always has spare bulbs, but it's no good. I'm not, and I had no money for any, so it had to go on the pile as it was. I included a ball of fine string. In the days when I could afford to collect flintlocks I'd have had a choice of several luscious miracles of firepower. I had one last look for Moll's frightening pistol in case she'd left it for me in some secret hidey-hole. No luck. To this day I don't know whether I'd have taken it if I'd come across it in some drawer. Maybe it's a mistake to look back and quiz yourself about motives, because they're a waste of time. I found a small hand fork and a hand shovel that goes with it. On to the pile.

I'd heard it tends to be cold in caves. I laid out two singlets, underpants, socks and my worsted suit. It's the only one I have, and hardly looked typical climbing gear, but it's made of the proper stuff. On impulse I added three unused hankies. Shoes bothered me. The plimsolls from this morning's jaunt were still wet through. I lit a fire and put them on the hearth, deciding to travel in shoes and change when climbing down to the tunnel. I added a box of matches. Funny how your mind works. I brought a propelling pencil with some spare leads and a few squares of white card, maybe thinking of floating a message out on some chance subterranean stream should that ghastly need ever arise. Which, of course, it would bloody well not. I was going to make sure of that, come what may.

There comes a time in planning when you find you are planning too hard. Your brain never leaves off. I found myself getting in this state. I started sweating for nothing and kept rearranging my heap of stuff senselessly, so I got control of myself and made a meal. Then I went out for a walk while there was some daylight still left.

I watched television for a bit. Then switched it off and listened to the radio. Then I watched a play I couldn't make head nor tail of. Then I tried to read, but found I was reading the same page over. Then I sang some madrigals, but my heart wasn't in it. I listened to a radio argument about the soaring costs of new bedding plants, and then watched the Wanderers get thrashed three-nil in a floodlit game, the duckeggs. I thought of candles, and added my only two to the heap.

Then it was dark, and I forced myself into bed.

I woke with the alarm clock going berserk. Three-thirty. For a moment I wondered what the hell I was playing at, setting it for that ridiculous time. Then I remembered. I had to go down a well.

My crate makes a racket at the best of times. I mean, even during the day in noisy traffic people turn, wondering what's coming. Nearly four on a pitchy morning it sounded like a helicopter. I keep meaning to get it seen to, but the cost's terrible.

I decided against the bike. On the grounds that I'd probably need every muscle fascicle doing its absolute thing today, I settled for the car despite its row. The trouble was, they'd recognize my motor anywhere. I'd have stood a better chance if Elspeth had lent me hers. Or Moll hers, or Sue . . .

I wasn't long reaching the Mount, cruising easily on to the down-slope towards the river. Most of our villages have no street lights, so I was relying on a vague, rather shifty-looking moon-glow as I cut the engine. With only wind noise and some wheel-swishing I coasted her down to the pub. Luckily, pub yards are traditionally open at the front. No gates or hedges. We rolled on to the forecourt, and I reached the side of the tavern wall before stopping.

I got out, pushing her slowly forwards until she was as far off the road as she would go. People might assume some early devoted angler had put it there, intending to return for a midday break from boredom. Most of my stuff was in a small satchel I used for carrying my materials as a lad, when I went out painting. The torch was in my pocket, and the pencil and some of the card squares. I sat on the car seat with the door open and changed my shoes for plimsolls. If there was any mud down there my feet would get wet anyway, and rubber soles were easier to climb in. I was shaking like a leaf. The cold night mist seeped into my bones. Sometimes you can talk yourself into a shiver, can't you?

Ready. I simply turned towards the hill and started up it straight from the tavern yard. There were a few obstructions, mostly large flint-stones and large tussocks of grass. A couple of times I walked straight into a gorse bush, but got off lightly. It was the line of gorse bushes that had tipped me off and gave me the final clue. They followed an obvious contour line as far as the hollow. There they ended abruptly, to recommence about a hundred feet down the hillside. Something had slipped them out of true: the magic landslip of 1847. What else?

No wonder there was a hollow. The uppermost half of the well was tilted. It couldn't be any other way. I imagined a nail, bent almost to right angles by some powerful force after it had been driven half into a piece of wood. The uppermost half now lay for the finding. And the well-head would be located exactly where the gorse-bushes began again lower down the hill.

I blundered into a gorse bush again. The moonglow was too feeble but I guessed I was at the lower half of the gorse line. Which meant that following it left would bring me to its abrupt end. And the well-head would be there. I felt with my hands, touching the spiky fronds at every step.

I wasn't spooked when I reached the end of the gorse line. Not really. But wells are funny things. In honest and kindly old

Britain wells and springs have always been slightly magic. And, often as not, the old folk would protect the magic of their own particular well by some rather odd — and quite evil — practices. It's no accident that our wells are often adorned with stone faces and completely sculpted Celtic stone heads. Don't dwell too long on how the fashion actually started. It isn't very happy reading. These stone heads, incidentally, are worth a fortune nowadays — if you dare risk the spooky vibes. Like most people, I don't admit to being superstitious. It's always somebody else.

I was at the end of the line, feeling round on my hands and knees round the tallest of the gorse bushes. I parted the grass on the down-side of the bush and reached underneath. There was a cold stone under my hands. I tried to be scientific, pushed my hands back under and felt around. There was another to its right. There was one a few inches displaced inwards to its left. And a third. And a fourth. They seemed heaped, rather than set in a circle. But wells are always circular. It took me a few more minutes of groping to fathom what had happened. The well had not been shifted sideways, as I'd guessed. It had just been laid down. Naturally, the stones had piled in the form of a small cairn. It was simply an earth-covered, stone-blocked cavern now.

I started picking at the first stone with my minute border fork. It was like trying to extract a tusk with a pin. I started being stealthy and silent. Within five minutes I was swearing and smashing at the bloody stone, probably making enough noise to wake the dead. I paused, wishing I hadn't thought of it in exactly those terms. That made me work things out more intelligently.

If the well-head had been toppled sideways by the sliding hill, then the surest means of gaining entrance would be through the great heap of stones at its mouth. Stones fall down, not up, I lectured myself severely. At this rate I'd be exhausted before I even found a route into the wretched well-head, let alone climbed down into the tunnel.

I walked round until I was standing overlooking the gorse bushes, then slid down, hanging on to the grass like grim death. I located the marker stone and wriggled back upwards until I was somewhere over the middle of the well's outline. There I started digging, using only the hand shovel. I was shattered when my blade struck something hard and it turned out to be a brick. I worked harder then, after the first moment of amazement.

I had the sense to splay myself to one side so that if the well caved in I wouldn't go tumbling in and get myself crushed to death by falling masonry; one foot was hooked round the stem of a gorse-bush as an extra precaution.

It took me the best part of two hours or so. Then, when I was telling myself I'd perhaps made enough of a hole to get through, I was helped by the incaving I had feared. The well side gave way with a rumbling sound, and the bricks I had exposed simply folded in. I only just saved myself from the falling in after the bloody things by grabbing for the grass and holding on. I lost the shovel, which was tough. That didn't matter much for the moment, because I was the jubilant owner of a hole some three feet in diameter into a medieval well which led straight to a valuable possession any antique dealer would give his limbs to own. I found my satchel and the torch. Now I was able to direct the beam downwards into the hole. Nobody could see it from the road.

I wasn't prepared for the filth which confronted me. There were deposits from wildlife several inches deep along the brickwork which now formed the floor of the well's lumen, possibly from badgers or foxes. I'd heard tales of the fury with which dog badgers attack an intruder. Maybe they'd be afraid of the torch-light. I tied a handkerchief round my face against the dirt, slipped over, and clung to the lip of brickwork with one hand, while shining the torch with the other.

The well descended in a slow curve into the hill, down and in. I let the torch rove and found small recesses with a single brick lip. Some form of primitive handhold? They seemed to be spaced about right for a climbing man. As long as there were plenty, and as long as they went all the way down, otherwise I'd have to risk the rope. I let my satchel fall. It hit the layer of filth and set up a smog of dung. I made sure that I could reach upwards again from the floor of the well before letting go. Careful old Lovejoy. Now nothing could stop me from getting out once I'd completed the task.

From above it had looked miles long. Once down there, it seemed that I'd only taken three or four steps before I was having to hold on to stop myself from slithering forward. A few more paces still, and I found myself actually climbing downwards, holding on to the projecting bricks in the shallow recesses and fiddling about with my spare foot to catch the next slot. It's easier said than done. I never know why people go climbing, anyway. After about ten steps on my brickwork ladder I thought maybe it was time I shone the torch to see in which direction I was now heading. Confident now, I turned from my position and shone the light down. Down.

Down, down it went.

Down into the bowels of the planet.

I whined feebly. There seemed to be nothing, nothing but a great hole whizzing vertically into the earth. And I was dangling from the merest foothold, one – *one* – single brick wide. I whimpered, and froze. Sweat poured down my face and prickled between my shoulders. I felt my hands ice up. My thighs quivered horribly. I even made a move to start up again, heading for fresh air and safety. Then I felt it. A glow began in my chest. From down below, deep in the hole, a radiance emanated. It warmed my chest and set my mind clicking again. My hands eased without being told. I felt the beauty of whatever was down there set up vibrations, with me in the very track of the waves. I found that my foot had begun to search for the next foothold almost of its own accord. I began breathing again, slowly at first but with regularity. I realized I'd gone down another step. Then another. Then again another.

I developed a rhythm, moving five careful, well-tested rungs, then shining the torch. Later, I realized I ought to have had the sense to count while going along, to estimate the distance. You can't think of everything. In fact, when you're terrified you can think of nothing.

I suppose I'd been slowly climbing down for about a quarter of an hour when I shone the torch and saw something there. It was a straight line going from side to side across the well's black base. Another three rungs and I could see there was another line, also dark and somewhat mottled, but parallel to it. At a rough guess I was about thirty feet above the lines when the rungs ran out. I saw the reason for the mottling. They were steel railway tracks, and bricks had fallen, partly covering them here and there.

The trouble is that common sense leaves you when you're near to what you want. It hadn't penetrated my thick skull that I would enter the tunnel at the top of the vault and probably break my neck the instant I forgot this elementary fact. Yet I nearly did.

It was only the vague worry of how to climb up again that stopped me literally letting go. I remembered the care with which I'd entered the well-head, and mercifully paused to wonder the same thing. I realized how close I'd been to falling. I got the shakes again and had to hang on for a minute.

I held on with my left hand and got the hammer out, clenching the haft in my teeth. I decided to bang in all the nails I had.

It took several attempts to get even one in. I dropped two, which left me seven. Some elementary mathematics took over. I spaced five more out in twos, one above the other, and wrapped the clothesline round each pair in turn. It would be less of a strain on them if my weight was shared by three pairs instead of one single long vertical column. God knows how long it took me, but in the end I was gasping and spluttering in the brick dust. And I'd had to hold the torch in my teeth while starting each fresh nail off. Worse still, every stroke of the hammer echoed and hummed up and down the well-shaft. Like being the clapper in a bell. My mind reeled from the racket. The hammer fell when I was clouting the last nail in, and thudded into something soft at the bottom. I gave up then, just turned the rope round as I'd planned and tied it in a million knots for safety.

In the descent I misjudged the rate of sliding and got a couple of rope burns. Added to that, I found myself wheezing from something musty in the air when I finally crashed down on the lines. As long as I stayed on the iron rails I would be all right. If they could bear the weight of a train they could carry me. I got my gear together and shone the torch about.

I was in a space, a bubble in the earth. It was no longer than ten feet and didn't reach quite to the tunnel walls. The brickwork of the tunnel vault disappeared behind an upslope of desiccated mud. Only the rails were exposed; it was rather odd. I remember thinking that at the time. Mud doesn't get flung upwards, does it? It lies there just being mud. The lines ran under the roof fore and aft. I was stuck. There was no sign of the little decorated carriage that I'd read about.

I shone and looked, shone and looked. There was an odd feel about the whole thing. I felt as if I'd come across a stage set with no play. I stayed straddling the rails, though the flooring of the tunnel seemed intact. I prodded it once or twice experimentally. It seemed just a tunnel floor. Then I noticed the rope.

It had rotted, but in its day it had been a good enough rope. Parts still felt waxy. It was coiled unevenly among the dust and the fallen bricks on the floor as if it had fallen after hanging down. Yet it must have been there a hell of a time to have rotted like that. I picked it up and noticed the iron stanchion ring still attached to a small length of it. Somebody had been here before me, but a century and a half ago. And he had come to a prepared spot, where a rope waited for him inside an old sealed well – a well with climb-holds. And, having escaped by hacking his way through into the well-shaft, he could pull across some odd bush or other, and from there it would be easy in the confusion to appear as if by a miracle near the nearest vent-hole. *And misdirect the rescuers?*

I sat down, my skin prickling with revulsion. Jonathan Chase had escaped according to plan, babbled of vent-holes, and deliberately directed the rescue teams away from his two entombed men. And he had lived a hero's life, even been decorated for his services and his bravery.

But if the Right Honourable had made his honourable way through this chamber, I reasoned in the darkness, and out through the well-shaft, then he must have entered it by some route that should still be visible. I shone the torch round again. From the angle of illumination the mud-caked bricks seemed indented near one rail. As if somebody had shoved anything he could find to fill a hole. It was on the inward direction of the rails, which meant that the carriage might be on that side. The shaft above me seemed to be at a slight angle to the vertical. That suggested the deeper part of the well lay on the incoming side too.

I cast about for my hammer, but couldn't find it. I took my satchel off. Holding my torch in my mouth was making me gag, and I started coughing and coughing again. For a moment I remembered firedamp, the silent odourless gas of the mines, and the terrible tales I had heard about it as a lad. There was only speed to counter that, speed in escaping. And I would be out of this hole like a bat in another instant. I made myself a fervent promise, and set to clawing the earth and bricks away from the indented spot. There was a space behind, a long hole just wide enough for a man. I took my jacket off and rolled it into a sausage shape. I wasn't going to leave it behind, and it would be impossible to push ahead or I wouldn't be able to see a thing. I noticed how cold it had become now that I had stopped really moving.

The small crawl-way Jonathan Chase had made for himself through the mud sloped up through the fall for a couple of feet then levelled off. With the torch I could see a space at the end of it. The whole course could not be more than twelve feet. I didn't like it, but twelve feet didn't seem for ever, or so I thought.

I ducked my head in and crawled forward with the torch leading the way. Easy. Not roomy, but easy. I reached the lip of the inner chamber. From the bobbing rays of the torch I could see by squinting ahead that it seemed at least as spacious as the one I'd just left. I caught hold of the crumbly lip to pull myself forward – and nearly fell into the lower half of the well. I screamed like a stuck pig, squealing and yipping with terror and dangling in space from a crumbling mass of rubble with my feet flailing in empty air. The torch was lodged in the aperture at one side where I'd just emerged, but I was in a mad scramble to get back. My leg caught on something hard. I felt the skin give down my calf. The other leg scagged on projecting iron and the skin tore. I had to do something quickly or my limbs would be shredded. My right leg flung wildly sideways. It struck iron, a firm rod of some sort. I rested it carefully on the metal, pressed, and let it gradually take my weight, or part of it. My fingers relaxed. I stood like a deformed acrobat, at a weird angle. I reached shakily for the torch. I seemed to be standing precariously on a single rail. The other had gone heaven knows where. Beneath me was the well. It wasn't bottomless. The light descended about sixty feet before water caught the beam and reflected it against the sides. Floating in the water, or stuck there on a muddy sediment, were the remains of two men. Presumably men, though now they were skeletal fragments crumpled under a dark brown slime.

My moan echoed hollowly. I fixed my position so I wouldn't slip and turned my head, holding the torch with my arm flexed underneath. I saw the carriage. Had I been facing the other way I could have reached out and touched it. As it was, I dared not let go or I'd fall.

The decorated bogie had stopped right on the edge of the well. It rested on two rails. The left one was shorn away and couldn't be seen. It was a small version of the hand-cranked wagon which plate-layers sometimes use for carrying their tools and metal supplies. A chair was rigged to the front part. It was almost as macabre to see the elegant chair in such a position. And on the chair was a glass case ribbed with dark wood. Even in the state I was, my heart gave a lurch. I looked at my right foot. The rail seemed continuous. If it held it could be a way across the well's five or six-foot gap to reach the carriage. Surely it would take my weight? You sometimes hear of several landslips, one after another. Well, everything's a risk.

I got myself upright, pushing carefully on the lip of the narrow aperture through which I'd just wriggled. I drew several deep breaths for reserve and stuck the torch back in my mouth. No daft nonsense about balancing. I crouched down and dangled my legs over the rail, straddling it. Then I shuffled along, swinging my legs and using my hands. It took twelve shuffles. Then I actually touched the glass case. It was beautiful. A feeling rose up inside warming the whole universe. I knew the Contrivance was in there. And, praise God, it was mine. I vowed a forest of candles to St Osyth in thanks and swarmed off the rail on to the wagon. There was hardly room to move between the side of the carriage and the sloping wall of dried mud, but I got there. A huge wooden sleeper, torn somehow from its bed and projecting from the mass of earth, almost slammed me backwards towards the gaping well by wobbling on to the carriage as I disturbed it. It fell with an almighty thump alongside the carriage, projecting over the horrid dark space below as if waiting for somebody to walk the plank.

Breathless, I reached for the glass case. I think the torch gave a flicker, but I couldn't have cared less. I'd actually lifted it from the seat when I suddenly knew I felt wrong. The place felt wrong too. Everybody can feel another's presence. You don't have to hear them or see them or be touched. You can tell. Just as you can tell if there's one person in a crowd staring at you without you looking. You just feel it. And I felt it now.

'Lovejoy.' Such a soft voice, almost a whisper.

The word boomed softly and reverberated around the chamber. I yelped and dropped the torch. At least, it rolled and fell. I can't remember. But a sudden thick dull splash put my light out and I was in there with nothing. Trembling, I replaced the case, with my scalp crawling, felt around where I was standing on the edge of the carriage. Nothing. I hadn't even my jacket, with its matches and candles.

'Lovejoy.' Softly again, wheedling. They'd followed somehow. And now they were in the outer chamber through which I'd passed. It was my only way out.

It was a man's voice. Brummie. Somebody laughed. My skin prickled. I would have fainted if I hadn't been so frightened of falling into the bloody water deep down there and dying, alone but for two skeletons.

'We've come to help you, Lovejoy.'

I thought of trying to explain, offer, bargain, promise, anything to stop them leaving me entombed down here. I couldn't have got further from help if I'd tried. I swallowed, third go.

'Time to pass it over, Lovejoy.'

Two voices chuckled, comfortably and at ease. They had a nasal quality. Hell-fire. Both Brummies were in the outer chamber. They'd probably brought more weapons than the Tower of London. I felt the sweat start down from my armpits and sting my chin. They seemed to have no light, but they weren't daft.

'I'm stuck,' I said. It seemed a voice from light-years off. It whined feebly, a real cringing Tinker-type voice. I vowed never again to criticize Tinker, if ever I got out.

'Balls, Lovejoy.' One of them chuckled again. 'They said you'd try all sorts. Just chuck the stuff out and we'll call it quits.'

That was a laugh. They were going to do for me. I knew it. They knew it. All the rest was chit-chat.

'I'm stuck under this rail. You heard it go, you bastards.'

More muttering. There were only two. I couldn't imagine Fergus doing any of his own dirty work, especially with his leg, and Jake always stays behind the army.

'Under what, Lovejoy?'

'A bloody railway line, you stupid berk.'

'We're not sorry.'

They seemed to be biting, though what good it would do me . . . I thought hard, seeing in my mind's eye the interior of this chamber as it had looked from the aperture when I had a light. I hadn't known there was a well. Surely they didn't, either?

'Look, lads. A deal, eh?'

'That's more like it, Lovejoy.' Mutter, mutter. 'No tricks, mind. We've heard you're a leery bastard.'

There was only one way to handle this, I thought, fear tightening my throat and making it hard to breathe. If I showed anything less than absolute terror, even the slightest glimmer of hope, I'd give the show away. My only ally was a hole. But one from two equals one any way you look.

'Don't be stupid. How the hell can I?' I muttered to myself, complaining loudly of their idiocy the way I knew was realistic. God knows, I was scared enough. 'I've no light or anything.'

'Careless lad.'

'What do you want me to do?'

'Hand the thing out.'

'I can't. I *could* see it. Before my light went.'

'What is it?'

'I don't know,' I lied. 'Some sort of box. My lamp fell before I . . . before I got trapped. This bloody sleeper fell on me from the side.' Well, it nearly had.

'Stay there.'

Boody fool. It just shows what sort of people are in antiques these days, doesn't it? I was narked even though they were going to crawl through the hole and kill me, the burkes.

I whimpered, 'If one of you just reached through you can take it. It's on the floor.'

'How far inside is it?'

'About eight feet.'

'Stay where you are.' Mutter, mutter. 'You go, Jim. Watch it,' I heard. 'He might have something.'

'We found all his gear,' the first voice said confidently.

A light blinded me for a second as a torch lit with a smart click. I glanced about swiftly. By standing balanced on the bent rail sagging its lunatic way across the deep well I could maybe create an impression of being on solid ground, though it would be difficult. Any time I could slip and fall . . .

'I can't move, you burke,' I snapped with a mixture of a Tinkerish cringe and anger. It was the best I could do. One seemed doubtful, muttering cautions. The other was perky and belligerent.

The light was abruptly blocked. It came through in one or two darts, equally swiftly doused. Somebody was in the crawl-way's aperture. I slid like I'd seen acrobats do on their rope, one foot before the other. My mouth was dry as a bone. I tried to blink but couldn't even do that. I felt the rail dip fractionally under my weight. I crouched for a second, but what if he had a torch and shone it downwards to look at me? He would see the well gaping beneath me and guess I'd tried to mislead him. And I'd be a goner.

'Pass it out, Lovejoy.'

146

The voice was so near I almost overbalanced and fell from fright.

'How the hell can I?' I snarled. 'I'm under this girder. It's my hand, trapped.' I wanted him to concentrate on the roof, the walls, the fall behind me. Anything but down.

'Stay there.' The light came in and blinded me, shining straight into my face. I swayed, my hand outstretched as if stuck somewhere out of his direct line of vision.

'I promise I won't move,' I quavered. It needed no acting skills. 'But promise you'll let me go if I pass it to you, eh, lads?'

'I promise,' his voice said again. I heard the second bloke chuckle.

His bulk blocked the light again. He called to his mate to shine his torch through. Small dashes of light struck into my chamber, but most was impeded by the first goon's bulk.

'Got you, Lovejoy.' I heard him come wriggling nearer.

The beam traversed my face and the walls behind me. They roved the ceiling and the carriage. I was only three feet from him. He wriggled out like a woodworm, head first. He carefully kept his eyes on me as he gripped the edge of the aperture, just as I had done, and swung lightly downwards. He dropped down, letting go. There was one slight difference. He simply kept on going. He went down and down. It was like a slow motion play. His expression changed, gradually turning from a domineering smile to one of horror. He simply sank without a sound, descending into the well. There came a ghastly wet thud. Something stirred sluggishly for a few seconds in the slime among the skeletons. I scrabbled back along the line babbling with terror and clung to the carriage. The image came of him rising covered with a terrifying macabre slime from the well's filthy mud and embracing me in a horrifying grip. I imagined his smiling face upturned, still smiling, as I scrabbled for brick after brick and dropped them down the well. I finished up hurling them down with all the force I could manage, mentally screaming abuse and hatred. The other nerk in the outer chamber must have thought the world had gone mad.

'Jim? Jim?' he was shouting. 'Are you okay?'

I paused, exhausted. 'He says stop there,' I bawled.

'Jim? Answer, Jim.'

'He says stop there.'

It was an inspired thing to say. I tried for utter weariness in my voice. Trying to say come on in would have tipped him off. He would go back for Jake or even Fergus. Or a hand-grenade. Or some foul thing to smoke me out. But telling him not to come in meant not only that Jim was boss in here, but was playing his mate off. Jim might have found something precious and was having it away. And leaving his mate with nothing

I waited almost smugly while the poison worked. Then I was more terrified than ever. A goon thinking himself whittled would come in full of aggro. If he had a shooter he would shoot before anything else. And I knew he had a torch. Jim's lamp was down in the well with him, its light dying fast.

I cringed beside the bogie, chattering with fear. If he came in I could chuck a brick but the force would be too weak. And the angle wrong. And bricks have corners, to catch on the sides and lose their force. Anyway, he'd see me move.

'Jim?'

'He says stop there. I surrender, honest.'

'Jim! Pass it out. The thing Fergie wants.'

'I'm trapped. Honest.' I sounded at the end of my tether, which was about right.

'I'll come through,' he threatened. He was narked Jim was saying nothing. And concerned. 'I have a shooter, Lovejoy.'

'Jim says stay there,' I told him desperately.

He called, 'Watch out, Jim.'

There was a sudden flash. For an instant I was puzzled. Then I heard myself screaming and screaming. The bastard had shot through the aperture and my shoulder was burning and smarting.

I fell down, probably a reflex. The torch-light was jerking about. Either he was trying to see what was going on in here or he was already slithering his evil way in, the bastard.

'Get the message, Lovejoy?' he said through the mud-lined hole.

I thought of hiding, but where? I even thought of suicide, but the only place was the terrifying black well. The huge sleeper nearly overbalanced as I tried to shuffle away from the aperture. I lodged myself across the end near the carriage, and it held. I felt it with my palms, splinters ripping into my hands. It was a massive piece of wood balancing on the edge of a great hole. I pushed it gently. It rocked. It only needed the slightest extra weight on that far end for it to tilt downwards into the well. And maybe the whole chamber would go in with it.

'Jim!' He was becoming impatient. 'You all right? What the hell you doing?'

'He says I'm to wait here,' I yelled, thinking like mad: a heavy piece of wood rocking. If one end falls sharply, the other rises. A lever? 'He's gone to find the other way out.' I needed him to come through but not yet.

The goon was puzzled and suspicious. 'The fiddle still there?' He meant the casket.

'Yes.'

'Right, Lovejoy. I'm coming in.' Christ.

The torch flickered again. I crouched on the carriage end of the sleeper and tore my trousers off. Sweat was pouring down me, tickling and irritating. My hair kept guiding rivulets into my eyes. I zipped the empty trousers up and tied the leather belt round their waist, making a bag with two holes.

I clawed every loose brick in reach and stuffed them into the trouser leg.

'What's going on?'

'I'm trying to get free,' I yelled. I was as terrified as I sounded. 'I can't. Jim left me here. There's another tunnel, a way out.'

A shuffling began and the light blocked in fits and starts. He was coming. Oh God. I ran out of bricks. The weight was crippling. My shaking hands managed to tie the trouser legs in a loop. I spread myself over the inward end of the sleeper and began pushing my ungainly bag along it until I ran out of distance. Frantically I turned round and pushed it further with my feet. At one point my heart stopped. The bloody bag nearly tumbled over but I got it balanced again. A flicker of light came. I could just see the bag almost at the limit of the sleeper and I felt my end trying to lift under me as the bag of bricks weighted the other end of the wood. As soon as I rolled off, the weight of the bricks should swivel the sleeper. Its own immense weight would add to the speed and it would flip like a giant seesaw but with one horrible difference. It wouldn't stop and rock back the other way. It would go on, down and down. It was a crude non-stop ballista.

I rose, shaking. So I had a pivoting wood sleeper, but now no missile. The exertion had been too great for my flabby body. My hands were uncontrollable. I retched a couple of times. I wobbled upright on my end of the home-made seesaw. Don't lose your balance and step off, Lovejoy, I begged myself. Please. But the missile?

There were no bricks left. Even if there had been, in the frightened state I was in I'd have piled them up wrong. There was only one heavy, dense projectile available. It had to be. With a groan of utter misery I groped back, touched the chair. The casket lid was gritty with dust and dried mud, but it opened easily.

I lifted the heavy metal object out gently, still balancing. The thrill of feeling it made my fingers tingle and steady. The goon was breathing stertorously, shuffling towards me along the crawl-way. He'd had the wit to bundle a jacket. He was pushing it ahead of him, probably as a shield in case I chucked anything, suspicious sod. I felt my precious object's contours. It was a silky model of an early engine. I didn't look, in the faint glow now coming from the aperture, just crouched and placed the silver miracle at my feet on the sleeper. We waited, both of us. Me practically naked, like a springboard diver waiting his turn at the back end of a diving board, and the precious diminutive gleaming silver machine, throbbing with the life instilled in it so long ago, on the wood between my feet. Standing there I was the trigger of my vast and clumsy home-made weapon.

The torch-light touched my eyes. I raised both hands, squinting towards the aperture.

'Don't shoot, don't shoot!' I squawked. 'Please, mate. Your pal's gone through there.' I pointed to my right. 'I'm stuck.'

The bastard held me like that for what seemed an hour. Of course, he could only see my top half from his position along the crawl-way, but that didn't make me feel any easier.

'Stay like that.' There was a pause. The swine was wondering whether it would be wiser to shoot me now.

'Jim told me to show you the other exit.' Pretty feeble, but it was the best lie I could invent to increase my paltry value.

'He thought another minute. 'Pass it out first, Lovejoy.'

'How the hell can I? My leg's stuck fast.'

'You said it was your arm.'

'Jim got that out.'

Another pause. 'Just stand still, Lovejoy. I don't trust you.'

He squirmed nearer, slower and more careful.

There was enough light now from the jerking torch for me to look at the sleeper. The gruesome sights in the deep well kept trying to drag my eyes past the wood and down to the horribly fascinating mess at the bottom. I made myself judge the distance from the well's crumbly edge to my silver missile. The length that would lash upwards was about the same as the aperture's exit was high, more or less. But any more or any less and the beautiful model would smash into the chamber wall. And he'd hear it go, and guess something was wrong. He'd see me move, anyway, and let fly. The torch went out. I had to remember the distances. Maybe the distance was too small? Maybe I'd misjudged . . . I almost bent down to move the silver piece back an inch. My mouth was dry as a rasp.

The torch came on suddenly, so near I felt I could have reached out and touched it. Too late. I stood with my trembling arms raised, blinded. I'd forgotten. How can you judge if a goon's in position if you're blinded? Oh Christ. I closed my eyes. I'd have to listen. But if his head actually projected into the chamber he would be able to look down and see his mate Jim decomposing below. Then he'd kill me. Never mind then what happened to the silver or to the goon. I'd be gone. So I had to step off and let the sleeper tilt upwards when he was all but within reach.

'Keep like that, Lovejoy.' Shuffle, shuffle.

I opened my eyes. The torch blinded me. It looked near yet no nearer. I couldn't gauge distances any more from dazzle. Then I heard a faint splash from the well below. A fragment of the aperture lip must have fallen. So it must have been pushed, by the goon framed in the aperture. *Now*. I simply stepped back off the huge wooden beam.

All hell seemed let loose. Wood tore my left shin with enormous force. The well quivered and shook. A brick clattered on the carriage. All in a second, dust filled the chamber and a terrible rushing noise came from somewhere far below. A deep thud came instantaneously, and a thick sucking sound. The torch went out. I opened my eyes, squinting and terrified, and crouched clinging to the iron rail in case the whole bloody floor fell away from under me. My mind screeched, stay still, stay *still*. Maybe the silver had somehow missed him and crashed into the dried mud and he was just waiting me out. A stand-off. I tried not to choke on the dust, but I had to breathe. That set me spluttering and coughing, giving myself away. Then I fell silent. The mud below stopped popping and sucking. The sleeper was probably sinking into it forever. I felt sick. There was no sound.

Silently I inched my way along the rail. The gap beneath felt like outer space. If the swine was still there . . . I touched the mud wall ahead and used it to support my forward weight balancing on the rail. I wobbled up straight shakily and stretched out into the blackness. The lip of the aperture felt covered by a folded coat. My touch produced no movement. Nothing. I carefully pulled at the coat. It came free, and I let it fall, making sure no precious silver object went into the well with it. That left only a long hole with a goon in it. I could hear nothing breathing. I reached out.

My hand touched my luscious silver, the cold, beautiful metal. It was embedded in something sticky and running with warm slime. Relief and nausea made me momentarily dizzy. Hard warm splinters of shattered skull-bone pricked at me. I pulled the silver free with difficulty. Still balancing on the rail and leaning on the mud-wall I tore off my shirt and singlet to wrap the silver in. I slithered back and regained the carriage, cautiously clutching the bundle and sat exhausted, my hands sticky with congealing mess, on the carriage chair as the Right Honourable Jonathan Chase had so many years ago. I'm not sure, but I think I blacked out for a while, even though all I wanted was to get the hell out.

The funny thing is it never occurred to me that I'd actually made it. All I could think of was that I was entombed deep in a hill and sick of trying to get myself not killed by everybody. Getting the goon out of the crawl-way was a nightmare of ugliness. I don't know what happened to the torch or his gun because I never found them. It must have taken me hours to pull him free. I stopped a million times to be sick. Hell can't be as bad, that's for sure. The silver had pierced his face, rammed through the facial structure and created a terrible porridge of bone slivers and tissue. His shoulders kept sticking as I pulled and pulled. When he finally tumbled, like a cork from a bottle, I was nearly carried down into the frigging well with him. He seemed all limbs. I just managed to get both arms wound round the rail when his falling body made me overbalance. The metal sagged but held, creaking and bouncing slightly. As his body glugged and squelched, far down, I thought a weary prayer for him. People have to do whatever lights their candle. I admit that. Pity that his had snuffed out, but that wasn't my fault, was it?

The way out was open and free.

19

The only difference in the outer chamber was that I could see the bottom of the well-shaft down which I'd climbed. Very vaguely, but definitely. My eyes must have become accustomed to the faint washes of light, such as they were. I could see the rail lines in the grey-black on the ground under the shaft. I never glanced back once I came out through the aperture. My clothesline lay in a heap, but there was a natty rope ladder dangling, twice as long as needed. They'd come better prepared than I had. I fell over it from trying to go easy, frightening myself because I still couldn't bring myself to trust the floor. They'd brought a pick and shovel. There was a spare torch, but I didn't need extra weight any more. And I wasn't too keen on inspecting myself, either, I knew I'd come through smeared with blood, brains, caked with dried mud. And some of the blood was mine. My feet felt swollen. To my surprise I was limping.

I unwrapped the silver engine and used the only legitimate water I owned. I peed on the object to wash it, then dried it on my socks. My singlets and shirt I left there. The engine just fitted into my underpants. I held one hem in my teeth, making sure it was evenly contained and wouldn't slip out of the leg holes. There was no question of resting. When you're in a tomb the first thing is to get out.

The distance between each brick foothold felt enormous at the start of the upward climb. My heart was banging like a train. I had to pause and hold on every second reach, and it wasn't just that I was going up this time, not down. I was simply done for. Time had gone, yet without me knowing how. In fact, I was so useless that I almost nodded off in mid-climb from weariness as the shaft curved towards the horizontal. The silver piece nearly slid out of the cloth, but I held it between my chest and the brickwork until I got myself straight again. I could see light ahead. Lovely, dazzling, glaring light. I crawled forward on my hands and knees, grinning, weary but jubilant.

Astonishing, it was still daylight. I caught on the edge of the hole, blinded by the brilliance of the grey overcast sky. One last haul got me up and sprawled panting on the stubby grass under the gorse bush. I could have wept with relief.

'It's Lovejoy. The bastard's naked.'

Fergus and Jake were smoking cigarettes further up the hill, and staring incredulously down at me. They appeared set for a long wait, judging from the scattered fag-ends and the sandwich wrappings blowing about. Both rose, Fergus on a stick. I almost fell back in the hole.

'You're in a fucking mess, Lovejoy.' Fergus wasn't beaming any more.

Jake asked, bewildered, 'Where's Jim and Cooney?'

With a squeal I turned and staggered at a low run as he moved at me, and plunged down-hill through the gorse line. If I could reach the pub ahead of them I'd survive. People would be on the road by now, surely to God. I heard Jake give a shout. Then they were after me, shouting and swearing at each other. Down on the road a car crawled by. I tried waving, but nearly dropped my prize. Anyhow, stopping to help a filthy blood-smeared maniac sprinting down a hillside is nobody's idea of a tea-time tryst. So I just ran and ran down, really only falling forwards and forcing my legs to be there to catch me. This way I kept going, but only just.

With two hundred yards to go to the pub car park I glanced back. Jake was nearer. I found myself slowing, though I tried to keep going. Weariness enveloped me. I'd not make it. I was gasping this to myself when Elspeth Haverill suddenly rose in my way, just rose out of the ground, her eyes wide. She gave a faint scream. I collided with her and we rolled over, down in the tussocky grass. I cut myself yet again, this time on her frigging clip-board.

'Fergus.' Jake had halted uncertainly when I looked at them. Fergie was limping after, eyes hard. Elspeth was trying to compose herself. She was frightened stiff.

'Lovejoy!' She gazed at me, open-mouthed. There were small

153

piles of clothing laid out in a row in front of her.

Fergus waved to his mate. 'Get it, Jake.'

I sat down, bone weary. I'd had enough. I thought of throwing Elspeth the silver, but she was winded by our collision.

'Right.'

They were moving down towards us slowly, Jake first, when I heard it. It was lovely. A beautiful sound of footsteps plodding and flopping along the hillside, and the rasping sound of middle-age in the torment of exercise. Round the hill, flabby and rotund, trundled six of Elspeth's runners. They were dishevelled and looked pathetic, but I'd never seen a lovelier sight.

I couldn't even rise to watch them come. They were on us in a few weak strides. They slowed to a stop and stood panting, staring. One pointed at me in astonishment, his belly heaving, and his sweating face a mottled purple. I must have looked in a hell of a state. The others edged closer. One, brighter than the rest, glanced at Jake and Fergus, back to Elspeth and me. Then he stepped closer and picked up a stone. Two others did the same. It wasn't much of an army, but for the first time in my life my side outnumbered everybody else's. Jake looked at Fergus. Fergus looked at Jake.

'Here,' I wheezed suddenly. 'What are you doing?'

Elspeth was fiddling with my middle.

'Putting this towel round you, Lovejoy.' Of course. I was naked.

I let her. We all watched Jake and Fergus turn and go. Their car was parked across the rear of mine. I couldn't have got it out unless they shifted theirs first, anyway. We saw Jake heave a cobblestone through my windscreen. He looked back at us defiantly. I bowed to annoy them as they pulled out.

'What's all this about, Miss Haverill?' the front runner asked.

'This gentleman fell down a crevice in the hillside,' Elspeth said glibly. In the forecourt below the car started. One or two of them thought to ask more but Elspeth wasn't having any. She clicked a stopwatch.

'I would remind you that it's *twice* round,' she instructed. 'Starting now.'

The team plodded off, some casting glances back at me. I watched Fergie's car out of sight, going towards town along the river road.

'I owe you, love,' I told Elspeth.

'What happened up there, Lovejoy?'

'Tell you later. Look. What do I do?' If I set off in my crate in this state I'd be arrested at the first traffic lights.

'Sit here and rest,' she commanded. 'You're exhausted. When

154

the others come back I'll take you home. We'll pretend you're one of my exercise team, and that you fell and hurt yourself. I have a sponge bag and towel. We can get some of that filth off in the meantime. What *is* it? Maybe my men can lend you some spare clothes, if they have any.'

'Why are you here?' I lay on the grass, clutching the silver still wrapped in my underpants. 'I thought the run was from the surgery.'

'Oh, I fancied a change.' She got a cold wet sponge and started on my legs. 'I knew you'd come here, you see. From your questions. I went to your cottage, then drove here and saw your old motor. So I fetched my runners along.'

'What if I hadn't showed up?' I asked from curiosity. 'What would you have done?'

'Mind your own business.' She squeezed the sponge over my middle and made me gasp. She tapped my silver. 'Is that toy train what you were looking for?'

I looked at the exquisite silver engine properly for the first time, holding it up against the sky from my supine position. Quite like an offering to a world full of beautiful space and air and light.

'Yes. Isn't it beautiful?'

'Quite nice,' she said critically. 'But it's bent.'

I said, 'So it is. Wonder how that happened?'

Elspeth got me home. One of the runners promised to drop my crate off at the White Hart for Tinker to collect. A sweaty track-suit was provided from somewhere.

'You know,' I explained as she drove, 'Poor old Jonathan Chase must have had a nerve.'

'Can't you put that toy on the back seat, Lovejoy?'

I was holding it in my lap. I trusted her, but said, 'It's too valuable.'

I wondered about the respectable Right Honourable gentleman. He had obviously arranged for an explosion to take place and cause a landslip. Of course, his plan was a risk. I felt a twinge of my subterranean fear return momentarily, and wound the window down for air. In fact, it nearly killed him outright. The plan was to halt the little carriage at the one fixed reinforced spot of the tunnel that had withstood the earth's subtle shifts from time immemorial. That was where the tunnel bisected the well-shaft.

The carriage had stopped. On cue, the explosion had caused the landslip. Chase had dug his way through to the well, pulled the bricks out and climbed up. At the top he had simply pulled gorse in the hole, to cover it up. And there it grew, year after year.

He'd had to have some luck, because his plans had gone slightly askew. I could tell that. The landslip had gone faster and further than predicted. But he'd made it, done his act, and successfully lived to finance the rival route. The clever, wicked old devil.

His two engineers would have been in on the plan. They had to be. But why those two tough men had ended up at the bottom of the well when the Right Honourable had managed to escape probably didn't bear thinking about. They probably got a percussion ball in each earhole, from one of those folding trigger pistols we antique dealers are always after. The truth was obvious. Jonathan Chase, pillar of Victorian society, was a scoundrel. And old Doc Chase, maybe not realizing how valuable the silver piece would be, and anyway fearful for his family's reputation — as if that ever matters — kept watch over what he knew to be the terrible evidence of his ancestor's perfidy. You couldn't blame an old bloke of his generation, though. It was only natural. I suppose it needs a scrounger like me to ignore reputations.

'What will you do with it?'

'Eh? Oh.' I thought for a minute and cleared my throat for a lie. 'Give it to the museum, I suppose.'

'Will you? Honestly?'

She looked so moved I was moved too. 'Hand on my heart,' I promised with sincerity.

She smiled radiantly. 'I'm so pleased, Lovejoy.' She squeezed my arm. 'He would have loved that.'

'In memory of him,' I said piously. Being praised is quite pleasant.

'Will there be a formal presentation?' She was already planning a new frock.

'Er, no,' I said, all modest. 'I wouldn't like people to think I was blowing my own trumpet.'

'You're really sweet, Lovejoy.' She turned to me mistily.

'Stop a second.' I actually felt sweet, grotesquely smug.

There was a phone-box at a cross-roads. I dialled emergency. The operator clicked me breathlessly through to a narky police-woman who wanted to start filling in forms.

'Hark,' I interrupted her questions. 'You've got a grouser called Maslow on your books. Tell him Lovejoy rang.'

'We don't pass on personal messages through this telephone exchange,' she told me with asperity. 'This is for emergencies.'

'This is for murder,' I continued. 'Say I'm prepared to make a statement of evidence.' Now I need not say anything about Sue being the other witness. When Fergie and Jake got their ugly mugs in the papers the Brummie mob would start asking nasty questions about their missing pair of nerks. Jake and Fergie would be for it either way. Poor lads, I thought, smiling.

Elspeth chatted happily all the way home. She assumed I had phoned my decision to the museum, and was so pleased. I didn't disillusion her.

The cottage felt as if I had been away for years. Elspeth gasped at the sight of all the furniture and the treens everywhere, but I ran a bath and didn't explain. We decided to go out and celebrate. Elspeth had enough money for us to have a real splash.

I was drying myself when this car came screaming down the lane in third gear. It stopped in the gateway, and Moll emerged, dressed in a smart new green suit. She knows I like green. See what I mean about women? There's no letting up, minds always on the go.

I honestly wasn't trying to keep out of the way, but it didn't seem my sort of scene. I'd had the silver model in the bath with me, soaping it. None of your scraping and sanding for precious silver, please. Mild soap and ordinary water is about the limit, followed by a cold but gentle towel. Having to leave the presentation case was a pity, but I wasn't going back for it at any price. I'd knock up a quick fake instead. That would really set it off, pretty as a picture. Imagine the millions of people who'd get pleasure from seeing it beautifully displayed in our Castle Museum. I finished wiping the silver surface dry while Moll and Elspeth nattered at the door.

'Lovejoy's rather busy,' Elspeth's voice announced, frosty.

'Not to me he isn't, dear.' Moll sounded confident and over-sweet.

'For everyone. *Dear.*' Elspeth was obviously going to stand her ground. I made no noise.

'I'm in a somewhat different category,' from Moll.

'That's quite possible, *Mrs* Maslow,' Elspeth shot back.

I slipped on my clothes and wrapped the silver in a dry towel. Time for Tinker to bowl up. The idle swine was still swigging ale somewhere, though I'd phoned him almost an hour ago on the way back. I'll cripple him, I thought furiously.

'Tell Lovejoy I'm here,' Moll ordered.

'If this is in the course of police investigations . . .' Elspeth's voice turned the sugar on.

'Lovejoy is my *partner.*'

I gasped from behind the bathroom door. *Partner* was beginning to have a nasty permanent ring about it. She must have read more into buying all that bloody treen than I had.

'He hasn't a partner.'

'Where do you think he acquired this houseful?'

It was time I left, even if it was on foot. I ducked and crawled between the furniture. There is a back door, but the hedge is thick

157

and there's no way through. I'd have to make it round the side and somehow cut out of my gate.

The sound came when I was crawling round my little unfinished wall at the rear of the cottage. The beautiful, melodious clattering of my sewing-machine engine. Tinker, with my crate, bless him. I was still blazing, but if I was quick . . . Get down there before they saw me. And before he turned into the garden.

A rapid sidle round the cottage wall, ducking beneath the sill to avoid being seen through the kitchen window, worse than any gangster in a shoot-out. Flattened against the side wall I peered round. The spluttering sounded nearer and nearer.

'It isn't a question of being obstructive, Mrs Maslow.' They were still at it, with Elspeth gaining the upper hand. She didn't seem to have let Moll in yet.

'Don't you think you are rather misunderstanding your functions?' Moll's voice. The chips were down. 'You're behaving rather like a wardress — '

It was warming up. I knew from the sudden easing of the engine's chug that Tinker had reached the chapel. Only one place to turn, about a hundred yards up. *Now.*

I clutched the silver in the towel and ran. On tiptoe, like a bloody fool, as if grass echoes. I drew breath and ran straight into the hedge as gently as I could. Luckily Moll's car blocked the gateway. I was round it in a flash and scarpering up the lane as my crate rumbled into view. Tinker was driving, and he had Lemuel with him. He knows I hate Lemuel in the crate, because he always leaves a liberal sprinkling of fleas behind. I spend a fortune on those sprays.

Tinker saw me waving frantically and screeched — well, creaked — to a stop. I hurtled up, signalling him to turn. He was already backing when I undid the door and fell in.

'Get going, Tinker,' I gasped.

'I fetched Lemuel for the aggro,' Tinker explained, desperately wobbling the gear stick. It's a bit loose. I'll have it mended when I get a minute. Luckily, we dealers always carry blankets. I wriggled under one and lay still, pleading, 'Hurry, for gawd's sake, Tinker.'

We rumbled forward.

'No scrapping, Lovejoy?' Lemuel quavered thankfully.

'It's all done, Lemuel.' Already I was beginning to itch.

Another car sounded ahead of us. A horn tooted. 'Sod it,' from Tinker. We stopped.

'Tinker.' Sue's voice. 'Is Lovejoy home?'

'Er, just dropped him off there, lady.'

'Thank you.'

And she was gone. 'Great, Tinker,' I told him, still muffled under the blanket.

'That all right, Lovejoy?' Tinker asked as we pulled away again. 'Here. What happened to the Brummies?'

'What Brummies?' I said under my blanket. 'There aren't any Brummies.' It was hellish uncomfortable bumping on the motor's tin floor. If only the springs hadn't gone. Sue usually brings cushions.

''Course there are, Lovejoy,' Lemuel croaked earnestly. 'That Fergie's got two frigging big hard nuts to do you − '

His voice was nudged to a thoughtful silence, probably by Tinker's elbow.

I could tell we'd reached the chapel. Tinker was just going to turn right when another motor came close to the van's side and throbbed in my lughole.

'*Stop,* Dill.' Maslow's voice, the bastard.

'Where's Lovejoy?' Oh, hell. *Tom* Maslow's voice now.

'He's, er, at the cottage, Mr Maslow,' Tinker said suddenly. We all hate talking to the Old Bill.

'With that bird with the big knockers,' Lemuel said, cackling evilly.

'That's enough from you.' The engine boomed and went off in smooth top gear, burning my taxes.

Lemuel fell about laughing. He and Tinker would be on about having tricked Maslow for months now. 'They couldn't find a bottle in a brewery.'

'Where to, Lovejoy?'

I stayed silent as we trundled towards the main road. The cottage would be like a carnival, what with Maslow wanting my evidence, and Sue charging in on the existing war between Moll and Elspeth. And from the Maslows' manner they had harsh words for Moll. Maybe Elspeth would catch it, as well, for not informing on me the way Maslow wanted. And Elspeth would fly at Sue for wrongly giving Moll her name that time . . . It was a right mess. The trouble is that absolutely none of it was my fault. Not one bit. I honestly don't know who gets me in these shambles, but it's not me, that's for sure.

'Where to, Lovejoy?' Tinker said again.

I was suddenly happy. I held one of the most valuable pieces of post-Georgian silver probably ever made. Me. I was here with it, embracing it. In my very own motor.

But then I remembered my promise to give it to a museum, the promise which had moved Elspeth so deeply. I'd been really magnanimous, maybe too magnanimous. After all, who'd been sick with terror deep in the earth, down a well full of unspeakable horrors, risking his life hour after hour? Yet I'd promised.

On the other hand, was my promise spontaneous? Given of my own free will and accord? Or had it been exorted from me? Wrung out of my unwilling soul by Elspeth's cunning playing on my emotions? Under the blanket I seethed with indignation.

'Lovejoy. Where the frigging hell are we going?'

Jill's place is a haven full of hardworking vannies, so that was out. Margaret's was too near the cop-shop. Lily would instantly phone Patrick, who would be so excited at helping to conceal me for a few days I'd not last an hour. Lemuel's is a doss-house full of fleas. Tinker's place is so grotty it's indescribable. Big Frank has so many bigamous wives that he's always being followed by divorce agents. I ran my mind down the list of friends. And suddenly Helen came to mind. I could see her now in the White Hart, smiling and smoking and stretching her lovely long legs towards the carpet.

'Eh?' Tinker was asking. 'You all right?'

I must have moaned. Helen could be trusted, if I owned up to escaping from Sue and the others. And Helen always had a good string of buyers for precious silver. Well, the bloody museum would want me to *give* it to them, as a totally free gift. Cheek. After all I'd done. And as for Elspeth, worming that ridiculous promise out of me so treacherously . . . I decided I'd go back to the cottage in a week or so. I like surprises.

'Drop me at Helen's, Tinker,' I said, and smiled under the blankets as we took off.